MOTIVE FOR MARRIAGE
Linda Markowiak

Harlequin Books

TORONTO • NEW YORK • LONDON
AMSTERDAM • PARIS • SYDNEY • HAMBURG
STOCKHOLM • ATHENS • TOKYO • MILAN
MADRID • WARSAW • BUDAPEST • AUCKLAND

ISBN 0-373-70755-X

MOTIVE FOR MARRIAGE

This edition published by arrangement with Harlequin Books S.A.

Printed in U.S.A.

Please God. Let Melissa be safe.

Nathan Perry snatched up the telegram lying on top of the pile of mail his housekeeper had left on his desk. The telegram was a day early. For the past eight years— ever since his two-year-old daughter had been placed in a witness protection program with her mother and step-father—the telegram had said the same thing: "Package Safe. Chet."

This year the telegram was longer: "Package safe, but moved to another warehouse."

Melissa *was* safe. For a moment that was the only part of the message that registered. Then Nate studied the rest of the telegram. *Moved to another warehouse.* What the hell did that mean?

Had the government been forced to give Melissa and Eve and Lloyd a new identity, move them to yet another place? As the years had passed, Nate had assured him-self he'd done the right thing by allowing his daughter to go with her mother. The proof had always been in these telegrams from his good friend Chet. *Package safe.* But now...

Nathan Perry knew what he had to do.

Pick up his package from the warehouse and bring it home.

ABOUT THE AUTHOR

Linda Markowiak has recently returned to northwest Ohio with her husband, Jim, and nine-year-old son, Stephen. She and Jim are happy to be back among friends and family. It was natural, then, for her to want to write a book about the North Coast with its pristine beaches and tiny, unspoiled islands. Though Linda—like Sara in this story—is no sailor, she has spent time doing some lazy power boating along the Maumee River.

Books by Linda Markowiak

HARLEQUIN SUPERROMANCE
629—COURTING VALERIE
717—FIRM COMMITMENT

Don't miss any of our special offers. Write to us at the following address for information on our newest releases.

Harlequin Reader Service
U.S.: 3010 Walden Ave., P.O. Box 1325, Buffalo, NY 14269
Canadian: P.O. Box 609, Fort Erie, Ont. L2A 5X3

I'd like to thank Ann and Dick Hamilton, Kent and Sandy Gordam and Andy Phillips for answering my questions about sailing and for "giving" Nate their fantasy racing boat, a Quest 30.

I knew I was dealing with a hardy bunch of sailors when I asked Dick how easy it would be for an experienced sailor to get caught in a storm on the lake. "Very easy," he replied. "Ann and I were in a bad one once. It was fun."

Again, thanks, everyone. May the wind be steady and true and the beer cold as you all sail your Quests into the sunset.

CHAPTER ONE

NATHAN PERRY shouldered his way to the front of the line at the airport, too impatient to wait his turn for a cab. He yanked open the door of the only taxi in sight and threw his overnight bag into the back seat. "Hey," a fellow passenger from the Chicago flight protested. "Get in line."

"Sorry," Nate mumbled. He hadn't really paid attention to the queue of people, except as obstacles in his path. He'd been shell-shocked, not really *there* for hours, ever since he'd got the telegram from Chet.

For the last eight years, the annual telegram had said the same thing. "Package Safe. Chet." And for eight years, Nate had fallen into a chair, weak with relief, flooded with memories.

This year had been different. He'd got home from work at 9:00 p.m. last night, and found his telegram there a day early, on top of a pile of mail his housekeeper had left on the table. He'd snatched it up. *Please, God. Let Melissa be safe.*

This year, the telegram had been longer. "Package Safe, but moved to another warehouse."

Melissa was safe. For a moment, that had been all of the message that had registered.

Then he studied the rest of the telegram. Moved to another warehouse. What the hell did that mean?

Maybe the government had been forced to give Eve and Lloyd and Melissa another identity, move them to yet another place. As the years had passed, he'd told himself over and over that he'd done the right thing, letting his daughter enter the federal witness protection program. The proof was always in these telegrams. Package Safe. But now...

"Where to, mon?" The cabdriver had a Jamaican accent and a friendly smile as he looked back at Nate.

"The Justice Department."

"I know where that is, no problem. Hey, are you with the FBI?"

"No," Nate said shortly.

"You look like an agent, with that haircut and good-lookin' suit. I know those guys over in Justice, too. My daughter dated a federal marshal." He pushed the button to show the fare for the proper zone. "He was a guy who knew how to crack computer codes. You got big business with the feds?"

"No." Nate leaned forward. "Listen, can't you cut the chat and hurry?"

The cabdriver's smile faded. His face disappeared from the rearview mirror. He wrenched the steering wheel left and the cab bounced out of place and shot into a narrow opening in the traffic. "How the hell was that for a hurry, mon?"

Nate didn't answer, staring out the window without really seeing anything. It was his first trip to Washington, but the city made no impression on him.

Instead, he was remembering his two-and-a-half-year-old daughter. The last time he'd seen her, Melissa had been on a weekend visit. He'd had to meet a client on Saturday, but Sunday had been all theirs.

Their last day together. He could remember it with perfect clarity. The temperature had been near freezing. He'd bundled Melissa in snowsuit, hat, hood and mittens, until she'd resembled a fat red hen, and carried her on his shoulders when her legs got tired at the zoo. At dinner she'd eaten nothing but french fries—out of her bag, then his.

Then, as he was buckling Melissa into her car seat, she said out of the blue, "Daddy, kittens say meow, meow."

"Hey." He smiled down at her. "You just said your first sentence! No more mama and dada and 'Melissa want.' This one had a noun, a verb. Kiddo, you're *great*." He'd planted a kiss on her forehead.

Reluctantly, he took Melissa back to Eve's. But Eve wasn't waiting on the porch with her new husband, Lloyd. So Nate walked Melissa to the door and rang the bell. At the time, he'd been too fixed on telling Eve about their daughter's first sentence to realize how strange it was that nobody was there to meet them.

Now Nate squeezed his eyes shut against the memories that came after.

The dark man who'd been there with Eve and Lloyd introduced himself as a federal marshal. Then had come the brief, terse explanation that Lloyd had seen too much, learned too much, in his job with the insurance company. The insurance company hadn't been legit, merely a money-laundering scheme for a big crime family. The Kallons. Surely Nate had heard of them?

Nate hadn't. But Lloyd Lapulski was going to testify against the Kallons, and then he and his family were going to disappear into the witness protection program. Surely Nate had heard of that.

Nate had. But he didn't really believe it. At first, he'd thought this was another attempt by Eve to discourage his visitation. Because—perversely—the harder he tried to be a father to Melissa, the more resentful Eve became. So it had taken a while for it to sink in that his ex-wife and daughter were actually going to be part of a program that up to now had just been an item on the television news. It took even longer to realize that Melissa was going to disappear from his life forever.

"You can't do this!" he had roared, first at Eve, then at Lloyd, then at the federal marshal who tried to explain that for Melissa's safety there was no other choice.

"Nate, see reason for once." Eve laid a hand on his arm. "For God's sake, we can't stay here. They might kill her."

Eve was dramatizing the situation again. She had to be. Nate waited for the marshal to say it wasn't *that* serious. Soon things would calm down, get back to normal. But the man was nodding in agreement.

Nate's hands fisted. "I'll take her home with me. You two can do what you want."

Eve laughed scornfully, but with a nervous high note. "How will you take care of her? When were you ever home from the office early enough to do squat for Melissa? *You'll* take care of her? What a joke."

He knew he hadn't been much of a family man, and Eve never hesitated to remind him of his limitations. But these visitations with Melissa, well, he'd got to know his daughter. He didn't want another fight with Eve. He just wanted Melissa. "Damn it, Eve—"

"Eve has custody under your divorce order. You agreed to that," Lloyd cut in.

"Well, I never agreed to let her take my kid and walk out of my life! I'm Melissa's father. I have visitation rights. From that same court order." Nate started to reach for Melissa. The little girl looked from one parent to the other and her mouth wobbled. "I'll call my lawyer. You can't do this. Please." Fiercely, he willed down his pride, pleading with Eve, with the two men.

"Believe me, Mr. Perry, it's the only way." The marshal stepped forward. "If you really love your daughter, you'll let her go and never try to see her again."

"I'm calling my lawyer, then Chet McMasters." Nate had gone to the other room. His attorney assured him it was perfectly legal for the government and his ex-wife to take his baby away and give her another name. Thoroughly rattled, he'd called Chet at home. Chet, an old friend of Nate's, was a lawyer at the Justice Department. His friend made a couple of calls then phoned back to assure Nate everything was on the level.

Nate had listened while his whole world came crashing down. Chet had managed to convince him of the urgency of the situation, told him Melissa's life could be at stake.

Then, as if sensing that Nate was still reluctant to let Melissa go, he'd made a promise. Once a year, he'd let Nate know his daughter was safe. No, he couldn't let Nate know more often than that. To bring up information on the computer too frequently could compromise the operation. But once a year, that would be all right. If everything was okay, he'd only say, "Package Safe."

Nate hung up the telephone. It was as if Melissa had died. As if *he'd* died. He thought fleetingly of all the hours he'd been working, how all along, everything he'd worked for was only for his daughter. For Melissa.

Once back in the living room, he talked Eve into letting him hold Melissa one more time. Under the watchful gaze of Eve, Lloyd and the federal marshal, he'd scooped his daughter into his arms. "Hey, kiddo," he'd whispered. Her dark curls were so soft against his cheek, like springy flannel. "Be safe, baby. And remember…" He swallowed. She would not remember. She would not be allowed to remember. "Remember what kittens say." He'd set her down gently and walked out the door.

And for eight years, no matter how complicated his real-estate development business became, how hard he worked or how successful he was, his whole life seemed geared to

February 15th, the day he'd hear about Melissa. Nathan Perry had played the game the government's way.

Now he wasn't as naive as he'd been the day they took away his daughter. Over the years, he'd found out a lot more about the Witness Protection Program. Most of what he'd learned wasn't favorable. The program was riddled with leaks. He'd worried about how safe Melissa really was, but he'd been too afraid of hurting her by delving deeper. But he was going to talk to Chet McMasters today, and he wasn't leaving Washington until he found out where his daughter was living.

"Package Safe, but..." Now Nathan Perry was going to do only one thing.

Pick up his "package" from the "warehouse," and take it home.

LIBBY JAMIESON'S hand shook as she set down the telephone receiver. Her attorney, Cameron Holling, was out of town for the day, so she couldn't ask him if there was a problem with the adoption, or why Judge Wyatt wanted a meeting with them. They were to be in court at 9:00 a.m. tomorrow, and Libby wasn't supposed to mention anything to Sara.

Automatically, Libby picked up a blue-tinted carnation and wopped off the stem at a forty-five-degree angle before sticking it in the foam base. Up to now, her plan to adopt Sara had been going perfectly. Libby had hardly seen her lawyer since she'd finished her duties as executor of her friend's estate and taken up her duties as Sara's guardian.

Now she was scared. A judge wanting to see you was something like getting stopped by the cops. You automatically assumed you'd done something wrong. And there'd always been those hints Julia, Sara's mother, had dropped. Secrets... Then those puzzling last words of hers, at the hospital before her death. But Julia had always liked attention, drama.

Of course, the reason for this meeting could just be to iron out a technicality. Still...

Get a grip, she told herself. *If you're late with the Smithson wedding flowers, you won't have the money to pay your lawyer, and that will create more complications than Judge Wyatt could dream up.*

Another bill. That was all she needed. It was always tough to wait out this time, to husband the funds she earned in the summer, when Harborside, Ohio, was clogged with both wedding dates and tourists. Holding her lower lip between her teeth in concentration, Libby broke stems of baby's breath. Placing some into the greenery, she took a step back and eyed the arrangement. Triangular. Competent and stiff, the fake gentian-blue of the carnations was an insult to the flower.

The doorbell jangled and Libby looked up, her heart going soft at the sight of Sara.

"Hey, Lib, guess what happened!" Sara blew a couple of black curls out of her eyes and flung her book bag on a tabletop covered with dried-flower bouquets. Her cheeks were red from the chilly late-winter air.

"Careful of my stuff," Libby warned automatically. But she was smiling. "Now. What happened?"

"Kathleen invited me to her birthday party. We're going *horseback riding.*" Her eyes danced as she took off her coat, scarf and mittens, leaving a trail through the shop. Her gold heart, with its tiny chip of blue topaz, glinted against the neck of her navy blue sweater. "I can't *wait.*"

Sara had never been on a horse in her life.

"If I have a good time, can I have lessons?"

Sara had been wanting horseback-riding lessons since before Julia's death. Neither her mother nor Libby could afford them, or the rental and stabling for a horse. Now the meeting tomorrow and the possible complications in the pending adoption flashed through Libby's mind. "I wish we could swing it." How terrific it would be to walk into Judge Wyatt's courtroom and say that Sara had everything she'd ever wanted.

She looked down at her hands. The nails were bluntly filed, more functional than beautiful. Like herself, Libby thought ruefully, thinking of her unruly, copper-red hair. The skin of her hands was chapped, cut in places from the hard stems of the flowers and misses with the clippers. Suddenly she felt the hot sting of tears behind her eyelids.

"Hey, Lib." A small, very cold hand stole over hers. "It's okay about the lessons. I was just asking."

Libby looked into eyes as blue as Lake Erie on a cloudless day. "I know, sweetheart."

Sara's skin was fair and freckled, with the high-contrast coloring of the Black Irish. But Libby, who loved beautiful things, loved Sara more for her irrepressible personality, her sense of humor, her maturity. Sometimes Sara seemed older than ten. But the girl had had a lot to deal with. Her father drank, and last year had killed both himself and her mother in a collision on the causeway.

"Wow, that's ugly," Sara exclaimed, her gaze on the arrangement Libby had just finished. She grinned. "What'd you do, dunk those flowers in toilet-bowl cleaner?"

Despite her anxiety about tomorrow, Libby chuckled. "Disgusting, huh?"

"Worse. Gross."

They looked at each other and giggled. Finally, Libby sobered a bit. "They're for Karen Smithson, and she wanted everything to match. The dresses, the flowers, the—"

"Cake," Sara finished, and she burst into laughter again. "Tidybowl cake."

"She's the customer."

"Right," Sara said in quick agreement. Libby always tried to be honest though reassuring about their financial situation. Sara understood it was important to please a customer of the shop.

Sara picked up a frond of Christmas fern. "So, can I help?"

Libby sighed. Sara had been "helping" around the shop since she could walk. Her mother used to bring her here so that the women could rehearse their lines for the community theater group they both belonged to. Tina Samms, a third friend, would often join them. "I don't suppose the help you have in mind is sweeping up this mess."

"I could make something. You know, for the wedding."

Libby made one last try. "Have you got homework?"

"Naw." She paused and looked away. "Well, a little. But I can help here a while."

Libby pointed with the clippers she held in one hand. "To the desk with you, fair maiden." She waved the clippers in mock threat. "Or off with your head."

"But Your Majesty, I wanna play with the flowers." Sara's blue gaze turned pleading. "I don't have *that* much homework."

Libby relented. It was hard to deny the kid when she turned on that preadolescent charm. But Sara's experiments cut into the slim profit margin of Country Tastes. "Well, okay. You can make a couple of small arrangements for the reception."

"Do they have to be blue?"

"Well, they didn't specify. Use a carnation or two, and see if you can use up some of this stuff instead of hitting the cooler for more."

"Cool!" Sara eyed the pile with delight.

For a few minutes they worked together, while Sara talked about everything from a food fight in the school cafeteria to how she wanted her own wedding to look. Libby glued foam bases for bigger arrangements. The tall gladioli the customer had specified looked stiff, so she tucked in a few daisies at a rakish angle. Daisies the customer hadn't paid for. But what the heck. She might get a referral or two out of this job. The high society of Harborside, such as it was, would be in attendance. She headed to the cooler for more material.

When she came back, Sara was admiring her handiwork. Libby looked at the arrangements and couldn't help a rush of pride. Karen Smithson might not appreciate these arrangements because Sara had broken the Rule of the Triangle, but if you appreciated art and flowers, you couldn't miss the rough talent the girl brought to the work. Libby smiled. "You, fair maiden, are good," she said softly.

"I like flowers." Sara hesitated. "I like living with you, Lib, and I feel really bad about bringing up those riding lessons again. I know Mom and Dad didn't leave too much—"

"Stop right there." Libby waited until Sara was looking at her. "I'd want you no matter what your parents left. We aren't using any of your parents' money until it's time for you to go to college. We agreed, remember?" She brushed the thick bangs out of Sara's eyes. Libby's voice softened to a whisper. "I always wanted a daughter. And I love you as if you were mine."

Sara blushed and averted her eyes. "I like it here," she repeated.

THE NEXT DAY, Libby put a damp herbal tea bag over each eye, willing herself to relax. Her eyelids were puffy, they always swelled when she hadn't slept well. She'd spent several hours before bed last night poring over the adoption paperwork, speculating on her mysterious meeting with Judge Wyatt. She'd called her friend Tina, who'd helped her rationalize.

Today she wanted to look her best, so she'd braided her hair into a chignon that felt ready to burst each time she turned her head, and now she was screwing around with these tea bags.

Two minutes later she was up and checking the mirror. Nope. They were still there, tiny swellings under each eye.

Deciding there wasn't any point in lingering, she put on her coat and walked to the courthouse. She was a half hour early, and some of the courthouse personnel were just arriving. She'd lived in Harborside all her life, and knew most of them. With a wave, she greeted the janitor, then headed for the clerk's office where Barbara Fielding was working. Barb and she had gone to school together, and were now both members of the garden club.

"Hey, Lib, just the person I wanted to see." Barb leaned forward over the counter. "Can we have a casserole for the meeting next week? Some of that brown-rice-and-herb medley?"

"Sure," Libby said quietly.

"What's up?" Barb asked immediately. "You seem sort of...subdued."

Libby quickly explained. Barb might just know what *i* Libby or her attorney had failed to dot in the adoption papers.

"I swear I don't know anything." The woman's expression was serious. "But you have my support...this *town's* support. Everybody's seen how Sara's become so talkative and bubbly this past year."

"Thanks." Libby felt comforted by the brisk, kind words.

"But, Lib?" Her voice lowered. "There's someone in the waiting room who's here on Sara's case, too."

Quickly, Libby craned her neck, but she could see no one.

"He was waiting on the steps when I got to work. I think he's a lawyer, an out-of-town guy. A way-out-of-town guy."

Barb leaned forward and lowered her voice once more. "I mean, the man's gorgeous, and I don't think he bought that suit of his off the rack."

Libby frowned, ignoring the invitation to gossip. "I've got Cam Holling. What would another lawyer want with Sara's case?"

"I don't know, but you'll be okay. This is Harborside, and Judge Wyatt won't take kindly to some outsider in a thousand-dollar suit telling him what to do."

That was true. And standing here worrying wasn't Libby's style. She'd done far too much of it these past sixteen hours. She made a quick decision. It was time to see what Mr. Gorgeous wanted with Sara's case. Plunking her tote bag on the floor, and slinging her jacket over a chair, she headed through the double doors into the waiting room.

She spotted the man in question immediately. Barb wasn't kidding. The man did look as if he was from somewhere urban and rich. And he was gorgeous. Libby's heart gave a tiny lurch, of nerves and something else entirely.

She hadn't been really attracted to a man in years, not since Brian, a slick charmer from out of town who'd shown his true colors eventually. The lesson had hurt. And the single men in Harborside were her buddies. Or maybe it was that she had never, ever been attracted like this. She certainly couldn't remember when the sight of a man had made her heart thump erratically and her mouth go suddenly dry.

He was tall. With hands in the pockets of his perfectly draped trench coat, he stood, half facing her, in front of a row of windows and stared out intently. The dim light of early morning streaming in brought out the shine in his wavy black hair. It was as black as Sara's. In profile, his features were almost aristocratic.

Damned if he didn't look like a lawyer. Somehow, this man was part of the trouble that brought her to the courthouse this morning. Libby took a deep breath and strode forward.

He turned to face her fully as she approached.

"Are you ready for me?" he asked. "My lawyer isn't here yet, but I don't mind getting started."

"You're not a lawyer?"

His mouth thinned with impatience. "Of course not. I'm the litigant." Then, as if just remembering his manners, he smiled and extended his hand. "Sorry. I've got a lot on my mind. I'm Nathan Perry. Are you the judge's bailiff?" A tilt of his head indicated the employees-only area Libby had come from.

She shook his hand. So he was a "litigant." She wasn't sure exactly what that meant. And she was irritated with herself, because she was sure that smile was designed precisely to charm, and she *was* charmed.

Without being blatant about it, he seemed to look more closely at her face and figure. Then his smile deepened, reached his eyes, became genuine...and devastating.

She was all mixed up—nervous, anxious about Sara's case, attracted to this handsome stranger—and as usual, overly conscious of her appearance. "I had to wear these tights," she blurted out. "I forgot to buy nylons again." *Oh, God, had she really said that?*

He chuckled, a sound as rich as a cup of espresso. Was there nothing about this man that wasn't perfect? "You look fine."

"Sure," she said lightly, hoping her cheeks weren't as red as they felt. "I'm Libby—Elizabeth—Jamieson, by the way."

He was still looking down into her eyes, so she could tell the precise moment that recognition crossed his face. Then his mouth tightened into a white line and his eyes narrowed. "You!"

"Excuse me?"

"*You're* Elizabeth Jamieson? The one who has Melissa?"

Melissa? Melissa...

All of a sudden, some things fell into place. Julia and secrets, her oft-repeated statement that things weren't what they seemed. And those last words of Julia's, just before she died: *Her name is Melissa. Tell Nate I'm sorry.*

OhmyGod. Sara must be, had to be...Melissa. And Nathan Perry was a litigant. *Nate* Perry. *Tell Nate I'm sorry.*

But what could all this mean? Libby wet her lips. "Just what is your interest in Sara?"

"Melissa," he corrected.

"Nate!" another voice called. They both turned as a tall, well-groomed woman approached, clutching a briefcase and wearing a trench coat that looked practically identical to the one Nathan Perry wore. "I knew I should have driven out from Toledo last night. These country roads—" She cut herself off as she reached them. "Sorry. You know I don't make a habit of being late."

Nate frowned. "But this was not the day to start, Marta. For chrissake, you know how important—"

"Sorry," she repeated briskly. "Has the judge called us yet?"

"No."

She shrugged. "Well, with judges it's hurry up and wait." She laid a light hand on his arm for a second. "Relax. You'll have Melissa soon enough."

Libby was confused, but one thing was clear. This Marta, whoever she was, was wrong. Nathan Perry would not have Melissa anytime soon.

Nathan shook his head slightly at Marta, indicating Libby. "This is Elizabeth Jamieson. And we have not talked," he added in a tone that suggested he and Libby had plenty to talk about.

"Oh. Really." An initial start gave way to a smooth introduction as Marta reached out a hand to Libby. "I'm Marta Wainwright, of Severn and Coxton, Chicago. We represent Mr. Perry in the matter of his daughter, Melissa."

His *daughter?* But Sara…Melissa's father had been Heywood Clark. Libby's mind searched frantically for any smidgen of information she had, any indication from Sara herself that Heywood Clark had been a stepfather. She could come up with nothing. But it was hard to think with her heart pounding against her ribs and her stomach feeling so tight.

Now Nate was looking at her, a strange, intent expression on his face. For a moment the courthouse walls and the other woman seemed to fade, as Libby was caught in his compelling blue gaze. "Yes. Melissa is my daughter," Nate said in a husky voice. "Tell me. Did you know?"

Know what? Libby thought half-hysterically. Know her name is somehow Melissa? Know you're somehow her father?

His gaze sharpened. "I asked, *did you know?*"

She could not look away. "No," she said softly.

He stared at her as if he was searching for something

beyond her denial. Finally he looked away, his shoulders slumping slightly.

The spell was broken, but the whole situation was unreal. In a numb fog, Libby heard their names called, went into the judge's chambers ahead of Marta Wainwright and Nathan Perry, explained to the judge that Cameron Holling was late and barely heard the judge growl, "Again!"

They all took seats around the conference table. The small conference area was paneled, intimidating, clearly a place where serious decisions were made. The judge sat at the head of the table, just underneath a huge plaque of the Great Seal of the state of Ohio.

Marta opened her briefcase and made a great show of arranging a stack of papers. Libby caught sight of the top one. Motion to Intervene in the Matter of the Adoption of Sara Clark.

Nate Perry sat still, straight. His hands were open, resting palm down on the polished oak table. She had a feeling that what he really wanted to do was fist them.

Nate Perry wanted his daughter. That much had penetrated her shell-shocked brain. But the situation still made no sense. Julia had been sort of dizzy at times, dramatic, but essentially a timid woman. Her husband had been a jerk, and Libby had always suspected Julia was afraid of him. At times, she had seemed anxious and sad.

But maybe Julia had been more than anxious. Maybe she'd had a good reason to be scared. Maybe her friend had kidnapped Sara—Melissa—from her father. Those kinds of things happened, she knew. But Libby had known Sara since the child had been about three years old. Didn't the FBI or someone track down missing kids? Would that kind of thing take seven years? And Libby truly couldn't imagine Julia as a kidnapper.

But one thing was certain. Libby loved Sara. She thought

of the nervous, quiet kid Sara had been a year ago, and knew that Barb Fielding was right. Libby *was* good for Sara; they were a real family. They belonged together.

The judge settled in at the head of the table and silence descended over the group. Marta had arranged every paper four times and had finally quit. Nate Perry looked as if he was beginning a slow boil he wouldn't be able to contain for long.

Where in God's name was Cameron? Libby hoped he was a good lawyer. The people in town used him, but she wondered if he would be intimidated by the formidable-looking Marta Wainwright of Severn and Coxton, Chicago. Cam was perpetually rumpled, and his idea of dressing up was to put on a corduroy blazer.

But appearances didn't mean a thing. Like Libby, Cam had chosen to come home to Harborside when he could have taken a job in the city. As far as she knew, Cam was competent. Looking at the single-minded determination on Nate Perry's face, Libby had a feeling that she would need more than just competent.

CHAPTER TWO

FINALLY, Cameron Holling arrived. As he settled into his seat, he whispered an apology in Libby's ear. She whispered back, "That's okay," but it wasn't. She felt as if she were going to explode with her unanswered questions.

At the head of the table, the judge pulled a set of papers toward him. "I've asked you all together because of an extraordinary situation. Yesterday I received a Motion to Intervene in Sara Clark's adoption, which is Mr. Perry's legal way of challenging Ms. Jamieson's right to keep Sara. I tried to reach you yesterday, Mr. Holling, but you were out of town."

There it was, out in the open. Nathan Perry wanted Sara. Libby realized that until that moment, she'd hoped she'd misread the situation. She looked up, across the table toward Nate. He was looking straight at her, too, and for a second, their gazes meshed. It was as if there had never been that brief moment of shared warmth in the waiting room. This man now had eyes as cold as ice, and as determined. There wasn't even the barest hint of a smile. *I want to win,* she read in his eyes. And it was obvious he was a man who was used to winning.

The judge cleared his throat. "Mr. Perry's story is extraordinary, but his attorney has provided all the documentation to assure me he's the natural father of Sara Clark, and that he hasn't been allowed to see his daughter, or even know where she was living. Eight years ago, while in the custody of her mother, the child entered the federal government's witness protection program.''

Beside her, Cam made a sound of disbelief, at the same time reaching for the documentation Judge Wyatt handed him. The judge explained the mechanics of the program and how Nate had had no choice in the matter.

Libby clenched her hands in her lap and waited as Cam looked over the paperwork. Across the table, she could feel Marta Wainwright's self-assurance. Finally, Cam gave an almost imperceptible nod.

It was true. Nate Perry *was* Sara's father. Studying him, she saw what she should have recognized instantly. He had black hair and sky-blue eyes that tilted at the corners slightly, giving him a look of intelligent curiosity. His cheekbones were a touch more prominent than most. No wonder Libby had found Nate Perry a handsome, appealing man. She was looking at a grown-up, masculine version of Sara.

According to the judge, Nate had lost his daughter eight years ago through no fault of his own. Sara would have been two or three at the time. For a second, Libby pictured what life must have been like for this man, and couldn't hold back the compassion that flowed through her.

Cam handed her a copy of Nate's motion, and Libby read it rapidly. It stated that Nathan Perry was the natural father of Melissa Perry, also known as Sara Clark, and that ''simple biology'' gave him a ''preeminent right'' as opposed to ''adoption by a legal stranger, Elizabeth Jamieson.'' He wanted his child returned to him immediately. As she read, Libby grew angrier and angrier.

''Simple biology'' be damned. If anybody was a stranger to Sara, Nate Perry was. Libby remembered all the things she and Sara had shared, this past year and in years gone by—the birthdays, the school plays, the community theater, the flowers, the square-dancing lessons that Sara loathed—the ones where the girls had to dance with the boys.

"You don't even know her." Libby looked to Nate, who remained still and impassive. Waiting. "You have no idea what she likes or dislikes."

He leaned forward. "Of course I don't. You heard the judge. Eight years ago my ex-wife and the government of the United States robbed me of my daughter. How could I possibly know? All I ever got was a telegram telling me she was safe. I didn't even know until last week that her mother had died almost a year ago." For a second, his husky voice went a note or two lower. It was the first sign that he was feeling anything but impatience at the legal formalities.

Libby took a deep breath. "You don't know that she loves celery sticks with peanut butter but won't eat brussels sprouts. You don't know that she likes cherry icing but won't touch chocolate."

Cam put his hand on her forearm, said, "Lib—"

But Libby went right on. "Do you know she hates carnations but is crazy about orange tiger lilies? Do you know her favorite play is *Once Upon a Mattress* and that when she was a toddler I had to read Beatrix Potter to her over and over, and you don't know anything about any of that…"

"Mr. Holling," the judge warned.

"Lib, be quiet," Cam whispered, more urgently.

Libby fell silent immediately, but she had so much more to say. Surely, if Nate Perry understood how much she loved Sara, he'd…

His hands on the tabletop fisted. "You don't get it, do you? I *want* to find out all those things about her. I want—" his mouth twisted "*—I want my daughter.*"

His mask slipped. The Nate Perry who obviously knew

how to charm, who could afford to hire Marta Wainwright of Severn and Coxton, Chicago, was gone. All of a sudden, he looked unsophisticated. Vulnerable.

Judge Wyatt cleared his throat again. "This is a very difficult situation. I'm sure that now you can see why I called you into chambers on an emergency basis. We'll have a hearing eventually, once Mr. Holling has an opportunity to prepare his case. But it would be better if we could decide some things informally now."

Marta Wainwright spoke up. "Of course. As long as Your Honor understands that the only discussion Mr. Perry will engage in is the one wherein we decide how soon he has custody of his daughter."

At the head of the table, the judge visibly tensed. Marta had been polite and formal, but the challenge was unmistakable. "Ah, Ms. Wainwright. We have much more to discuss." He gave her a small smile. "Frankly, as the judge presiding in this courthouse, I set my own agenda and choose the topics for discussion."

"Certainly, Judge." Not looking at all repentant, Marta fell silent.

"Good," the judge said after a moment. "I'm assuming that, due to this extraordinary situation, Sara has no idea that her father wants her back." He looked at Libby.

"No," she said slowly. "I'm sure she doesn't even know she *has* a father. If she knew anything about being in the witness protection program, I think she would have told me." Libby avoided Nate's gaze. "To Sara, her father was Heywood Clark, who was killed a year ago."

She took a deep breath. "Actually, Your Honor, I'm kind of worried about how she'll take the news. Mr. Clark wasn't, well, always nice to Sara."

"What does that mean?" Nate asked sharply.

Libby had been facing the judge, but now she looked briefly to Nate. "He drank."

Nate's features seemed to turn to stone. Marta whispered something in his ear.

The judge leaned back in his chair. "Mr. Perry, I want you to know some of the facts. First, this is a small town, and I am acquainted with Ms. Jamieson's family. I knew her father before he passed away. But we've never been close friends or socialized with each other. Actually, I know almost everyone in town, so I've gotten used to putting personal issues aside. I can be impartial in this matter. Anyone have a problem with me continuing to be the judge here?"

For a moment, Marta Wainwright looked as though she might well have a problem with it. Then apparently thinking better of crossing the judge again, she shook her head.

"Fine. Now, Mr. Perry also needs to know that Sara's home life was far from perfect, and Ms. Jamieson has been kind to her since the child lost her parents almost a year ago. After all, without Ms. Jamieson's intervention, Sara would be in foster care right now. You ought to thank her for that, at least."

Thank her? Libby felt bitter laughter rise within her. They were trying to take Sara!

"But Mr. Perry is her father," Marta said.

The words hung in the air. Libby turned toward Cam. Why was Marta doing all the talking?

The judge wiped a weary hand across his forehead. "I'm a father myself, and I respect the connection you have with your daughter, Mr. Perry. In the law, your rights are protected. But I've got to think about Sara's best interest. Ms. Jamieson has confirmed what I suspected—that Sara has no idea that you exist. And I can't let you simply uproot her and move her to Chicago. After I received your motion yesterday, I was up all night, researching, talking to other judges."

Marta Wainwright smiled. "I brought case law, Your Honor, that I'd be happy to share with the court."

Cam whispered in her ear. "I'm not quite sure what the law is here, Libby. I'll have to do some research, too."

Libby nodded. Chalk one up for Marta Wainwright, she thought. The woman had obviously come armed with cases supporting the rights of fathers. But neither she nor Cam had known what was happening, so there'd been no way to prepare for their side yet.

A shiver of fear went through Libby.

The judge made a note in the margin of his paper, then spoke. "Sara needs to be told, and as soon as possible. But gently, for her sake. And we need to arrange for Mr. Perry to see her."

"When?" Nate asked. There was no mistaking the eagerness in his voice, and Libby felt again that unwelcome pang of compassion.

She swallowed. "I could talk to her."

"If this is for her best interest," Cam said, "we should let Sara say what she wants."

The judge smiled for the first time. "Oh, I don't think we'll let a ten-year-old girl call the shots." He picked up the motion Marta had filed. "This motion is rather combative, Ms. Wainwright. We do things a little differently in Harborside, but I'll give you some time to get used to my courtroom. What I'd like to see, from both the attorneys, is a suggestion to their clients to cooperate with each other. Maybe Ms. Jamieson and Mr. Perry could break the news to Sara together, and we could schedule some visitations for Mr. Perry."

Marta Wainwright bristled. "Mr. Perry needs to return to Chicago. He has a property-development business. Right now he's in the middle of building the Iris Complex, a multimillion-dollar resort on Lake Michigan—"

"Marta," Nate interrupted, his voice a clear warning. He turned to the judge. "I'll work with Ms. Jamieson on a visitation plan, and I can stay in town as long as necessary." He glanced toward Libby, his mouth grim with purpose, before turning to the judge. "Apparently I need to pass some sort of test. Of fatherhood, I guess. So be it. I've been passing tests all my adult life. And I'll do anything you ask in order to have my daughter back."

The judge smiled, a man-to-man smile. The knot in Libby's stomach tightened. Nate Perry had obviously said what the judge wanted to hear. Marta might lack the instinct for dealing with Wyatt, but Nate had it.

What would Sara think about all this? Libby had no idea. For the first time since she'd met him, Libby tried very hard to judge Nate objectively. There was no doubt that the man was prepared to go to great lengths to get his daughter back. Even his apparently big-business dealings in Chicago would be put on hold. What other steps would he take? Libby wondered.

Would Sara like him? He was rich. From a big city. With a lurch, Libby remembered the horseback-riding lessons Sara wanted so badly. If Nate ever heard about his daughter's wish, Sara would be learning the feel of the English saddle within a day. How could any ten-year-old girl resist?

"I need to talk to you," she said to Cam in a low voice. "Might we have a moment, Judge?"

"Of course. This is a shock to your client. A year ago, there was nobody for this girl. Without Libby, Sara would have been in the foster-care system. And now we learn she has a father." The judge shook his head. "I'll leave you to talk. Try to come up with a visitation plan. If you can't,

I'll order one when I come back." The judge rose and left the room, shutting the old oak door behind him.

"What do I have to do?" Libby whispered as soon as Wyatt had left.

"I don't know," Cam admitted. "You know how much the judge hates to be crossed. He's already decided Marta's a pain, so if we're cooperative about visitation, I think we'd have a better chance at the final custody hearing. It'll buy us some time. I'll look into this guy. We might uncover shady business practices. Or maybe he's a woman- izer...keeps bad company...not a good influence for Sara."

Libby glanced across the table, feeling sick to her stom- ach. She didn't know about business practices, but Nate didn't look like the kind of man who lacked female com- panionship. After all, in the waiting room she'd been charmed by the guy. And she'd thought herself immune to charmers.

She looked more closely at him, trying to see under the surface of the polished businessman. He was sitting there, waiting. Not in conference with his attorney, not looking over his papers, just waiting.

Nate caught her glance. "Well?"

Cam looked up. "Do you want to propose something with regard to visitation?"

Marta started to speak, but Nate cut her off. "No. What- ever Ms. Jamieson decides is fine." He hesitated. "The thing is, a child belongs with her real parent, and I've got plans—" He stopped, started again. "Ms. Jamieson, you know her better than I do. I'll defer to your judgment. I don't want to hurt Melissa."

At his words, Libby was suddenly ashamed. Nate *was* Sara's father, and even if he hadn't seen his daughter in eight years, he'd have strong feelings for her, wouldn't he? After all, she considered Sara her daughter, and Nate's legal challenge had brought out every mother-bear, protective instinct she had.

And didn't Sara deserve to know her father?

"I'll never relent on the custody case," she said. "I love Sara, and I'm convinced she's better off with someone she knows, in a town she's familiar with."

"But visitation?" Nate said.

"Yes."

At the one word, Nate Perry smiled—a slow smile that lit his blue eyes and took Libby's already twisted insides and tied them in knots so tight she was afraid they'd never unravel.

NATE NEEDED a place to live in Harborside, and he figured he might as well be right on the water. He parked at one of the state parks at the edge of the lake, and checked over the small list of houses for rent the real-estate agent had given him. Looking out past the dock, he watched the water. Lake Erie was shallow, and its waters were rougher than Lake Michigan's. And the islands in the distance appeared more numerous. Erie was legendary for its fast-forming storms. Nate had already picked up a chart in town. He intended to learn the waters as soon as possible. Sailing was his passion, so if he was going to stay in Harborside for a while, he was going to sail.

He chewed over his list. There were cottages on the fringes of Harborside, but most were used only seasonally, and were therefore not adequately heated. Besides, few would have electrical systems that could handle his computer, copier and fax machine. There was a restored Victorian mansion for rent in town. Nate had considered it, thinking the place might impress Judge Wyatt. But he really wanted something on the water.

He loved the water. When he was a kid, he'd walk down

by Lake Michigan, hands in his pockets, the wind blowing off the lake buffeting his body. He'd watch the sailboats—white sails, rainbow sails—and he'd think about the people who lived in the glittering towers overlooking the water. And he'd dreamed. Oh, how he'd dreamed.

Now he had his own condo at one of Chicago's prestigious addresses—a complex he'd developed—and he had his own sailboat at the yacht club. On the water he felt free and loose.

If he had a home on the water, he could teach Melissa to sail.

There was one more place to consider. From the car window, Nate saw it in the distance—a condominium, a white sugar cube that stood very close to the water's edge. Bittersweet Point, the developer had called it. The place must have been bitter, because after building only one two-unit structure, the developer had gone bankrupt.

It was a familiar scenario. Real-estate development was a risky game and the stakes were high. Huge amounts of money were made and lost. Bankruptcy happened frequently, and unexpectedly. A number of Nate's colleagues who, one month would be attending every party, supporting the ballet, providing scholarships for ghetto kids, would suddenly lose everything. And when they lost their money, their wives and girlfriends left, too. Nate had seen that situation many times. Nothing survived.

Nate put the rental car in drive. The joke among the high rollers of Chicago real estate was that on every deal you "bet the farm."

Nate no longer bet the farm. As soon as he could stop taking such big risks, he had. But those first years had been scary as hell. No wonder he'd been such a lousy husband and father. He'd worked around the clock, scared to death that he'd lose everything, including his family. He'd been even more terrified that he found the game too enjoyable, that somehow he craved the excitement of being in a business where everything was on the line. That he'd be like his father.

Hell. He'd been so preoccupied with his thoughts that he'd passed the overgrown access road to Bittersweet Point. He pulled over and swung the car into a U-turn.

The gravel access road twisted among the trees. The trees here were smaller than those a few miles inland, deprived of nourishment in the sandy soil, bent into sinewy submission by the wind. Their bark was wet from a recent rain, branches glistening black against a sharp blue sky. Twining through the undergrowth were the bittersweet vines. The bittersweet had been picked at by birds. But here and there were flashes of brilliant orange.

Automatically, almost without realizing that he was doing it, Nate began to weigh the site's attributes. He broke through the trees onto a wide, rough beach. Getting out of the car, he walked to the water's edge.

The beach faced a tiny cove, and on the opposite shoreline were shabby, comfortable homes. Melissa lived in one of them with Elizabeth Jamieson. Marta had obtained the address from the judge's office. It was the third house. You couldn't miss it. Who would put that shade of blue trim with that butter-yellow house? Libby Jamieson didn't follow the ivory/taupe/slate color scheme that his decorators were all slaves to. There was a clothesline out in her backyard, and it was hung with towels and sheets, in a brilliant rush of color that reminded him of the twenty-thousand-dollar antique Amish quilt that hung in the lobby of his condo in Chicago.

In contrast, the sugar cube at his back was stark and ugly, a blight on the unpretentious beach. If he rented this horror, he could sit behind the windows of his living room and look across the cove and wonder what his daughter was doing every minute of every day.

And wonder about her caretaker, Elizabeth Jamieson. Libby, they all called her.

When he'd first met her, Nate had been instantly attracted. He'd always been partial to redheads, and Libby's coppery hair had been a flyaway halo around her face. She wasn't beautiful. Pretty, but definitely not beautiful. These days, he had his pick of beautiful women, and every time he had a beautiful woman on his arm, it proclaimed to the world that he was somebody. And her clothes! What a contrast to the sophisticated, very expensive up-to-the-minute fashions his Chicago women friends wore. He smiled, remembering Libby's too-bright skirt.

Then he remembered her confession about forgetting to buy stockings, and he chuckled aloud. At her comment, he'd had to physically restrain himself from a detailed perusal of her legs.

Nate picked up a stone and whipped it out over the water, trying to make it skip. But it sank like a...stone. God, now he was reduced to dwelling on clichés and smiling over a frizzy-haired, small-town woman.

Okay, so he was attracted. He wasn't about to act on the attraction. Libby Jamieson was the enemy, whether or not he imagined that she looked at him with sympathy, whether or not she had agreed to allow him visitation with Melissa.

Just before she left the courthouse, she'd given him a school picture of Melissa, and Nate had felt his throat tighten painfully. They'd been arranging the next month of his life, careful not to look too directly at each other. She'd hesitated, then asked him to wait a minute. Blushing, she'd chattered inanely while she rummaged in the funny-looking satchel she carried.

Finally, she'd found her wallet and extracted something.

"Here, this is for you," she'd said softly as she'd handed the small snapshot to him. "I thought you might like to have Sara's picture."

He'd taken the photograph, so overcome at the unexpected gesture that he hadn't even managed a thank-you. It was the first likeness he'd seen of his daughter since she was two and a half years old.

He'd been stunned at the changes eight years had brought. Of course, he'd known Melissa wasn't two and a half anymore, but... And his daughter was so beautiful, she took his breath away. Her face was less round than he remembered, her hair straighter. But she still had those blue eyes. "Sara Clark" was embossed in gold script under the photo.

Brought abruptly to the present, his mouth twisted. Sara. He whispered the name, wondering if Eve had picked it or if some anonymous government bureaucrat had chosen his daughter's new name. Well, Sara didn't know she'd ever been Melissa, so Nate had best get used to the idea that she probably would want to be called Sara.

There was plenty to get used to.

This cold white condo, which he'd rent. This town, so small and out-of-the-way that he hadn't been sure if his cellular telephone would work. The fact that, contrary to his dreams, he wasn't going to be able to just sweep Melissa—Sara—up into his arms and take her back to Chicago.

And he'd have to get used to dealing with Libby Jamieson, because, like it or not, she was important in Sara's life.

The real-estate agent had said she'd leave a key under the mat on the deck. The two units were side by side, with matching decks that touched each other and were separated only by a wooden privacy fence. Nate headed toward the building.

"Hello!"

Nate stopped, startled, and turned toward the sound.

A blond boy, maybe fifteen or sixteen, sat on the deck of the second condo. Nate peered up at him, over the solid wood railing. The kid was smiling.

"Hello," Nate said politely, unhappy at being disturbed. He hadn't thought to ask if the place next door was rented.

"Are you renting this place?" the kid asked.

"Maybe."

"Cool!" The boy smiled. "You'll really like it here. The guy who was building these things was going to build like a hundred more, but he never did. I heard you drive in, and I almost said something to you, but you went right down to the beach. You didn't come up here, like anybody else would. So I watched you. You've got a good arm." He stopped. "With the stone," he explained.

Nate headed for "his" deck. "The stone sank."

"Whatever," the kid said cheerfully.

"Whatever," Nate repeated, not wanting to encourage the boy's chatter.

"Why don't you come over? My mom would make you coffee."

"Thanks, but—"

"She's nice-looking."

Nate gave a mental groan. Just what he needed. A talkative, matchmaking kid next door with a nice-looking mother. Now that he was on a level with the teenager, he glanced toward him and froze in shock. The boy was in a wheelchair. A blanket was over his knees, and a few pages from a sketch pad in his lap fluttered in the wind.

The kid grinned at him. "Didn't notice at first that I'm in this chair, did you?"

"No," Nate said honestly, startled at how easily the boy spoke of his disability.

"Man, that is so cool. Whenever you meet someone, you

have to deal with it. They look at you, but not *at* you. But we were talking before you noticed, so you couldn't think anything about it. You sure were chewing over something deep." He paused. "So, you were going to blow me off and go inside, weren't you? But now that you see I'm in a wheelchair, you'll feel like you have to stay and talk." He looked very pleased with himself.

Nate felt a flush light his cheekbones. He shoved his hands into his pockets. The kid was perceptive, that was for sure. He settled for introducing himself. "I'm Nate Perry."

"Trevor Samms. You got a wife?"

Back to that already! But the damn thing of it was, Nate actually felt himself smiling. "No wife."

Trevor waved a hand in the air. "Terrific. Sure you don't want that coffee?"

"Trevor, you and I might be neighbors. We'll get along a lot better if you understand I'm not interested in marriage."

"Who said you were? And even if you *were* married, you could still look. I hear a guy never stops looking unless he's dead."

Nate's mind immediately conjured an image of Libby. Sure, he looked, but he'd never marry again. His four-year marriage had been hell enough that he hadn't been tempted to marry again. Not once in the nine years since his divorce. He lifted the mat, but the key wasn't there. Damn. Before he knew it, he'd be stuck having coffee with the good-looking Mom Next Door. Not that Nate didn't feel sorry for the kid. Trevor probably was lonely. But Nate had his own problems, and plans to make.

He straightened, conscious of Trevor watching him. "No key," he said, though he questioned why he was offering any explanation.

Trevor shrugged. "Mrs. McCurdy forgets things. Not exactly God's gift in real-estate agents." He gave Nate another one of his two-hundred-watt smiles. "To continue the inquisition, you've got no wife, but have you got kids?"

Until Nate had told his story to his attorney and the judge, only a handful of people knew he was a father. And then he'd had to fill out all the personal and financial information the court had required. He felt his mouth harden. "Look, Trevor—"

"Call me Trev. Now, have you got kids? A cute daughter you'd like to keep out of my evil clutches?"

"I have a daughter. Her name's Sara," Nate said shortly.

"Does she live with you or your ex-wife?"

Nate pulled out his car keys. He'd skip the tour. He already had a good idea of what the place was like inside, anyway. "If I'm going to live here, we've got plenty of time for all these questions, don't you think?"

The kid's nose wrinkled. "Sure. Hey, that's right. You and me, man. I just know we're going to be friends."

Not likely, Nate thought. Was everybody in Harborside so nosy? Well, it didn't make any difference. He'd be back in Chicago before he had a chance to get to know anybody except Sara. And that was just as well. Nate had always done best when he'd kept his eye squarely on the task at hand.

And he always, always went it alone.

CHAPTER THREE

THE THREE OF THEM gathered in Libby's living room. Sara had picked up on the tension in the air, and sat very close to Libby on the sofa. Across from her, Nate sat in a high-backed wicker chair. His broad shoulders covered all the curlicues on the back. The chair itself had groaned alarmingly when he'd settled himself into it.

Nate's gaze was intent. It had seldom left his daughter's face, as if he wanted to memorize every line of nose and chin.

Libby said nothing. She had wanted to be here when he told Sara that he was her father. She had no idea how Sara would react. Heywood hadn't been much of a father, and maybe Sara would welcome this handsome stranger with the intense blue eyes, a man who looked so much like her. But Libby was damned if she'd make it easier for Nate to tell his story. After all, this man had the power to change her and Sara's lives forever.

Now Nate sat forward, his knees apart, his hands clasped between them, his eyes on his daughter.

He cleared his throat. "I don't know what Ms. Jamieson—Libby—has told you about me, but..."

"Nothing," Libby said quietly.

"Nothing?" His gaze slid to hers momentarily.

"Just before you came, I explained that you're interested in Sara's adoption, and you want to tell her about that interest and what it might mean for all of us.'' She tried to keep the censure out of her voice.

''Well.'' Nate cleared his throat again. He looked down at his hands. But when he began, his voice was stronger, surer, than Libby had expected. ''You see, Sara, ten years ago, I had a daughter. Her name was Melissa. Her mother and I didn't get along, and we divorced. But I saw my daughter as often as I could because I loved her very much.'' He looked into Sara's eyes, as if willing her to believe that fact.

''So?'' Sara asked rudely. Libby forgave her lack of manners. The girl's back was rigid. Libby took her hand.

''You're that little girl, Sara. Your name used to be Melissa Perry. You're my daughter.''

For a moment the silence was unbearable. Sara did nothing. Then she whirled in her seat to face Libby. ''That's not true.'' She looked terrified as her gaze flicked from Nate to Libby. ''My father is...my father was Heywood Clark.''

Libby put her arm around Sara and held her close. The child felt small and fragile and her shoulders quivered. ''It's true, Sara. Your mom was Julia Clark, but Heywood was your stepfather.''

Sara pulled back to look at her. Her face was so pale that every freckle stood out. A kind of strangled giggle came out of her throat.

Nate spoke again. ''It's a long story. God, that sounds dumb, but—I rehearsed what I would say, but I just couldn't quite imagine telling you, so...'' His voice lowered, softened. ''You're my daughter,'' he repeated, and there was a kind of desperation in his voice.

Libby felt a twinge in her heart.

Sara frowned. ''You can't be my father. How can you? You never even lived with us.'' She turned to Libby. ''My mother never told me anything about this, and she would have said something, wouldn't she?''

Libby took Sara's other hand, so that she held them both. ''I know this is hard to understand, but Cam and Judge Wyatt have checked out what Nate says, and it's true. Nate is your father.''

''And I love you,'' Nate added. He started to stand, as if to move toward her.

''No!'' Sara cried, shrinking into the back of the sofa.

''Okay,'' he agreed immediately, sinking into his chair again with an absurd little squeak of wicker. His mouth settled into a grim line.

For a moment, nobody said anything. The three of them sat in a frozen tableau, Libby and Sara together, Nate across the room. Then Nate explained about the witness protection program, about how he'd thought all these years that he had been keeping Sara safe by staying away.

His story still felt unreal to Libby. And if it felt that way to her, how must it feel to Sara? And how frightened she must be. She'd had so little stability until this past year. Libby had had no idea, before Sara had started telling her things a few months ago, just how rough life had been for the little girl.

Nate finally finished. ''I know you'll have questions for me, and I'll answer every one.'' He smiled a little, more a nervous gesture than an expression of warmth. ''I promise to tell you the truth.''

''I don't have any questions,'' Sara said, her chin coming up.

''Okay,'' Nate said again, carefully.

''Wait.'' Sara took one quick look at Libby. ''I do have a question. Why are you here?'' Her tone made it clear that she could think of no good reason.

"Because I want you back, to live with me. I want for us to be a family again."

There was a breathless pause as the full import of what he was saying settled over Sara. Then she stood. "I don't want to live with you. No way. *No way*." Her wide eyes sought Libby's. "I don't have to, do I?"

Libby didn't know how to answer, to be both reassuring and truthful. "I want you to stay with me, and I've told the judge that. He's the one who'll decide. But for now, everybody thinks you ought to get to know your father." She had a harder time saying her next words. "For you to give him a chance."

"Is that what you want?"

No, Sara. What I want is for Nate Perry to go away and leave us here, together in Harborside, with my house, my shop and my friends, where nobody's ever given a thought to the witness protection program and fathers don't come out of nowhere demanding their daughters. "What I want," she said instead, "is to make the best of a difficult situation. I want you to stay with me, and Nate wants you, too. You see, baby, everybody wants you, so no matter what happens, someone will be there for you."

Across the room, Nate cleared his throat. "I wanted you to come back to Chicago with me right away, but the judge had other ideas. Now I can definitely see he was right. We should take some time, get to know each other. I have a plan—"

"Forget it," Sara cut in. A red spot had appeared on each cheek. "The judge will decide, and *you* have plans, and Libby says it's okay that you want me, and I thought *she* wanted me, and you're nobody, *nobody*..." Her mouth wobbled as she stared at Nate. "And I wish you would go back where you came from and..." She stopped, obviously searching for the worst word she could think of. "Or you can go to...to hell."

Libby was on her feet, reaching out. "Sara—"

"Leave me alone!" Sara stormed from the room, and Libby could hear her pounding feet on the wooden stairs, and the crash of her bedroom door slamming.

A long silence settled over the two adults. Finally, Libby rose. "You'll have to excuse me. I need to try to talk to her."

He rose, too, but didn't respond. Instead he turned to look out the window. His profile was perfect, but it might have been carved from stone. His shoulders were high, held almost too high, as if he was braced for another blow.

Libby left him to go upstairs, her heart heavy. Just a few days ago, life had seemed so good. Standing in the hallway outside Sara's room, she knocked, and when there was no answer, tried the door. It didn't give. Sara had never locked the door before.

"Go away," Sara said from behind the closed door.

"Can I come in? We need to talk, sweetheart."

"We already talked. And *he* wants to take me away and you don't care if I go."

"That's not true." Tears pricked the back of her eyelids. "I was trying to be fair, that's all, and I didn't mean for you to think for a second that I don't care. I want you very, very much. I love you. Do you remember when I told you that you were like my very own daughter?" She had said that last when she'd given Sara the little blue topaz heart for her birthday that the girl always wore around her neck.

The old lock grated, and Sara wrenched the door open. "Is that true?"

"Oh, yes."

Sara threw herself into Libby's arms and sobbed. And Libby, though she was sure it wasn't a good idea to cry in front of Sara, couldn't stop the tears that coursed down her own cheeks.

Suddenly, Libby thought of Nate. She hadn't heard him leave the house, and now she imagined him downstairs, waiting. What was he still doing in her living room? Hadn't he realized that his plan had failed and it was clear that his daughter wanted nothing to do with him?

Maybe he was relieved that he didn't have to deal with this messy scene upstairs. After all, he was the man who'd hired Marta Wainwright of Severn and Coxton to breeze into Harborside and turn her and his daughter's life upside down.

After a few minutes, Sara's sobs turned to sniffles. Libby smoothed a lock of Sara's hair and gave the top of her head a quick kiss. "Listen, sweetheart, we'll talk some more. Let you get used to things. Maybe have Cam tell us what to expect when this finally goes to court. Would you like that?"

Her features solemn, her cheeks tear-stained, Sara pulled back a notch and nodded. "It's just...I'm in the play at school and in *Fiddler on the Roof* this summer. And you said I could stay forever." She swallowed. "I'm...scared. My dad...he got drunk and stuff. I mean my old dad... Oh, Lib—" Her voice caught. "I don't even know what to call that man who says he's my father."

"I know," Libby said softly. "You've got a lot to get used to, but you'll have plenty of time. The judge has given us all lots of time. And for now, why don't you call him Nate?"

For some reason, knowing what to call her father seemed to calm Sara.

Libby added, "Nate might not be anything like your old dad, if you give him a chance. But right now, we have to decide some things about your...Nate. He's still downstairs. Do you want to talk to him, or should I tell him to come back some other time?''

''Some other time.'' The words were whispered.

''Well, I guess I'd better go tell him that. Will you be okay up here?''

When Sara nodded, Libby sighed and headed for the stairs. For a man who loved his daughter, Nate had managed to make her miserable. Maybe if he realized how miserable she was, he'd go. Maybe all the way back to Chicago.

He was waiting for her at the bottom of the stairs. ''Is she all right?'' he asked immediately.

Libby nodded. ''I think so. Your coming here was a shock, but she'll be fine. I'll talk to her some more. After you leave.''

''I planned exactly what to say to her. But somehow, I never expected her to hate me.''

Libby hesitated. She had no reason to offer this man any comfort. Or any hope. ''Right now, she's just confused and scared. You'll have to show her you're different from Heywood.''

He raked a hand through his hair. ''You blame me for upsetting her.'' The words were weary.

Libby was silent. Who else was to blame?

''There was no way to tell her gently,'' he said. ''I knew my news would shock her, but what choice did I have? She has a father. Would it be better if that knowledge were kept from her?''

''I don't know.''

He nodded. He was standing so close to her in the little entryway. Libby would have liked to step back, but she couldn't do that because the stairs were right at her heels. Nate was just so...large. Her house had been built with enough nooks and crannies to satisfy her love of shapes and forms. Now every part of the space seemed too small.

"You must hate me," he said abruptly.

"No," she said, and it was the truth. She ought to hate him. But in truth, she wasn't sure what she felt. She was afraid of his legal power. He was Sara's father and he had money. He also made her uneasy with his intensity and determination. He was obviously stubborn, and she, as a determined and rather stubborn woman herself, understood just how single-minded the type could be.

But she didn't hate him. She couldn't hate someone who cared about his daughter that much, even if what he was doing was selfish and unfair.

She swallowed. "I think in time Sara will be willing to see you."

"You think?"

Hope sprang into his eyes. The last thing she should do was make things easy for him. But she said, "Why don't you come for dinner tomorrow night? We could rent a video or something."

"I don't want you to go to any trouble." His body was taut, as though he was physically restraining himself from showing his gratitude. His eyes were so very blue, she thought suddenly, as blue as the line where the sky met the lake.

"Ah, no trouble. You don't have to have meat, do you?"

"Meat?" He looked startled at the question.

"For dinner, I mean. Do you have to have meat? I'm a vegetarian and I like to make more unusual things, you know, like couscous. Of course, you can't get couscous at the Three Nets Grocery here in Harborside, you have to drive to Toledo, but I have some in the cupboard..." God, she was going on and on again. The man always managed to make her nervous, even when they weren't talking about Sara. *Especially* when they weren't talking about Sara.

"Sure, fine."

"Okay. Well, I guess I'd better check on Sara."

He was standing in her front hall, so only two steps brought him to the front door. Nobody used the front door; everyone came around to the kitchen. But Nate wouldn't know that. Libby reached over to pull open the door. Her hand and his touched the knob at the same time. Both jerked away.

Then Nate opened the door. A sharp, lake-scented breeze rolled into the hallway.

Nate's eyes searched her face. He hesitated for a second, then said, "Look. I just want to know something. Why are you doing this, making things easier for me?"

"The judge wants us to do that. He said we should co-operate for Sara's sake." Libby ignored the voice in her head that said cooking dinner for Nate might be going beyond even Judge Wyatt's expectations.

His face closed immediately, and he nodded slightly to himself. "Of course. You make a meal, and that little fact creeps into your testimony when we go for the hearing. Marta wants a fight. But you, for Sara's sake, invite me over so that my daughter and I can get to know each other, while I'm so unyielding I look like a jerk to the judge—"

"Stop right there." Libby held up her hand. "Let's get one thing straight. I'm making my offer for Sara's sake. The judge is right. She needs to get to know her father, regardless of which one of us she lives with. And I won't have her hurt by you." Now he looked as angry as she was. Fine. Her voice lowered. "And someday, when you do get to know her, maybe you'll explain to your daughter just what makes you so cynical. It's not the world's most attractive fatherly trait."

He yanked at the zipper of his jacket. "Thanks to a woman, I really wouldn't know much about fatherly traits, would I?" None too gently, he pulled the door shut behind him as he stepped out onto the porch.

He didn't trust her. He didn't dare. The more you wanted something, the tougher you had to be. And the only person you could count on was yourself.

THE NEXT MORNING, Nate sat on a red vinyl seat in the Shoreline Diner and poked his fork into one of his sunny-side up eggs. The eggs were delicious, the yolks a dark orange. But there was no small-town friendliness in the Shoreline this morning. The waitress had been sullen when she'd taken his order.

"Mr. Perry?"

Nate set down his coffee cup and looked up at the young man in the suit and topcoat who stood next to the booth. "I'm Nate Perry," he replied.

The young man held out his hand deferentially. "I'm Kevin Smithson, vice president of Harborside Savings and Loan. I heard you were in town."

Of course he'd heard, Nate thought as he stood slightly and shook hands. In the week he'd been in Harborside, Nate had discovered that practically everybody he met had heard he was in town and what he was doing there. Nate knew exactly why the waitress had refilled every coffee cup in the Shoreline except his.

And it didn't matter, he assured himself. He didn't make friends easily. Success attracted admirers, but not friends.

"Can I sit with you a minute?" Smithson asked.

"Sure."

The young man slid into the booth opposite and gestured for the waitress. She slapped a jelly ball on a plate for another patron with much more force than necessary. "Got a bee in your bonnet, Phyllis?'' Kevin asked when she finally approached with her coffeepot and order pad.

"Never you mind," she sniffed, her glance pointedly directed at Nate, so he couldn't mistake who she was snubbing. "The usual, Kevin?"

"Naw, make 'em blueberry today."

She finally offered a smile. "Branching out, are we?"

"Karen's after me to eat more fruits and vegetables." Both of them laughed. Kevin gestured to Nate's cup. "Think you forgot to top off that one, Phyl." Phyllis had the good grace to blush as she filled the cup Nate pushed toward her.

"Thanks," Nate said after Phyllis left. "I figured one cup would be my limit today."

The young man smiled in return. "Rough on you, are they?"

Nate felt his mouth tighten. "I can handle it."

"Sure you can." Kevin picked up his cup. "From what I'm hearing, you can handle just about anything."

Suddenly, the man across from Nate didn't look quite so young. There was an intelligence about him, a serious purpose, that made him appear more mature.

Nate took another bite of egg. "So, what's on your mind?"

Kevin sighed. "Bittersweet Point."

"Ah." Nate chewed thoughtfully.

"Maybe you'd like to do a little business while you're here."

As soon as Kevin had mentioned Bittersweet Point, Nate knew what the other man wanted. The bankrupt developer of Bittersweet Point must owe this small-town bank a lot of money. To Harborside Savings and Loan, Nate must look like a savior.

"Not interested," Nate said flatly.

"You don't even know what I'm proposing," Kevin protested.

"I'm here for one thing, and when I get it I'm heading back to Chicago. I don't have the time or inclination to take on a project here, and once I'm in Chicago, I don't want to have to return to Harborside to supervise a development."

Kevin's eyes narrowed slightly. "You might be here longer than you planned, according to what I heard."

"I've already been here longer than I planned." The younger man flushed, and Nate felt unexpectedly sorry he'd snapped at the guy. It wasn't Kevin's fault that Nate was forced to hang around Harborside. He'd already acknowledged that the judge was right. He could hardly drag Sara back to Chicago with him. Especially since she'd made it clear that she wanted nothing to do with him. Suddenly, Nate pushed his plate away. The eggs didn't taste so good, after all.

As always when his emotions threatened, Nate focused on what he was good at. "Look," Nate said. "The site has environmental problems. You'll need an expensive waste-handling system to avoid polluting the lake. And if that damned white cube I'm living in is any indication, you've got aesthetic problems as well. You've got a fabulous, pristine beach in an area of Cape Cod–style homes. Those cubes won't appeal to upscale buyers; that type of client knows when something isn't well integrated to its site."

Kevin's short stack of blueberry pancakes arrived, but he ignored them. Instead, he simply sat back and listened as Nate continued.

"However, as I've driven along the shore, I've noticed how much of the water's edge is taken up with marinas and older homes. Bittersweet Point is one of the last large undeveloped stretches of beach."

Kevin nodded. "Right. Harborside hasn't exactly been on the beaten path of new development—that's gone more toward Catawba Island."

"Of course, you need to look at the demographics of the major urban areas. The Toledo market might be saturated, and you'd need to determine if Bittersweet Point is too far out—" Abruptly, Nate stopped.

"Thought you weren't interested," Kevin finally said, leaning forward. "You could turn this place around, you know. There are environmental problems. Okay. Who better than you to solve those problems? Didn't you win an environmental award?"

Actually, Nate had two of those awards. He'd got them because he'd put money and thought into making his resorts tread as lightly as possible on the vulnerable shoreline of Lake Michigan. And no matter how much he'd told himself that spending the extra money was really good for business, he knew that hadn't been his only reason. Nate needed no reminders that he had a soft spot for the beaches and the water. He couldn't afford a soft spot.

He also couldn't afford the time and energy to undo the mess at Bittersweet Point. He was already trying to run his business by long distance. In Chicago, the Iris Complex was entering a critical phase. And of course, his first priority must be Sara—finding time to get to know the daughter he'd lost so long ago.

"Sorry. I'll pass this time," he said to Kevin.

There was a small silence while the younger man dunked a forkful of pancakes into a puddle of syrup. Finally, Kevin spoke in a thoughtful tone.

"This is an interesting town." He chewed a bite of pancakes. "Harborside's small, and some of our people have to commute to Toledo for a job. Bittersweet Point, done right, could bring a lot of jobs to town."

"Maybe you'll find the right developer closer to home."

"Anyway," Kevin went on as if Nate hadn't spoken, "the townsfolk are very loyal. They'd take kindly to somebody who brought jobs to this community. I'm not saying they'd be more loyal to an outsider than to one of their own, but it wouldn't hurt, if a person wanted something, to have made a few friends, you know?"

Of course, Nate thought. How slow he'd been to catch on to what the other man was offering—a chance to shore up Nate's case with Sara. Surely that was worth some risk. "If you ever need a job and you want to live in Chicago, look me up," he said.

"I take it that's a yes to taking over Bittersweet Point."

"Yes," Nate said.

"Just like that?"

"Just like that." The project *might* make money; Nate hadn't done enough study to be able to tell, yet. But if Bittersweet Point couldn't be built profitably, if they had cost overruns... Nate took a long swig of coffee. Thanks to the Iris Complex in Chicago, he was leveraged more than he liked to be. Nate was no gambler. He wasn't in any trouble, just a little beyond his comfort level regarding short-term cash flow. But Nate knew he had to accept the other man's offer. Sara was the most important thing in his life. And he needed all the help he could get.

"You know," Kevin said abruptly, "everyone around here's worried about Libby. She was born here, and after her mother died, the ladies in town kind of pitched in to help her father raise her. But me, I'm from Toledo, and I've been married before. My daughter lives there with my ex-wife." He paused. "You think I came to see you because of the money the old developer owed the bank. But you're only partly right. I've been thinking, if my ex-wife pulled something, so that I couldn't see my little girl, I just..."

Nate looked into the other man's eyes. He always knew when he was being flattered or built up in a negotiation. This wasn't one of those times. Kevin Smithson actually had a smidgen of understanding about what he was going through. He smiled in gratitude, even though he usually didn't like to show his feelings. But somehow, sitting in a diner in a place he'd never thought to be, it felt all right. He was hungry again.

Nate picked up a slice of cold toast. "Do you have any idea how Libby Jamieson feels about the development?" Why was he asking, anyway? He didn't care what Libby felt about anything.

At the other man's puzzled expression, he added, "Well, I know the back of her house faces Bittersweet Point."

"Well, I'd guess Lib would feel the same as most, glad something's going to be done with that mess."

Nate nodded, relieved. Somehow, to his surprise, he wanted, well, approval from Libby. She was unusual and pretty, and he felt the stir of desire every time he thought about her. If circumstances were different, and if she were willing, they might have acted on that desire. But to seek her approval of himself, of what he did for a living...

That didn't sit right, because Nate Perry needed approval from no one.

CHAPTER FOUR

HE BROUGHT FLOWERS to dinner. Libby blushed as she caught sight of the bundle in his hand. She recognized the distinctive paper wrap. The peach tulips were from her own shop.

Nate held the bouquet against his chest. "I thought Sara might like tulips."

"Oh." Libby blushed more furiously at her mistaken impression that the bouquet was for her. "Sure she would." She gave a light laugh. "And of course I appreciate the business."

"Yours *is* the only flower shop in town." Then he hesitated. "I guess it wasn't too imaginative, to bring her flowers when she probably sees them pretty often. But I didn't know what else she'd like."

Sara didn't see flowers "pretty often." She saw them every day, when she helped out at the shop. But Nate obviously didn't know that. "Well," Libby said, "she doesn't get flowers from her father every day. She'll like them, Nate."

He cleared his throat and held out his other hand. There was a bottle in a paper bag. "And I brought a bottle of wine. You *do* drink wine, don't you?"

"Well, yes." She was puzzled at his tone.

"You don't eat meat," he said by way of explanation. "I thought maybe you were a...a health nut or something, and you wouldn't approve of alcohol."

"I'm not a real health nut. Just a nut, as everyone in town will tell you." She tried a smile on for size. All of a sudden, she was uncomfortable again. And there was no reason to be uncomfortable.

Unexpectedly, he smiled, too. The warmth of it felt as if someone had suddenly turned on a light in the room. With a start, she remembered that moment at the courthouse, when they'd first met and he'd had no idea she was the one trying to adopt Sara. He had charmed her that day. Heck, he'd bowled her over for a moment. But there was no way she could allow that to happen again.

So she said the one thing she knew would kill that incipient warmth. "I'll see if Sara's ready."

He nodded, the smile fading immediately.

Libby ushered him into the living room and headed upstairs. Usually Sara would be downstairs, complaining if dinner was late. But since coming home from the shop today, she'd been holed up in her room.

Sara met her on the landing. "I'm scared," she whispered. She smoothed down her denim skirt. "What'll I say to him?"

"You'll be fine." Libby gave her a quick hug. "We've talked about this. It's just dinner. You were scared when you came to live with me, and sad because of your mom, and everything worked out."

"It worked out okay."

"You'll have to give him a chance." Any animosity Libby felt toward Nate must remain hidden from Sara. If—when—she won the custody suit, Nate would still be a part of Sara's life. Libby owed it to Sara to make getting to know her father as easy as possible.

So she herded a reluctant Sara downstairs. In the living room, Nate had forgone the squeaky rocker to sit on the edge of the sofa. When Sara came into the room, he rose.

"Hello, Sara. You look very pretty." Like an actor in a bad play, he held out the flowers.

Sara came close enough to take them, then backed up a step or two. "Thank you," she said stiffly.

"Tulips," Nate said then, a kind of eagerness in his voice as he nodded toward the flowers.

"Yes. I see that."

"Libby told me you didn't like carnations."

Libby had told him that at the courthouse but given the tension that day, she was surprised he remembered.

Sara said nothing.

"Actually, she said you liked orange tiger lilies, but she didn't have any. I got the tulips at the shop."

"I know. I unpacked them last Saturday and put them in the cooler. It's one of my chores." Sara shrugged.

Nate winced.

It was excruciating to watch Nate's awkward efforts and Sara's refusal to give an inch. Libby knew she needed to do something. "But they're pretty."

Sara tossed her head.

There was a pause. *Do something,* Libby thought. In a moment, Sara would be running for the stairs again.

Before she could think of something to say, Nate moved toward his daughter. Sara flinched. He swallowed, and for a moment Libby thought he was going to touch the girl. But he didn't. "Libby's right. The flowers are pretty. Like you, Sara. You were always pretty. Smart, too."

Sara stared up into his eyes.

Nate's voice dropped. "You said your first words very early. You were an early developer, your mother used to say."

Libby felt her throat swell. So Nate had some memories of his daughter. Certainly not as many memories as Libby had, and not as recent, but... She wondered suddenly if he had been there for his child's birth, if he had held his red, wrinkled baby daughter in his arms and hoped for so much for her.

It took her a moment to realize that the other two weren't speaking. Sara looked as though she might bolt. Nate's mouth was tight; having gone this far, he was obviously out of his depth.

No way were these two ready to be left alone to get to know each other. "Sara, I could use your help with dinner."

"Oh, sure," she agreed with an alacrity that at any other time would be comical in a ten-year-old.

Disappointment flashed across Nate's features.

"You, too, Nate," she invited with a lightness she didn't feel. "How are you with a salad?"

"I don't think there's much to mess up in making a salad. I can handle it."

In the kitchen, she gave him the lettuce while she checked the dish in the oven. She asked Sara to set the table. But the silence was grating. "How about some music," she suggested, poking a disk containing rock oldies into the player on the counter. The bouncy music helped fill the uncomfortable silence.

Sara seemed determined not to talk. Libby asked Nate about his work, then his home in Chicago. When he described his condominium, Libby noted that, although she was pretending not to, Sara was listening.

"Anyway," Nate continued as he washed lettuce under the tap, "I have space at the yacht club for my sailboat."

Libby slid the pan out of the oven. The top looked crusty, although she'd followed her mother's recipe. She set it onto a trivet. "So what kind of boat do you have?" she asked, knowing she sounded falsely bright.

"A beauty." Nate paused for a moment and his voice

unexpectedly softened. A tiny smile touched his lips. "A Quest 30."

Sara stopped, fork in hand, to stare at Nate. Her eyes were round. Harborside was more a power-boating town than a sailing town, but both Sara and Libby knew a thirty-foot Quest was a colossally expensive racing yacht. A couple of kids at Sara's school had fathers who sailed, and in Harborside everybody talked boats. Boats were the true status symbols in town. Libby saw the slowly dawning knowledge on Sara's face that her father was rich. She felt a deep twinge of foreboding.

"That's quite a boat," Libby said, nervously taking note of the obvious. She slipped on her oven mitts again and took the rice medley out of the oven. "Has it got a name?"

There was a pause. In the background, a sixties group sang of falling in love.

"It's got a name," Nate said finally.

Something in his tone seemed strained again. Libby set the casserole down on the counter. Her face was flushed from the oven.

Nate was facing his daughter. The chorus faded out. "I call it the *Melissa*."

"Oh." Sara's breath whooshed out with the one word. "But that...that was my name, wasn't it?"

"Yes."

"Oh," she said again, faintly. Her hand gripped a fork.

Nate gave Libby a questioning glance, a sort of *what now?* Libby shook her head. *Give Sara some time,* she tried to say with her eyes. But she herself was shaken.

She put the food on the table. Sara sat down quickly in a chair across from Nate. That meant the two adults sat together, facing Sara. Libby's kitchen table was a large, scrubbed pine rectangle, so she was sitting at what should be a comfortable distance from Nate. But it wasn't comfortable. In profile, she could see those aristocratic features of his. There was no doubt about it. The man was a work of art.

"Have some rice medley," she said abruptly, pushing the casserole dish his way. A flyaway lock of her hair fluffed up. Impatiently, she tucked it behind her ear.

"Thanks." He eyed the dish doubtfully before spooning a tiny amount onto his plate.

"What's this?" Sara asked, poking her fork into a slice of meat loaf.

"Meat loaf."

"I *know* that. I mean, why'd you make meat loaf?" Sara turned to Nate. "We always have salad and honey-bran rolls when we have rice medley. Libby doesn't make meat." Those were her first voluntary words to her father.

Nate didn't seem to miss the significance of the small exchange. He smiled at his daughter.

The flash of warmth for Sara still lingered in his eyes when he looked at Libby. She blushed to the roots of her hair. Why had she made meat loaf, anyway? She figured Nate probably liked meat for dinner, and he was a guest, that was all. "I thought you might not like rice medley, that was all," she said.

"I'm sure I'll like rice medley. And I like meat, as well. Steak, roast beef..." He looked at Libby. "Meat loaf..."

"McDonald's?" Sara asked hopefully.

"Well, okay, McDonald's."

Sara smiled. Libby might have smiled, too, at the tentative pleasure on Sara's face, but again she had that little flash of foreboding. "Well, the meat loaf's my mom's old recipe. She died when I was a baby, so I like to make things of hers, just to remember her. Only, they don't always turn out. I don't know if she was a bad cook, or if I am." She knew she was chattering, feeling awkward at sharing personal information with Nate.

But as they ate, Sara seemed to thaw noticeably, a couple of times volunteering information to Nate about *Oklahoma!,* her school play. Nate seemed completely focused on his daughter.

But Libby couldn't concentrate. She kept thinking about Nate, wondering what kind of man he was inside and chiding herself for caring.

She started when she realized both Nate and Sara were looking at her. "Sorry, I didn't hear you."

"I said, Sara seems to like the shop," Nate said.

"Yes, she's always been there. She used to come in with her mom, when Julia and I rehearsed our lines for the plays we were in. Then, when the store closed and we had to go to the theater, her father would pick her up."

Oh, Lord, Libby thought with an inner groan as she saw Nate's mouth harden again.

Sara seemed oblivious to the slip. "Now that I'm grown-up I have to do chores."

Nate frowned in earnest now. "Chores? You mean work in the shop?"

"Oh, yes. Every day after school. I have to sweep, and refill the cooler, and dust sometimes, and once Libby made me wash the windows. When I get home, I have to clean my room and everything..." Her voice trailed off dramatically.

"Libby makes you do all this?" Nate sounded stunned. And disapproving.

"Oh, for Heaven's sake." Libby's nerves finally snapped. Now Sara liked her father enough to complain. "Yes, she has a few chores. She's too young to stay alone after school. Besides, I like her with me. And Sara didn't tell you she makes flower arrangements, which she loves to do. And she didn't tell you that when we washed the windows, we had fun—" Libby fell abruptly silent.

Nate stared at them both. "Fun. Washing windows."

Sara shot Libby a look that might have been a belated apology. "Sure. I mean, I guess it was fun."

Nate looked completely mystified. Libby focused on her plate. "Yeah. We were standing on the sidewalk, and it was a warm day and we kind of had a, well, I guess you'd call it a wet-mop fight. We must have looked a real sight. Our clothes wet and clinging..."

Slowly, Libby raised her head, dreading Nate's response. After all, grown women didn't chase kids down the sidewalk brandishing a soapy squeegee. Sara had ducked, laughing, into the doorway of the sporting goods store, her fingers still curled around the handle of a bucket. It was one of Libby's most precious memories, but Nate would never understand. Steeling herself for disapproval, she looked straight into his eyes.

And was flooded with warmth. He wasn't smiling. But his eyes shone with a pure blue flame, bone-deep and primal. The warmth of that gaze spread along her limbs to her toes, to shoot back and settle, low in her belly, in the very heart of her. She started to tremble. And was the first to look away.

Beside her, Libby felt Nate shift. She could sense his surprise, then his discomfort as he turned to his daughter.

Swiftly, he was in control, giving Sara his full attention. Watching them, Libby decided she must have imagined that look of his. There were facts about life that were inviolate. One of them was that men like Nate did not look at women like Libby with, well, sexual desire. Yes, she was imagining things because she'd had fantasies lately about sexy blue eyes and a perfect mouth, and a man who was all wrong for her, in every way possible.

She stood. The meal was over.

Sara stood also, and Libby had to remind her to take her plate and glass to the sink. Nate got up with his. "You don't have to do that," she protested. "I was reminding Sara."

He didn't reply, just helped her clean the table in silence. Sara went upstairs to get a few rocks and shells to show her father. Plate in hand, Nate surveyed the kitchen. "Where's your dishwasher?"

"I don't have one."

"All the antiques and vases and things arranged everywhere and you don't have a dish—"

"Look, enough said. We don't live your kind of life. And it's not as if I'm trying to save these hands or anything." With defiance, she held her hands up for inspection. "They get ruined working with the flowers, anyway. What's a little dishwater?"

With hardly a glance, he went to the table again. Libby automatically turned on the warm water. Nate wasn't interested in her hands, and why should he be? She was sensitive about how they looked, but there was no choice in her line of work. She'd held them up, almost daring him to criticize. He probably had his own nails buffed regularly. But she already knew how different his life was from hers.

"Here." Sara came into the kitchen with a heavy, overflowing box. "Do you like rocks?" She put the box on the table with a thump.

Nate hesitated. "Sure. I like rocks."

"Cool. What's your favorite?"

Again the hesitation. Nate probably couldn't name a single one. Libby couldn't help a mean little smile. "Surely you have favorites, Nate. Which is your favorite igneous rock, which your favorite sedimentary?"

"Which is *your* favorite, Sara?" Nate hadn't missed a beat.

"This iron pyrite. Fool's gold," she said promptly, holding out a glittering stone for his inspection.

"Is there a rock shop in town?" Nate asked.

Sara shook her head. "No, you have to go to Toledo."

"Why don't we do that? Go to Toledo?" Nate's voice was eager. Too eager, but Sara didn't seem to notice. Libby looked across the room, to where the light from her old globe chandelier brought out the blue highlights on two heads of glossy black hair.

Sara put down the fool's gold. "Yes, let's. But could we go to the mall or something? I *love* the mall."

"Sure. The mall. Next Saturday?" He looked to Libby for confirmation. "After chores, of course."

There was no reason to refuse. "Yes," she said, and he smiled again. It wasn't his cool, practiced smile, but a real one. Almost more powerful for its rarity.

Later, as soon as Sara had gone to bed, Nate rose to leave. If Libby had needed any reminder that Sara was the reason he was here, she had it in his eagerness to leave. Well, it was for the best. She knew she was susceptible to sophisticated charmers. And her best friend, Tina Samms, had married one, and the jerk had left her high and dry years ago. So Libby should be glad that Nate was giving her a reality check. She ought to be grateful; instead she felt a twinge of disappointment.

"Thank you," he said, shrugging into a leather jacket. "Your dinner was delicious." In his tone, she heard the studied charm of the Chicago millionaire, and suddenly, she couldn't stand it.

"Come on. You hated the rice medley and I know the meat loaf was ghastly."

There was a long pause. "But your table was...pretty,

with all those little colored bottles. You're making this so easy for me—for Sara—when you could be..." He shoved his hands in his pockets. His voice had deepened, and she had no doubt of his sincerity now. "Thank you for that."

She swallowed and nodded.

"Look. Why don't you come with us Saturday? Let me buy you a pizza. No pepperoni." He smiled that damn devastating smile. He added quickly, "I want to buy some things for Sara. I never have, you know. And I don't know her sizes, what she likes."

Of course, she thought. He wanted her there for Sara, and to make things easier for him.

"Okay."

"Good."

At the door, Nate lingered. "Would you mind if I came over tomorrow? I'd like to see Sara after school. I know the plan was Wednesdays and Saturdays, but..."

Libby hesitated, wondering what would be best for Sara. But this evening had gone so well—better than she'd hoped— "Okay. Come whenever you can."

He nodded. There was another pause. Then, "Look, I just want to know," he said, "why you're doing this for me. If Sara gets to know me..." His voice trailed off, but she knew what he was going to say. If Sara got to know him, his claim for custody would be all the stronger.

"For Sara." It was for Sara, and only for Sara, she reminded herself.

"Really? Well, I just..." His voice trailed off again. In the dim light he looked oddly vulnerable. That vulnerability touched her, because while she armored herself against the Chicago millionaire, she couldn't seem to armor herself against the father, or the man.

"People don't do things for such selfless reasons." At the bleakness in his tone, Libby's heart ached. In Nate's world, that must be true. Libby pressed the tips of her fingers into her own palm, against the calluses there. She had her flowers, she had Sara, she had so many memories. She had a *life*.

She swallowed. "Harborside isn't like that. I'm not like that. I love Sara too much to be selfish. And I think you love Sara too much to be selfish, too."

He gave a harsh chuckle. "Most people would hardly describe me as selfless."

She hesitated. "Don't get me wrong. I'll take you to court over Sara, because she's become my daughter, and I'm convinced she's better off in Harborside. After all, what do you have to offer her in Chicago?"

"Ballet, singing, all the lessons she wants. The arts. The best schools."

"Everything money can buy."

He didn't seem to notice her sarcasm. "Right."

"Will you have time for her, Nate? You've got your business, and you'll be a single parent. When you're in Chicago, can you make time?"

He looked confused, and that shocked her. Surely he realized that his life-style would change dramatically if he had Sara. She'd given him food for thought. But now something in that rare less-than-sure expression made her add, "I know you love her. I do, too. Whatever happens, I'll do what's best for her."

He swallowed. "I appreciate that. I do appreciate what you've done for her."

She nodded. The tension between them was thick. She looked up, into his eyes, into a face that was all shadows and angles.

Unexpectedly, his hand came up, stilled, then hovered in the air. He leaned forward slightly.

Dear Lord, he was going to kiss her! Of its own volition,

Libby felt her body sway slightly, hungering for Nate's touch.

He didn't kiss her. Instead, he dropped his hand to his side, opened the door and went through it into the night. Libby shut the door and leaned against it. She was light-headed and dry-mouthed, and scared to death at her own response to nothing more than a look and a gesture that meant...nothing. *Fool's gold,* she said to herself. The man was fool's gold—glitter on the outside, hard as iron within.

TREVOR SAMMS SCOOTED his wheelchair around and pulled open the refrigerator door, then reached into its specially made shallow recesses for a can of soda. The light from the refrigerator dimly illuminated the room, so he left the door open to light his way as he searched through the cupboards for some chips or pretzels or packaged cupcakes or maybe all three. He was starving.

"Trevor? Is that you?"

His mother was silhouetted above him, in her nightgown, leaning on the balcony railing that overlooked the kitchen below.

Trevor smiled. Who else would it be, with the fridge door open? "It's a madman, come for onion dip," he said in a stagey whisper. "Then he'll hold us at gunpoint, till we break and tell him where we've stashed the gold..."

"Cut it out." Tina Samms tried to sound stern, but Trevor knew she liked his sense of humor. Most of the time. He decided to press his luck, and changed his tone, making it deep. "No, I'm the guy next door. Nate Perry. Handsome, rich, come calling..."

"Trevor." Now her voice contained a clear warning.

Trevor stopped. It was fun to bait his mom sometimes, but she didn't like the guy next door. She spoke to Mr. Perry, but only when she had to. It embarrassed Trevor, how his mom snubbed their neighbor, because he could tell Mr. Perry was aware of it. 'Course, he could see why his mom didn't like him. Mr. Perry was going to develop the Point, and then they wouldn't be able to afford to live here. And Mr. Perry was trying to take Sara away from Libby, who was his mother's best friend.

Libby didn't like Nate Perry either. He'd heard her say that to his mom, when they thought he was in his room with his headphones on. Libby had got mad about the condos too, said Nate was being self-centered. Trevor had listened, because for some reason he wanted to know everything about Nate Perry.

Libby had shown his mother all the stuff Mr. Perry had filed with the court, and his mom had kind of choked and said he gives about four times as much to charity as she earned.

"Do you want some company?" His mom was starting down the stairs.

"Naw. You've got a lot to do in the morning." His mom was making all the costumes for the community-theater production of *Fiddler on the Roof.* She made her living doing alterations mostly, but Libby made sure she always got the orders for the costumes at the theater. And she covered Country Tastes on Saturdays so Libby could take the day off.

"You've got school in the morning," she returned.

"I won't be up long. Honest." Lots of times he had trouble sleeping. But, though he suspected his mom was aware of it, he didn't feel like talking about it.

"Well..." She hesitated.

"Go to bed, Mom. Really."

She hesitated a second longer, then turned away. From her bedroom doorway, she yelled, "Close that refrigerator door!"

Trevor slammed the door real hard so she'd hear it from upstairs. Then he piled his lap with chips, a container of dip, Oreos and cupcakes, not bothering with a plate or bowl. He could reach the dishes, though, if he wanted to. Unlike their last house, he could reach everything in the kitchen, because originally the place had been built for this super-rich old guy in a wheelchair.

Handicapped accessible, the For Rent advertisement had said. And the condo was a great place. He and his mom had known going in that when the right developer came along, they would have to move. Their unit would become part of a large complex and would eventually be sold. Now Nate Perry was that developer. In a town like Harborside, everybody knew who he was, and they all knew things would change at Bittersweet Point. Only really wealthy people would be able to afford to live here.

His mom was mad about that, and blamed Nate Perry, although she'd admitted Mr. Perry wasn't personally responsible. He was just a businessman.

Trevor knew who was really to blame. Jonathan Samms. His father had left them six months after Trevor's accident, and he hadn't seen his son since, or paid a dime of child support. So he was the one ultimately responsible for the fact they'd had to rent the place before this, so small, with such tight turns and doorways that his mom had had to help him get on the toilet.

Most of the time Trevor didn't mind being stuck in the wheelchair. He'd had four years to adjust as the counselors called it. And everybody, including him, thought he'd adjusted just fine. But he'd silently hated the chair, really and truly hated the chair, when his mom had had to help him in the john. He made jokes about her strength, when she was grunting with the effort of helping him move, but he hated that part when she saw him...bare. He knew who was really responsible for *that*, too.

Trevor would sure like to tell his dad... What? Maybe he'd ask him stuff, instead. Stuff like why wasn't Mom good enough for you, and why didn't you wait around to see how good I can handle the chair, and why...? Sighing, he pulled on his sweatshirt. Then he stuck his pop can between his thighs and opened the sliding glass doors to the deck. He wouldn't get a chance to tell his father anything anytime soon. Nobody knew where Jonathan Samms lived.

The deck was warmer due to an early-spring heat spell. For a few moments Trevor sat at the edge of the deck, watching the dark water.

"So. Can't sleep?"

Startled, Trevor glanced next door. Sitting on the steps of his own deck, with his feet on the sand below, was Nate Perry. Mr. Perry had both hands wrapped around a bottle of beer.

"You startled me," Trevor said.

"Like you did me, that first time."

Trevor felt himself begin to grin. "You figured you owed me."

"Something like that."

Trevor was kind of in awe of Nate Perry, because he was a rich guy from out of town who had cool high-tech stuff. But he liked the guy, too. He'd started conversations with Nate Perry a time or two. Mr. Perry didn't talk much, but he didn't blow Trevor off either.

And the way he'd come back for his kid after all those years... Well, Trevor had got a big lump in his throat when he'd heard that story, and had to blink his eyes real hard. His mom might be upset because of Libby, but all Trevor could think was one sentence, over and over. *He came back. He came back.*

"I just came out to look at the way the moon makes the waves all silvery," Trevor said, and then he felt dumb because he thought that wasn't something he should admit. He should talk about cars or something, not sound like a Hallmark card.

"Me too."

"Oh." That made Trevor feel good somehow. "I just like looking at the water."

"Yeah," Mr. Perry said. "I know."

The way Mr. Perry said that, Trevor just knew this big-time rich guy liked the way the moon went in and out among the clouds and glowed on the waves. Trevor was feeling better and better. He didn't know any other grown-up guys well except Mr. Murphy who always whined if he didn't get the leads in the community plays, and Mr. Carlyle, who used to mow his mom's lawn.

"I don't suppose," he ventured boldly, "you've got another beer on you."

"Oh, I don't think so, Trevor." Trevor thought he heard the hint of a smile in Mr. Perry's voice.

"Just seeing how far I could push you." Trevor popped the top on his soda can. "Mom won't let me have one, either. Want to come over for some chips? Dip? Cupcakes? There're two cupcakes in the package." It would be so cool if Mr. Perry came over.

"Thanks. I'm okay right here."

"Oh." Some of the magic went out of the night. But Mr. Perry didn't go inside after that, as Trevor had half suspected he might.

For a few moments they were quiet, each on his own deck. Trevor figured they were hanging out, the way he'd seen grown-up guys do, clustered around one pickup truck or another on Raft Street, just standing around, a foot on the bumper, beer cans on the hood.

Trevor wondered what a guy like Nate Perry thought about on nights he couldn't sleep. Maybe he thought about Sara. Or maybe he only thought about his business in Chicago, or developing Bittersweet Point. Suddenly, he burned with curiosity. "When you can't sleep, do you think about her?" he asked out of the blue.

"What?" He saw the beer bottle in Mr. Perry's hand hit the sandy beach without a sound.

His reaction puzzled Trevor. "Well, I know Sara's your daughter."

"Oh. Sara."

"Who did you think I meant?"

"Nobody in particular."

His mom used that tone of voice when she wasn't going to tell him something no matter how he pestered. Trevor frowned and drained the last of his soda. "Sara's okay. I mean, for a little girl." Sara talked too much, but she wasn't bad. And Trevor tried very hard not to be jealous of her because she had a father who wanted her so bad he was going to court to get her. Heck, he'd have to be jealous of just about every kid he knew, if he wanted to be jealous of kids with dads.

Nate Perry couldn't be his dad. And he didn't want a dad. One had been more than enough. But Mr. Perry could be kind of a...friend. Trevor frowned as he used his teeth to open the package of cupcakes. That wasn't the word he wanted. Well, maybe it could just be more like a big brother. What did they call it on TV? Male bonding. Yeah, that was it.

"You could call me Trev." He'd made the offer when he'd first met Mr. Perry, but Mr. Perry still called him Trevor, like everyone else. But Trev sounded more masculine somehow.

"Okay. Trev it is."

Cool, Trevor thought. Awesome.

CHAPTER FIVE

NATE'S EUPHORIA about Sara's agreement to go shopping lasted only until he was in the entrance of Libby's house. When he arrived, Sara's greeting was subdued. Libby told her rather sharply to change her jacket for something warmer, so he guessed they'd had a few words about the trip already this morning. Had Sara changed her mind about going? He'd thought things were going so well, at dinner this past Wednesday. He'd been looking forward to the outing more than he had anticipated anything in a long time.

He wished things were as easy with Sara as he'd imagined they'd be, when he had been in Chicago, making plans. His daughter with him, living in the bedroom he was having redecorated for her. No more feeling empty, and the end of his ever-present fears for his daughter's safety. He'd planned the very best for Sara—the best schools, trips to Europe, dancing lessons, all those things he couldn't afford before.

"Ready?" he asked as she finally came into view for the second time, in a hooded jacket.

"Ready," she said, her gaze not quite meeting his. Damn. She was his daughter. If he only knew what to *say* to make things perfect.

She marched ahead of him down the walk.

He raised his eyebrows at Libby, and moved aside so that she could go down the walk in front of him. He was glad she was coming. There was safety in numbers. She could put things right if he said or did something stupid. Today Libby was clad in faded jeans that hugged shapely legs, and a soft peach-colored sweater. Nothing outlandish. The color was great with her red hair, and the turtleneck collar hugged the long, slim line of her neck. He was definitely attracted to her, but she showed no attraction to him. There didn't seem to be a flirtatious bone in her body; he found himself respecting that about her.

As she passed him, he saw that one dangling silver earring had become caught in a strand of her hair, and he could have sworn he caught the scent of her, of spice and greens...

He willed down his reaction. "So Sara's upset with me?" he asked in a low tone.

"Not really." A light frown crossed her features. "Her friend Kathleen asked her to go horseback riding today. Sara wanted to go, but she'd made a promise to you."

Oh. Sara hadn't wanted to go with him. He'd thought all week about this outing, and Sara hadn't wanted to go. Libby must have made her, and he hated the thought of that.

Libby smiled. That smile was so real, so genuine, and again he felt that funny little kick in the gut. "I thought she should keep her promise. And anyway, ten-year-old girls are flaky sometimes, you know."

He didn't know, but it was obviously one of the things he was finding out.

At the mall, Sara perked right up, and he began to see what Libby had meant. Were all kids this moody?

"So, where to?" he asked, pleased that his daughter was finally showing some enthusiasm for the outing.

"The Pumpkin Coach?" she asked hopefully.

Walking beside him, Nate thought he felt Libby hesitate.

But he couldn't be sure. Since he'd never felt so conscious of a woman before, maybe he was misreading her.

"Okay," he agreed.

At the store, Sara went right over to a navy and red rugby shirt and matching slacks. The set was cute. "What's your size?" Nate asked, pulling one off the rack that even he could see was way too small.

Sara rolled her eyes and giggled.

But Libby looked at the price tag and frowned in earnest. "Nate—"

"Here's one that looks like it might fit," Nate interrupted, holding the outfit out to Sara.

Sara took it. She shot Libby a look. "Um, how about some sneakers?" she asked, a little shy, a little bold.

"Sneakers it is," Nate replied. Sara grinned at him. It wasn't one of her shy smiles, it was a grin, wide-open and genuine, and it felt so incredibly good. He felt a smile of his own forming, and for some unearthly reason, he looked to Libby, as if to share it.

She pushed a flyaway lock of hair behind her ear, and she didn't return his smile. "Nate, Sara really doesn't need new shoes, but if you want to buy them, there's a discount place—"

"Aw, Lib, I wanted those silver ones with the glittery laces." Sara gave Nate a pleading look.

That decided it for Nate. "Pick any you want. No, wait, take a pair of each color." He grabbed a pair of hot-pink shoes, a pair of yellow. Piling them up to her chin, he added a pair of neon blue ones for good measure.

"Wow! Thanks! Marie has some like the pink ones. I can't *wait* to wear these." At Nate's direction, Sara picked out some other things—jeans, a purple leather purse—just the thing, he guessed, to go with silver sneakers—and other stuff besides. Girl stuff. Daughter stuff. In Chicago, he'd imagined giving Sara lessons and a fine education. He'd never quite imagined himself out with her, buying her things so...directly. Sara disappeared into the fitting room.

Nate felt on top of the world.

"Nate, listen," Libby said urgently as Sara departed.

He liked how she made his name sound, all low and husky. Then he shook his head, as if to clear it. He had some dangerous notions about this woman. Like that urge to tell her about himself that had hit him as he was leaving her place Wednesday, to say things he'd never shared with anyone. It was a siren call that seemed to come from her, that whispered, *you can tell me anything.*

He'd told Eve a few things about himself, about how scared he felt about the business, about his father's gambling, how it was so hard, sometimes, even to touch her, his wife, with any spontaneity. The next time they'd fought, she'd thrown that admission in his face.

Sure, he thought. Tell Libby things. *Tell her your deepest, darkest secrets so she can use them in court to keep your daughter away from you.* His euphoric mood disappeared.

He shot her a quick, covert glance. She was fiddling with the laces of one of a pair of sneakers on a shelf. He'd been in business long enough to know when someone was working up to something, and Libby was definitely working up to something. Well, he was buying Sara things that made the girl's eyes sparkle. And he was damned if he was going to let anything spoil the occasion.

"So, what's the problem?" he asked a trifle impatiently.

"This place is kind of expensive." She laughed a little, nervously. "I mean, I know you haven't shopped for a girl before, and there are a lot of other shops that offer better values—"

"This was Sara's choice."

"Well, but—"

"I can afford it." All this fuss about a kid's clothes, he thought with rising irritation.

She flared a little, tossing her head, two pink spots on her cheekbones. "Sure. Rub it in."

He put a hand on her forearm. The peachy angora was even softer than it looked, and he had a hint of the warmth of the skin beneath. He pulled away immediately. "I'm not trying to show you up," he insisted.

"Well, it wouldn't be too hard, would it?" She looked at him with a mixture of defiance and defensiveness.

"Just what's that supposed to mean?" She wasn't going to try to spoil this for him, was she? She had so much. She had Sara.

She pressed her lips together, then gave a quick shake of her head. "You know what I earn. More to the point, you know what I don't earn, to the penny. I assume you read the financial and personal-information papers I had to file with the court, just as I read yours."

Nate had, and he'd been appalled at how little his daughter had been living on. Eve and Lloyd had left Sara a small inheritance, but Libby hadn't touched it. He felt a spurt of reluctant admiration. She certainly needed the money, and as Sara's guardian, she could have spent it on his daughter's care. But she was saving it for Sara's education, Marta had told him. Sara wouldn't need Eve's money now. But he smiled at Libby, softening in spite of himself at how much she cared about his daughter.

"Look," he said. "I'm not trying to buy her, I'm trying to buy things *for* her. This is about my daughter, not about court."

She flushed and gave him a half-formed return smile. There was nothing flirtatious about it, but her expression was so unexpectedly sexy that he had to look away. She had the most artless way about her. It set him to hatching never-to-be-executed plots for coaxing her into bed.

He shook his head. He hadn't been celibate in the years since his divorce. But he picked women carefully, women who were interested in the things he was—decent conversation, a handy date for charity functions, an honest, mutually satisfying sexual relationship—and never, never any discussion about the future. It had been a while since he'd been involved with a woman. So perhaps abstinence was responsible for his reaction to Libby.

"Libby?" Sara had reappeared, in a nautical-looking dress, her gaze focused on Libby. "What do you think?"

"It's cute." Libby glanced at the price tag. "But not *that* cute, sweetheart." She sighed. "Though I expect your father will be happy to buy it for you."

Sara's gaze flickered uncertainly from Libby to Nate.

"It's only money," Nate said.

"I think that's my line." Libby's tone was dry as she took a pair of silver lamé sneakers from Sara up to the sales counter.

Nate felt his mouth tighten. Okay, so money was important to him. Didn't Libby understand that with money you could buy anything, even peace of mind? A couple of minutes later he stood before the stack of clothing piled on the sales counter and pulled out his credit card. The sales clerk was smiling. Sara was smiling. That was all that mattered. He was going to leave the boutique, and then they were going to go to shop after shop, anywhere Sara wanted, and buy whatever she wanted, and Libby's disapproval be damned. After all, how could you spoil a kid you hadn't seen in eight years?

In the toy store, he coaxed Sara over to the display of dolls. She murmured something about not playing with dolls much anymore. But he stood beside her at the glass case and watched her carefully, and could see her take in a breath over a porcelain-faced Victorian lady, with a red velvet gown and a tiny, real-fur muff. "We'll take that one," he said to the salesperson.

"Oh," Sara breathed. She hesitated. "I don't need that doll. I wouldn't dare play with something so fancy anyway."

"But you like it?" He heard the eagerness in his voice.

"Yes. Oh, yes."

"Good." He pulled out his credit card again and went up to pay.

It was while the clerk was ringing up the sale that he remembered the train, his Lionel toy train. God, he hadn't thought about that train in years. He'd been about Sara's age when he'd owned it, just young enough to imagine that the train would be spared when everything his family owned was auctioned off...for the second time, thanks to his father's gambling debts. The train had had coal cars, boxcars and cattle cars...oh, and two tiny mountains, a switchback and some fuzzy trees made out of green-colored moss, a bridge...

His mother had understood. She'd wanted his father to keep the train set out of the auction. His parents had fought over the issue, and Nate had hated that part the most, holding his hands over his ears in bed one night as they yelled about that train, hurling wild accusations at one another.

Of course, the train had been sold along with everything else they owned, and of course his father had said next time he'd buy his boy *two* trains, and of course, three years later his father had hit it big again with the numbers, and offered to replace the whole setup, even bigger than before. Nate had refused. He was too old, he'd said, and his father had clapped him on the back and said he was a man and didn't need any old toy train.

He shook off the memory. He had money now, and rock-solid investments, and major holdings in real estate. Land. Solid and real—as long as a man worked hard and kept his wits about him. He'd learned to depend on himself for the things that were important. Sara would know nothing but stability. He forced a smile. "Thirsty?" he asked Sara.

"Real thirsty." Her gaze included Libby. "And I'm kind of hungry too…?" The last was drawn into a question, and he realized that Sara was still uncertain around him, looking to Libby for security. The thought hurt.

"Great. We passed a McDonald's at the food court."

Libby was quiet as they headed that way. Nate and Sara got in line for hamburgers and french fries while she went to the wok place for stir-fry. Nate was buying Sara way too much. Perhaps he really didn't mean just to impress the court, play up for Judge Wyatt the contrasts between what he could provide and what Libby could give Sara. But that's the spin Marta Wainwright would put on things. And regardless, if this buying spree continued, it couldn't be good for Sara. She needed to get to know her father, what kind of person he was inside. She still knew so little about him. Nate seemed to be drawing Sara out but sharing so very little of himself.

Cam had had a fit when he'd found out that Libby had let Nate come over every day after school. He urged her to do no more than comply with the schedule. Her friend Tina had done the same, cautioning Libby more than once not to let Nate get the upper hand.

But Sara needed this time with her father. Libby shook her head, telling herself that, no matter how extravagant, today was their first shopping trip. Nate would learn to slow down. It had been an intense week. Maybe what they all needed was some breathing space.

She looked toward the table in the middle of the food

court, where Nate and Sara were now sitting. Two black
heads were leaning toward one another, so close they almost blended. The girl was so beautiful, a delight to be
around. The man was so perfectly proportioned that in contrast, she felt plain and...ordinary. She'd always liked life
in Harborside, *liked* being ordinary. Now all of a sudden,
life just didn't seem fair.

Balancing the foam plate in one hand and holding a too-
hot cup of tea in the other, she sighed and headed over to
them.

"Libby! Guess what?" Sara jumped up from her seat
just as Libby was preparing to set her plate on the table.
Libby moved, but not quickly enough. Sara bumped her
arm hard. The flimsy plastic plate buckled, sending pea
pods flying. The rest of her lunch tumbled down the front
of her sweater.

As tea sloshed on her hand, she jerked back with a cry
of pain, which promptly sent the contents of the cup arcing
through the air.

Nate leaped to his feet, his handkerchief outstretched.
"Did you burn yourself?" His voice was deep with concern
as he used the handkerchief to make a firm swipe down the
front of her sweater.

Libby felt herself blush. What a mess she'd made! "I'm
fine," she managed to say. All of a sudden—midswipe—
Nate froze. Then, through her mortification, she realized it,
too. Nate Perry had a hand on her breast.

Heat raced from her cheeks to her toes in an embarrass-
ing, thrilling combination of sensation that finally settled
low in her belly. Through layers of wet sweater and bra
and a corner of handkerchief, she could still feel his hand
there, his palm cupped, the pads of his fingers pressed
against her nipple. She started to tremble.

Nate still hadn't moved. Slowly, Libby brought her face

up to look up at him; he looked down. His eyes were brilliant, locked on hers.

Sara said, "Geez, I'm sorry!" and Nate jerked his hand away and shoved it, handkerchief and all, into his pocket. He looked away.

Sara was rattling on. "Gosh, that's *soy sauce* on your sweater, Lib. I don't think soy sauce comes out, does it? I mean, if you take off your top and soak it in cold water when we get home…"

"It's okay." With more of an effort than she should have required, Libby pulled herself together. Nate's touch was accidental. He'd been trying to be a gentleman. He didn't ever need to know how he'd affected her, how she'd had that hungry, tingly two-second flash of utter…lust when she'd felt his touch.

"Now," she said, forcing a smile and sitting down again with Sara. "Donate a french fry to the cause of my lost lunch and tell me what got you so excited in the first place." She resisted an urge to swipe futilely at the stain on her sweater. Nate, she noticed out of the corner of her eye, had retaken his seat next to Sara and now appeared fascinated with his Big Mac.

"Well, Nate's going to get me horseback-riding lessons!" Sara turned a dazzling smile on Nate. "Isn't that just s-o-o neat?" She sighed dramatically. "I've wanted those lessons for s-o-o long." When she looked at Libby, there was no uncertainty, no waiting for Libby's approval, only an expectation that Libby share her joy.

Sara *had* wanted the lessons for the entire year she'd been with Libby. "That's great, sweetheart." Libby almost meant it. Heck, she *did* mean it. She reached over and squeezed the girl's hand. "Thank you," she said softly to Nate.

He nodded but didn't look directly at her. He wasn't still embarrassed, was he?

All right. So things had seemed a tad weird in that moment when they'd looked into each other's eyes. So for a second she'd thought he'd felt something too. Well, even if there *had* been something sexual between them, to a man like Nate it couldn't be anything special. Cam had told her what he'd found out about Nate's personal life. He was seen regularly at society functions, and each time, it seemed, he had a different woman with him. Glamorous, beautiful women. Nate had probably had his hands, his lips, on the bare flesh of many a woman... *Oh, God.*

"And," Sara added, popping a french fry into her mouth, "Nate's getting me a horse."

"Renting you a horse, sweetheart," Libby corrected automatically, blessing her ward's chatty nature.

"Buying me a horse," Sara insisted, her eyes very bright. "We're going to a horse farm and I get to pick out my horse. What he's going to rent is the stable space. Right, Nate?" She waved her cheeseburger at him for confirmation.

The hard planes of Nate's face softened. "Right. And we're going to make sure you get a new saddle, the safest equipment—"

"Right. A saddle maybe better than Kathleen's. Oh, I don't mean a lot better, just kind of better because sometimes she's mean to me because she's got a horse and I don't." Sara paused, her forehead creased. "Well, maybe not better than Kathleen's. She did invite me to her birthday party. And I don't want her to get her feelings hurt. Just a saddle and bridle and stuff that's only as good as Kathleen's. Okay, Nate?"

Nate. Nate. Nate. Suddenly, it was hard to remember that less than a week ago, Sara had been wondering what to call the man who'd appeared in her life wanting to be her father. Things were moving too fast. Sara's cheeks were flushed, her eyes too bright, her tongue going at too frenetic a pace even for her.

Sara was being seduced.

Libby paused, the end of a french fry still poised mid-dunk in a puddle of ketchup. She understood. What woman, young or old, could resist the fantasy of a sinfully handsome stranger who came to town with big, big presents and an urge to be a daddy? Lord, even she herself sometimes— her mind turned abruptly from the thought.

Maybe Cam and Tina were right. Libby looked over at Sara. The girl continued to talk to Nate, cajoling him into buying her what fast-food places called apple pie. Neither father nor daughter seemed to notice that Libby wasn't saying much at all. Neither of them would like what she was thinking now. But Libby knew that when you loved a child and were responsible for raising her, you had to do what you thought was right.

She made a decision. It was almost guaranteed to be met with opposition from both Nate and Sara, but Libby had made up her mind. She looked over at Nate. He was listening to Sara's chatter, telling her nothing at all about himself. Nate Perry was definitely not going to like what she had to say.

WHEN NATE DROPPED them off a couple of hours later, Libby stayed behind as Sara got out of the back seat. "See you next Saturday!" Sara sang out.

Libby rolled down the window. "Here's my key." She handed it to Sara. "It's late. Can you go in and get ready for bed, please? I'll be in soon, but I want to talk to Nate for a minute."

"What about?" Sara asked. Immediately, her smile

faded, and her gaze flickered from Libby to Nate and back again.

"Nothing special. Don't worry, sweetheart," Libby reassured her. After a slight hesitation, Sara smiled a little uncertainly and headed up the walk.

They sat for a moment in the dark. Libby had left the window down. The sound of tree frogs was a constant, underlying noise. Nate waited for Libby to begin.

Finally, she spoke quietly. "Nate, you're buying Sara too much."

That again! Nate never got truly angry, not out-of-control angry. He hated that. But this woman had a way of pushing his buttons. "My choice," he said shortly.

She stared straight ahead. "I think you should do other things with her, things that don't cost money. Ride bikes, take walks. Tell her what kind of man you are, what your own family was like. She has grandparents, for example, and I've never heard you mention…"

"My parents are dead." Nate heard the flatness in his tone, as if he didn't care that Sara wouldn't know her grandparents.

"She's going to have questions—"

"And I said I'd answer them, the very first time I saw her," he cut in, his temper rising in spite of his best efforts to control it.

"But you didn't act as if you meant it, and today you didn't give her time to think about anything but the next item on her wish list. You don't start conversations. You just buy her things."

There was a small silence. It was true; he'd known Sara wanted the doll, and he could relate to her wanting it the way he'd wanted the train. But the thought of telling his daughter tales of his own childhood caused his gut to clench. He preferred to keep some things to himself. What was the point of sharing all that…that pain, anyway? The most difficult truth of all was that he felt a lot more uncomfortable around Sara than he'd ever expected to. He didn't dare admit it to Libby. Her attorney would have a field day with his cross-examination.

"Anyway," Libby finally went on quietly, "I'm thinking that I made a mistake, making visitation so open-ended. Until the court makes some other decision, you'll need to come at your designated times." She took a breath. "Wednesdays after school and Saturdays until noon. And please, slow things down. We don't even know if horseback riding will hold Sara's interest, so maybe you could just rent the horse for now."

Nate made a grab for self-control. Eve had done this. After their divorce, when she'd figured out that Nate genuinely wanted to be a father, she played games with his visits. She threatened him with court action. Sometimes when Nate went to pick up his daughter, neither mother nor daughter had been home. But Libby was not Eve. He had to remember that.

"If I want to buy her a horse, I'll buy her a horse," he said between clenched teeth. "You want to play games? All right. I'll ask the court to give me more visitation." He was tired of negotiation. Negotiation was part of business, but this was his *daughter* they were talking about.

Libby rapped a fist on her thigh. "You're seducing her!"

Seducing. The word conjured images. Strong images. Emotions. Touching Libby's breast. That surge of sexual desire that had been like a flash fire. Seducing, she said. "So this is really about my feeling you up at the mall?" His voice was harsh with disbelief, anger, his choice of word deliberately crude.

She turned toward him swiftly. "How dare you! How

dare you suggest that I'm using Sara because I'm angry at you.''

For a second, they just stared at each other. She was breathing hard; her eyes were wide and shiny in the dark. He could see her breasts rising and falling.

And suddenly, he believed her. She wouldn't use Sara, not deliberately anyway. She had nurtured his daughter, protected her. She had given him Sara's picture, his first image of his growing daughter. It was easier to see Libby as an enemy; he was sure he'd have to fight her for Sara. But she'd play fair.

She'd play fair.

And at that realization, in the space of one heartbeat, anger turned to desire.

He put his hands on her shoulders and drew her toward him. Libby sensed his intent; he didn't move with lightning speed, but with sure purpose. As if by their own volition, her feet came off the floor, her thighs shifted, she turned toward him more fully.

The gearshift pressed into her legs. In the dark, she saw little, felt a lot. Warm breath fanned her face. And then his lips made contact. She heard his sharp intake of breath.

He was good; she'd known he would be. Practiced. She hated that, even as she felt herself responding. He settled his mouth over hers with a heat that made her tremble. She was shy; it had been years since she had kissed a man. She didn't want this. She was dying for this.

Almost tentatively, she opened her mouth, and the stroke of his tongue was like a whole body caress. His hands held her cheeks as he took the kiss deeper.

Then he groaned, and suddenly he wasn't practiced at all. His hands gripped her head more firmly. As he tipped her face closer to his, his lips asked...demanded...then took, and there was a kind of desperation that she didn't understand. It was that desperation that undid her, that sent a surge of longing through her that was more powerful than anything she'd ever known. The noise of the tree frogs outside got louder until she dimly recognized the roaring sound as her own blood in her own ears.

But, oh, God, she shouldn't be kissing Nate. With an effort, Libby raised both hands and shoved at his shoulders. "Damn you," she whispered.

Immediately, he let her go, but stayed close, resting his forehead against hers, his breathing harsh. His hair was a brush of thick silk against her skin, his eyes an inch from hers in the dark. She closed her eyes, overwhelmed by his nearness. He said absolutely nothing, and then with a long, charged sigh, he straightened.

She had no idea what he was thinking. As usual. And she was embarrassed, knowing he had to have felt her response, her yielding to the demand of his mouth. Embarrassment turned to anger. She wanted him and she didn't even know him, and what she did know about him told her to shield her heart. "This doesn't change anything," she said softly. "I won't change my mind about Sara."

He leaned his head back against the seat. "I know. We need a plan."

"A plan?" She was incredulous. How could he kiss her like, well, like that, all heat and sizzle, and then talk about plans? The tips of her fingers and toes still tingled, and he wanted to make *plans?*

"A plan. Look, maybe—" he cleared his throat "—we should start with honesty."

She made fists of her hands. "As in...?"

"I think you wanted that kiss, for instance."

Libby nearly choked. "You arrogant..." Words failed her.

"Male?" he prompted quietly.

"I suppose they all want it," she said bitterly.

"They?"

"Your...women. All the women you sleep with."

He slapped his hand on the steering wheel. "You make it sound like I have a damn harem."

But he hadn't exactly denied that there were other women in his life. Bitter laughter welled in her and threatened to break through. What did she want from him? For him to say, *There won't be any other women now that I've met you?* Come on, she knew the type; she'd had experience with the type. And she didn't love him, didn't care what he did, as long as it didn't hurt Sara.

She reached for the door handle, pulled it open. Her lips felt tender, her legs weak. But her will was strong, she told herself. "We'll never come up with a plan," she said.

"Then it looks like I'll see you in court."

CHAPTER SIX

THREE WEEKS LATER, Nate sat in his Chicago office and gave his assistant, Jeffrey Rand, his full attention. There were problems with the Iris Complex. Iris was a Chicago lakeside development of boutiques and trendy dockside cafes that also featured an indoor sports complex and sky-high, revolving lounge. From the beginning, the resort had had complications—legal problems with the city code, labor trouble. Projects this big always were major management headaches, and this was the biggest project Nate had ever undertaken.

Jeff was writing something on the pad on his lap. A young man in an expensive suit, Jeff was ambitious, a kid on the make. Because Nate needed to be in Harborside, he'd been forced to give Jeff too much responsibility. Jeff had made a few minor decisions so far, and done well. But Nate was still worried. For one thing, ambitious kids tended to gamble too much, risk too much.

"Anyway, the upshot of all this is that the bricklayers are unhappy about the overtime situation," Jeff was saying. He glanced at his memo. He was about halfway down a long list of problems.

"I'll talk to them," Nate said wearily. He was so tired these days, and so torn. He needed to be in Chicago. But Judge Wyatt required him to be in Harborside, so he was commuting constantly, a real hassle because of Harborside's isolation. And the groundbreaking for Bittersweet

Point would begin soon, and he'd have tons of work there, too. Well, there wasn't a choice.

"I already talked to them." For the first time, Jeff smiled a little.

"What happened?" Nate tensed. The guys on the job site were tough, mistrustful of management. Only twenty-six, and with a baby face, Jeff took a lot of ribbing.

"I gave them more money."

Nate groaned.

"A quarter of a percent more." The kid's tentative smile turned positively brilliant.

Nate hid his surprise. He couldn't have done better himself. Jeff had been a good pick as an assistant, though Nate's associates hadn't been sure at the time. He was too raw, they said. He'd come from a tough part of town, he had no polish. But Nate had seen something of himself in Jeff. A burning desire to get ahead. So, despite certain misgivings, he'd hired the kid.

"That's fine, Jeff," he said.

Jeff's smile faded a little. "Sure."

Nate wasn't certain exactly what he'd done wrong. "Look," he said finally, when the silence got too long, "Marta's waiting, and Marta's fees don't stop just because she's in my waiting room reading *Cosmopolitan*. Why don't you use your head on the rest of that stuff, see what you can do on your own and give me a call in Harborside early in the week."

Jeff jumped up, obviously pleased now. "Terrific." He opened the door for Marta Wainwright on his way out.

"Nate. Still afloat financially?" Marta grinned as she breezed into the room, elegant in a blue silk suit and pearls. Putting an enormous leather briefcase on a low table, she sat down in one of his wing chairs. When her skirt hiked up a fraction, she ignored it, giving him a good look at her legs. Marta had never made it a secret that she was interested in him. Nate too had been thinking about a relationship off and on for nearly as long as he'd known her.

But his reaction to her now was rather puzzling. He hadn't been involved with a woman in quite a while. He was available, and so was she. Yet the view of her legs, the fairly obvious invitation, didn't interest him at all.

"I've got the motion to increase visitation you wanted me to draft." Marta rummaged in the briefcase, producing a yellow legal pad and a sheaf of paper.

"Right." Instead of taking the papers from Marta, Nate got up from behind his desk and walked over to the window. He couldn't see Lake Michigan from here, and today the city skyline looked gray and smudged and huge, tower after tower, all the way to the horizon.

Two days ago, he'd been sitting on the steps of his Harborside condo in the dark, talking with Trev Samms—the boy always assumed Nate wanted company. The contrasts of his real life and those days in Harborside were starting to get to Nate, confusing his thoughts, making him lose focus.

From behind him, he heard Marta snap her briefcase closed. "We're asking for some visitation in Chicago, for Sara to come for a whole weekend or two, more when school's out, if the court action is still dragging on come summer."

Nate felt his gut clench. How would he make conversation with Sara, all alone for days at a time? He'd tried to beat Libby at her own game by taking her suggestion that he spend his time with Sara doing simple things. But Libby must have said something to Sara about his more limited visitation, or maybe somehow Sara blamed him, because she'd been much more subdued on the six visits he'd had with her since their shopping trip.

The last time, he'd taken her for a sail on his rented sailboat. He'd tried to show her how to tack at one point, and Sara had held the lines in a death grip and finally asked him to take them back. He'd been disappointed, sure that sailing was something they could share. Sara had been nearly silent on the trip back to dock and then the ride to Libby's.

He turned to Marta. "I had to cancel this Wednesday's visit so I could make the trip here." It was merely coincidence, Nate told himself, that he'd decided he had to come to Chicago right after the sailing incident. And coming here hadn't had anything to do with Libby, with that kiss he'd shared with the enemy, that soft, sweet-smelling enemy who had aroused him so much with one kiss that his hands were still shaking on the steering wheel as he'd driven home. That had never happened before. "What will canceling one time do to my chances of getting visitation increased?"

Marta stood and poured a cup of coffee from the pot on the coffee cart his secretary had just brought in. "Well, it's rather ironic that you're asking for more when you didn't take advantage of what you had. But the judge just needs to understand that you're a hell of a lot more important guy than anyone in Harborside. I'll explain. I'll handle it."

Nate moved from the window and sat down. "This isn't working, Marta. When Sara talks to me at all, she keeps mentioning this play she's in at her school, and all her friends. And the fact that she's in *Fiddler on the Roof* this summer. She doesn't seem interested in my business or anything in Chicago. She seems to have a lot going on in Harborside. I feel like some kind of heel around my own daughter for wanting to uproot her."

"Crap," Marta said sharply. "That's crap, Nate. Keep

talking like that, and you'll never get custody of her. You've got to talk like a winner."

His father had said that, too. Act like a winner and you'll be a winner. And sometimes, it had worked for his old man. When he was a kid, Nate had actually believed the wild promises his father made, had actually believed that this time, *this time,* his father would make a fortune and then he'd quit playing the numbers, betting at the track, all of it. Nate had actually believed, over and over again, that his mom would be happy, and there'd be money so that he could stay at the prep school with all his friends... Nate's hands fisted on the desk. "I've got to figure out something. If only Sara were older."

"If she were older, her custody would be pretty much up to her. Her choice," Marta said.

Nate knew Marta was right. If Sara were old enough to decide for herself, she'd undoubtedly choose Libby as her guardian. But maybe if she were older, she'd be able to see how much Nate wanted to be a good father to her. Well, he might be a long way from winning the heart of his daughter, but he was working on it. It would be so much easier if he didn't have to deal with her guardian.

A guardian who had that shy, almost wondering way of kissing, who'd smelled like a garden, whose curves had set him on fire.

Nate knew how to behave in business. To his father's advice—act like a winner—he added: work hard, figure out a can't-lose strategy. Winning had become a habit. Nate was used to having it all.

But there was no way to have it all, not in this situation. Unless...

Yes. A plan. And it was so damn simple, after all, that Nate couldn't believe he hadn't thought of it before. His mind said *yes.* But for a moment, his gut clenched. He felt as if he was standing on the edge of something, afraid he'd fall... No. He'd keep his head. This was a plan, a strategy.

"File the motion, Marta," he said decisively. "I'm going to need some leverage for a little negotiation in Harborside."

"I DIDN'T THINK he'd really do it." Libby slapped the copy of Nate's motion onto her kitchen table among the piles of fringe and satin, sending a few glittering sequins flying.

Tina Samms had read the document through twice already. Libby sat down across from Tina and automatically picked up a red satin Western-style shirt in one hand and poked her middle finger into a thimble. She was used to having her hands busy.

"Nate Perry's a jerk," Tina agreed sympathetically as she tacked a length of fringe on a denim skirt.

"He's not a jerk." Sometimes she wished he was. It might make the upcoming court hearings easier to take.

Tina looked up from her work. "No? Then tell me what to call a man who wants to take Sara away, even though she doesn't want to leave you."

Libby started to attach a line of fringe to the yoke of the shirt. Her stitches were big, uneven, but that didn't matter. This was unpaid labor for the school play, and the audience would be seated too far away to see what an unsettled woman could do to a line of hand stitching.

"The thing is, I don't think Sara's nearly as unhappy about her...Nate as she lets on." Her thread tangled, and she yanked. "She really looks up to him. I went out to see her ride the horse he's rented for her, and Nate stopped by to pick her up from the stable for his visit. You should have seen the smile she gave him. Wide-open. For a second there, she was really glad to see him." She sighed. "But then she wanted to show him some trick she learned, a tight double turn, and the horse, Penny, wouldn't cooperate. I got a little scared, afraid she couldn't hang on to that horse, but Sara just kept trying, until Nate told her she should let it go."

Libby frowned, remembering. Just as she'd been about to say something to Sara, Nate had intervened. When Sara had dismounted, and come with drooping shoulders and slow steps through the gate, Libby had given her a hug and told her she could try again another day. Sara had looked to Nate for reassurance, too, but Nate was rummaging in his pocket for his keys and didn't say a word. Well, maybe because he hadn't been looking into his daughter's eyes, he hadn't noticed how much Sara wanted his approval.

Tina was sorting through the sequins. "But she still wants to live with you." When Libby didn't answer for a moment, she looked up. "She *does,* doesn't she?"

"Well," Libby said slowly, "she wants to be in her school play, but that's only two weeks away. She'll be in *Fiddler on the Roof* with me this fall. But last night when we were doing the dishes, she said that Nate has a housekeeper. That Nate builds shopping complexes. Sometimes, she's just...overwhelmed, and I can't blame her. Remember when we were kids, Harborside didn't seem exciting at all?"

Tina played with a sequin. "How could I forget?"

Twenty-five years of friendship meant that many things didn't need to be said. They had both lost mothers when they were young and the loss had been an instant bond between them. Neighbor ladies and teachers had tried to fill the gap in feminine wisdom, but mostly it was Libby and Tina, going it alone.

Bored at first, because both of them were interested in art and drama and Harborside offered nothing in either category. Then scared of boys and growing to womanhood without a mother to talk things over with. When she was fifteen, Libby had been so frightened of a boy who'd coaxed her into a tree house for a kiss and a grope that she'd punched the kid in the nose and pushed him out of the tree. He'd been furious, told her nobody wanted to kiss a girl with hair the color of a copper-pot scrubber anyway. His friends had taunted her in the school hallways for days afterward. Tina had stuck to her like glue.

And Libby had stuck by Tina when, at age seventeen, Tina met Jonathan. Jonathan was older, new in town. He was just out of the service, with a glamorous flyboy image. Tina hadn't had a chance.

Impulsively, Libby put down the shirt and covered Tina's hand with her own. For a second, Tina tried to keep sewing, tiny stitches that were her trademark. Then she stopped. "Oh, Lib, it was all a long time ago."

"But still…" Libby kept her hand where it was, over her friend's.

"Yeah." Tina's bottom lip trembled. Jonathan Samms had left four years ago, shortly after Trevor's accident. Since he'd left, Tina had had a struggle financially. Married too young to pursue an education, she'd also needed to work at home to be with Trevor. A couple of years ago, she'd finally given up on tracking down her husband to collect overdue child support. Her heart wasn't really in the task, anyway. Tina had stubborn pride.

But she was a good friend. She'd tried to warn Libby about Brian Karsten, who'd come to town a few years after Jonathan. He was studying lake pollutants. Libby had just finished art school and had come home to bury her father. Brian was worldly, good-looking, intense. One afternoon, he'd held her for hours as she'd talked about her dad, and that night he'd made love to her. Her first time. She'd waited for the right man.

But at the end of that summer, that summer she'd grieved for her father and come to love Brian Karsten, he'd sat her down for a talk. It had been fun, he said. But surely she knew he wouldn't be in Harborside forever. Surely she'd heard of summer romance. It was good, it was intense, and in September it was over.

Tina turned her hand in Libby's until they were palm to palm, then squeezed and let go. "Well," she said finally, "some people don't think I got much out of twelve years with Jonathan. But we had Trevor, and I'll bless Jonathan for that until the day I die."

"And I guess in a way Nate gave me Sara." Sara of the effervescent chatter. Sara, who'd inherited the most spectacular set of genes. Sara, the reason she couldn't really call Nate Perry a jerk. But just how long would she have Sara? Sure, Sara was anxious around her father, as anxious as she'd been a year ago for Libby's approval. But that only meant she cared about him, didn't it?

Even more unsettled, Libby got to her feet. "How about a cup of tea?" she suggested. She lit the burner under the kettle and got out the tea canister. "And how about some chocolate? I think I need it." But after Tina agreed, Libby realized she didn't have any sweets in the house. Then she remembered the chocolate chips she stored in the freezer, for those times she baked for one town function or another. Pouring some into a small bowl, she brought them back to the table with the tea.

"Look at us," Tina said after they had both had a few icy chocolate chips. "Two thirty-somethings still drowning our sorrows in chocolate."

Libby couldn't help smiling, her heart a little lighter. "And when Harborside didn't have what we needed, we remade Harborside. Who'd ever have thought this town would have so much live theater?"

"Who'd ever have thought we'd come to love it here?" Tina added.

Home. Friends and a good life and Sara—at least for now. A waxy chocolate chip finally melted on Libby's tongue, almost more bitter than sweet. Bittersweet.

"Your Nate Perry *is* a charmer, though." Tina took three chocolate chips and popped them in her mouth before picking up her needle again. "Trevor's really shot with him. Even calls him by his first name. It's Nate this, Nate that."

"Really? Nate buddies it up with Trevor?" Libby was surprised. For Nate to befriend a fifteen-year-old boy seemed out of character.

Tina frowned. "Not exactly. But if Nate's out on his deck and Trevor spots him, he's gone, right out there to talk." She paused. "The thing is, you know how Trevor can't sleep sometimes."

Libby nodded. Trevor didn't get as much exercise as many boys his age. It made him restless. That was Tina's theory, anyway. What remained unspoken between them was a conviction that, despite Trevor's unrelenting cheerfulness, something was on the boy's mind. But every time his mom pressed, he always teased her until she gave up trying to find out what it was.

Tina made a small knot. "Well, he goes out to sit on the deck in the middle of the night. And sometimes, Nate's there."

"Really?" Libby didn't want to examine why any conversation about Nate seemed so important. These days she was hungry to hear his name.

"I've eavesdropped a time or two. I don't mean I listen in. But I've looked down on the deck from my bedroom window, and it's the weirdest thing. Trevor sits on our deck and Nate sits on the other one."

"But they talk."

"Well, I guess so. I've never known Trevor not to talk. Trevor can't go next door. There's no ramp. But Nate never comes over, either."

"Well," Libby said slowly, "I think Trevor maybe needs to talk to an older man. He has no father at home, and so far, no one has seemed to fill the gap for him."

"I know. I used to wish so hard for somebody. But a guy like Perry? A guy who's going to make this place into a resort so expensive, Trevor and I will have to move out. How could they have anything in common? Beyond all the glitz, what is there to the man?"

Libby had the most absurd urge to rise to Nate's defense. He was intelligent, he went to work every day, worked incredibly long hours, from what Cam had been able to find out. But she knew what her friend meant. Both she and Tina had a healthy disrespect for glamour boys. She just couldn't picture Nate befriending a kid, even one as outgoing as Trevor.

"He's rich and successful," Tina continued, picking up a rhinestone. "But you'd think Trevor could see beyond that. I've taught him values, you and the folks in town have pushed those values, and I can't see what there is about this shallow guy from—"

"I kissed him," Libby said abruptly, and immediately felt the heat rush to her cheeks. Oh, God, she'd promised herself to forget that kiss, never to mention it to a living soul, not even to Tina.

Tina's mouth formed a little O of surprise, and the rhinestone in her fingers dropped, bounced, landed in the bowl of chocolate chips. "You *kissed* Nate Perry?"

Libby swallowed and nodded. "Actually, he kissed me. But I kissed him back."

Tina stared. "But you didn't sleep—"

"No!"

"Thank God. Libby, think. This guy's going to take Sara if he can. He's brought in a powerhouse of an attorney, set himself up in town like he's never going to leave you alone and now he's filing this motion for more visits. So far, the judge hasn't gone for anything Nate's proposed. Hasn't it occurred to you that Nate is using you, kissing you, hoping maybe you'll get confused about what you really want?"

"Of course it has." Libby plucked the rhinestone out of the bowl. "Believe me, it's never going to happen again."

"Good." Tina seemed relieved. She even smiled a little. "Don't worry about it, kid. It's just physical, right? Just hormones."

Just sex. Libby couldn't look at her friend. She hadn't been with a man for ages. Of course she had fantasies. A nameless, faceless, oh-so-gentle-but-demanding man who undressed her with exquisite care, who put a mouth to her breast in a sweet caress, who whispered his own need against the hot skin of her neck. A man who, these days, seemed to have shining black hair and sky-blue eyes.

TWO WEEKS LATER the man with the shining black hair and sky-blue eyes stood in one of the attorney conference rooms at the courthouse. He'd dismissed his lawyer, asking to speak to Libby in private. Libby, too, had asked Cam to wait outside. The two attorneys had grumbled together, their shared outrage at being shut out by their clients making them congenial for once.

Sara was out in the waiting room with Cam. The judge had asked her to come down for the hearing, and he planned to see the girl in chambers later. Sara was tense, although both Libby and Cam had tried to reassure her.

Last night, Sara and Libby had had a long talk. Sara was upset about the court hearing. She had come to kind of like Nate, she told Libby with eyes averted. But she was kind of scared, too. After all, Heywood—which was the name Sara used now in referring to her stepfather—had been mean, especially when he drank.

Sara now had mixed feelings about Nate. Sometimes she was effervescent, thrilled to see him. Sometimes she was wary, sizing him up. And even on the days when Sara was glad to see Nate, she was careful to keep some physical space between them. Libby wondered if Nate had noticed.

Now Libby stood, too, across the oak table from Nate. The table was a broad expanse of golden wood that held nothing but Nate's motion. He'd said they could settle the motion, if she'd hear him out.

"Well?" she said finally, as the silence lingered. He was studying her with nerve-racking intensity.

Then, "Has it occurred to you that we could take care of all our problems if we got married?"

Whoa. Libby wasn't sure she'd heard right. "Married? Married?" She sounded shrill.

Nate smiled for the first time, a cool smile. "Believe me, I never thought I'd be doing this, either. But marriage would mean we could both have Sara. And Sara would have both of us."

"Yes, but…married?" She couldn't seem to stop repeating the word. Why couldn't she be cool about this the way Nate was? Just say, "Of course I can't accept, but thank you for offering to share your life with me," as though she received proposals of marriage all the time. Heck, it wasn't even a proposal, not really. Nate's words were a far cry from some guy on bended knee with a velvet box.

He was still studying her. "Sara needs time to get used to me. Things in Chicago are heating up, and I need to spend time there without worrying about the spin some lawyer's going to put on my every move. Sooner or later Judge

Wyatt will make a decision.'' He paused. "I'm sure Cam Holling has told you that you might lose. I'm her father. You're not even a blood relative. And Sara seems to be coming around slowly, getting to trust me.''

Libby bit her lip. He was right. "But Sara wants to live with me, and I'm the one who's been caring for her. And I have more time to spend with her. Marta Wainwright shouldn't be too confident, either." *So there, Nate. You might just lose.*

Nate knocked a fist lightly on the table and then leaned forward. "I won't deny it. We need to be honest. In this case, I've gone against every negotiating instinct I have. But I know now how I should have handled things from the beginning.''

Honesty. That was what he'd talked about after the kiss they'd shared. She'd wondered if he'd been in the least affected by that kiss. Well, now she knew—she couldn't forget it, but he didn't even mention it. "We should have got married when you first tried to interfere in Sara's—in my—life," she agreed sarcastically.

"Right.''

"Wrong.''

"Why not?''

For a million reasons, she thought. Nate had to be able to name at least ten of them. For a moment, she was nonplussed. Nate was a master negotiator. This must be a strategy—put your opponent off balance. She *was* off balance, but she gave him a reason. A big one. "For one thing, I don't love you, and you don't love me.''

Still with that huge table between them, he looked her right in the eye. "True.''

She felt the oddest pang of disappointment. Of course he didn't love her. She didn't love him, so she didn't want him to have feelings for her. It just hurt to have him say he didn't care, so...blatantly.

Nate spoke again. "You don't have to worry about anything. Marta will draw up a prenuptial agreement. Your shop will be protected."

"*You'll* be protected, you mean. I doubt you want my little shop and its big debt load."

"We'll both be protected."

Sure, she thought. She'd been talking about love, he'd been concerned about his business. *Protect your things, Nate, those things that mean so much to you.* As if she wanted resorts and restaurants and shopping complexes.

Well, he wanted honesty. She could be honest, too. "I don't want anything you have. You might not believe that, but it's true. I'm more concerned about...other issues. For example, I don't believe in marriage without love." She braced herself for a cynical comment. "I suppose to a man like you, that seems hopelessly old-fashioned and naive."

Unexpectedly, he shook his head. "I loved my wife for a long time." Nate stopped, swallowed. "But I've learned. You can't trust love, it doesn't last. And believe me, love alone doesn't get you very far in a marriage. You need shared goals, mutual respect, commitment. We've got those things. We both love Sara. I admire the job you've done raising her, and while I think you could do a hell of a lot more with that shop of yours, you've got talent I recognize and respect. And this might not be a love match, but I take promises seriously."

She'd been shaking her head, daring him to deny the power of love, but his words stopped her for a second. Nate wanted to provide a home for her. She shook off a nagging thought that they had different ideas about what home meant, and Nate wanted big things for Sara, while she only wanted the child's happiness. But there was no denying that they both loved Sara.

And he *was* the kind of man who kept his promises. That much she was certain of. If his reputation in business wasn't enough to convince her, his quest to reconnect with his daughter did. Nate might be a loner, and he might be a glamorous charmer, but he kept his promises. It wasn't love, but it meant a great deal.

He was studying her. "My idea makes a hell of a lot of sense."

In the weirdest way, it did make sense if she used her head. If she ignored her heart and the voice there that said, *It's not supposed to be this way.*

She'd long ago given up on romance. She'd come back to Harborside after art school in New York, glad to have the chance to pursue her business. For years she'd done the flower arrangements for weddings, tried hard to make the occasions lovely. For other women.

She was happy. And if, long ago, she'd dreamed of a man who liked to walk in the rain and fix the car, who knew what was really important in life, who'd shyly give her a chip of a diamond, well, it was a nice fantasy. But nobody could run a shop like hers and make it pay in a small, out-of-the-way town like Harborside unless she was practical. And Libby was nothing if not practical.

Nate was waiting for her to agree. She shivered. Her fantasies about him were darker, more urgent, more...sexy. He'd been very outspoken about love, but he hadn't mentioned sex. If she were going to seriously consider his idea they had to discuss sex. She opened her mouth to speak. "I don't want to live in Chicago," she said instead of what she'd planned. But she blushed as though he could read her thoughts.

"I understand, and actually, I think it's best if I commute, stay in Chicago during the week, come to Harborside on weekends.''

"What kind of marriage is that?"

He smiled again, as though he sensed her weakening. "The kind for people who aren't pretending to be madly in love. Sara can come with me sometimes when school's out, but basically she'll get to be at home with her friends. It's a great solution.''

"We'll have to talk this over with Sara. I won't marry you unless she's comfortable with the idea," she warned. But it *was* a good solution. Surely it would be a relief to Sara if there was no pressure about the pending court hearings.

"We'll talk to her together." He paused. "Let me anticipate some of your other objections." He raised a finger as if ticking off imaginary items. "One. You don't want my money. Fine. But I'll pay my way, and I can afford to be generous." He raised another finger. "Two. We can live in your house. It's not my idea of how to live, but it's, well, kind of surprisingly comfortable. Did I miss anything?''

Sex. You missed sex, Nate. He was going to make her be the one to say it, damn him. Maybe he assumed she was dying to hop into bed with him. Or maybe he wasn't interested in sex…with *her*. For a moment she wondered with a kind of mad, welling humor which would be worse—him wanting her, or not wanting her. She turned and paced, until she realized she was acting like Nate, pacing and analyzing. This was ridiculous. She might be a bit naive, but she wasn't a shy virgin, either.

"And sex?" The boldness in her tone didn't match the warmth in her cheeks, but she held his gaze.

"It will be good."

It will be good…good. The word echoed along her nerve endings, starting tiny fires.

His dark, espresso voice dropped another note. "You felt it when I kissed you. I wanted you. I still want you. I'm tired of denying it."

Oh, God. For a moment, thoughts of love, thoughts of their differences went right out of her head. A man like Nate Perry wanted a woman like her, a not-so-pretty woman with two broken fingernails and frizzy red hair. And suddenly, she wanted him, too, with a hunger that was real, fierce and demanding, a desire too long denied. She took one step, two, her gaze on his.

His eyes lit with triumph.

Libby froze. She knew better. Every defense she had sprang to life. This man would hurt her if she let him. "No," she said before she had a chance to change her mind.

"Libby." His voice was low, seductive.

It scared her, how much she wanted him. How on earth could she even think of sleeping with him, a man who didn't believe in love? "I said no!" Her voice shook.

A few swift strides took him around the table. Now he was close. "Come on. Marry me," he said urgently.

Sara needed Libby. Sara needed Nate, too. But how to protect her own vulnerable heart? She took a deep breath. "All right, if Sara agrees and if you want a loveless, *sexless* marriage, I'll say yes."

He looked at her for a long moment, with that compelling gaze. She'd just accepted a proposal of marriage from Nate Perry!

He reached into the trouser pocket of his suit, produced a jewelry box and handed it to her without a word. Her own hands not quite steady, she took it and opened it.

Inside, a ring lay on a bed of white satin. Libby reached out and lightly touched the stone. It was an aquamarine, set in an antique setting of twining vines and cunning golden flowers.

So there was a velvet box, after all. Libby felt the hot prick of tears behind her eyelids. Somehow the ring seemed to symbolize something, if only Nate's promise to take care of her and Sara. For a man like Nate, used to being alone, marriage—any kind of marriage—must be a real leap of faith. She wondered if he really had any idea what a leap it was. For the first time, she felt a faint hope that Nate's crazy scheme might work, that they might be able to work out some way to live together in harmony. "Is this a family piece?" she asked, trying to mask how the gesture touched her.

He gave a harsh chuckle. "Hardly. I bought it in Chicago."

"Rather certain I'd say yes, weren't you?"

He shrugged. "When all's said and done, you're a sensible woman. And when I have a plan, I believe in being prepared. So I thought I'd buy something that suited you."

"Oh." The ring was pretty. No, beautiful. When the full implication of what he'd said dawned on her, her breath caught. He couldn't mean—

"I wanted something unique."

"Oh," she said again.

He took her hand, touched her callused palm, slipped the ring on her finger. "Believe me, Libby, you are nothing if not unique."

Later, she would have cause for regrets, she was certain. But for just a moment, her hand tightened around his.

CHAPTER SEVEN

A FEW DAYS LATER, Nate was driving with his new bride, following a winding route that hugged Lake Erie. Tina was watching Sara for a few days so that he and Libby could honeymoon. Nate had wanted to go somewhere tropical— the Caymans perhaps. He might not believe in love, but it was natural to want his wife. And he was sure if he just got her alone, the tropical moon and nature would take their course. After all, their one kiss had been incredible, a rush of sensation that had been nothing like he'd ever felt before. And he'd known from the way she'd clutched at him and met his mouth with hers, that she felt it too. But Libby had refused the Caymans.

Finally, she'd agreed to a ride along the coast, a stop at a motel. "Two rooms," she'd said firmly. "And only because if we don't go somewhere, we'll be gossiped about at the Shoreline Diner."

Nate had tried to mask his annoyance. God, she was stubborn. Waiting for declarations of undying love, no doubt. Didn't she understand that he'd given her everything he had—his daughter, his protection, anything she wanted?

It had seemed so simple, hatching his plan for marriage from his office perched over Chicago. But in Harborside, he was learning things didn't always go according to his expectations.

Take Sara, for instance. He'd thought it would be hard to convince *Libby,* but that *Sara* would be all for their marriage. After all, they were marrying for her, so why would she object? They'd all sat down on a bench in the courthouse park, right after they'd left the courthouse on the day he'd proposed to Libby. Sara had listened carefully as Nate had told her that he and Libby would be getting married as soon as possible.

"But where will we live?" she'd asked him, her brow wrinkling. He'd explained about his plan to stay in Chicago during the week, come to Harborside to be with them on weekends.

"That's really weird," Sara had said, frowning in earnest. "I mean, you'd be married and everything, but you'd be in Chicago? How is that being married?"

Libby had shot him a helpless look, then talked about how much she and Nate loved Sara.

"But..." She'd turned right back to him. "You two never even went anywhere, like on a date to the movies or anything. My friend Cynthia's mom is divorced, and she goes on lots of dates, but Libby and you never did. And you never even kissed or anything." She paused. "I mean, I've never even seen you kiss. So, *have* you ever even kissed each other?"

What was he supposed to say? He kept forgetting that Sara was half grown-up. Of course she'd have questions. But there was no way to begin to explain all the complications of his relationship with Libby. So he said nothing. After a long, uncomfortable silence, Libby had stepped in.

"Sweetheart, there are all kinds of ways people show that they respect and think about one another, and your dad and I do respect each other. Nate and I have talked things over, and we think we can be a family, just not the kind of family Kathleen has or your other friends have."

"But a real family?" At the hope in his daughter's voice, he'd vowed then and there to make this marriage work.

Libby had hugged Sara, quick and hard. "A real family. A family made for the best reason of all—because we both love you."

Sara had sat still for a moment, obviously thinking things over. Then she had shrugged. "Well, I guess that sounds okay. Definitely weird but okay."

The rush of relief that went through Nate was totally unexpected, and scary in its intensity. He welled down the feeling, telling himself that his plan was good and sound and rational. After all, it was just a wedding—a marriage— for Sara.

The wedding itself had been simple. A civil ceremony. Libby's friends in attendance, Tina Samms looking worried and on edge, then snubbing him afterward. Trevor, shaking his hand. Flowers everywhere, exquisite arrangements, Libby with blooms in her hair like a forest maiden. Sara in delphinium blue, smiling. His daughter always kept that tiny heartbeat of space between them, but after the ceremony, she'd given him a smile that had lit her features. That smile alone told Nate he'd done the right thing.

Now he had to keep things running smoothly. He'd never give a woman power over him again. So he'd keep his condo in Chicago, concentrate on Sara and business like before. He was married, but nothing much had to change.

So why was his mouth suddenly dry, his stomach tight?

"You're quiet," Nate observed.

"So are you," Libby said back, in some ways feeling as awkward as any bride. But she knew so much less than most brides about her husband. For example, did Nate even have any friends, among the developers he partied with, the guys at the yacht club? If so, he'd never said.

Unexpectedly, Nate's hand on the wheel relaxed. "I don't talk that much. But you usually do."

"Okay, rub it in."

"Talk to me." He turned and gave her a lopsided smile. "You're making me nervous."

"I make you nervous?"

He nodded, growing serious immediately. "Let's just say I don't acquire a wife every day. I could use a bit of a distraction."

Wife. She was a wife before she and her new husband had had a courtship. Heck, they'd never even been on a date. "Well, I could talk about Sara. *Oklahoma!* is opening at the elementary school in two weeks, and I know Sara wants you there. She has a big part, you know."

"I'll be there."

"Right. Let's see...I'm doing a garden party for the Smithsons. Karen Smithson read about Vita Sackville-West's white garden in England and wants me to mimic it. So I've got a big order in with my Toledo wholesaler. Whites are challenging to work with. You need form and foliage contrast, because you don't have color to help you." She sighed. "I'm not complaining. She's a good customer. You have no idea how difficult it is to keep the cash flow evened out in a business that—" She cut herself off, thoroughly embarrassed. "I guess you do know, don't you?"

"Yes."

"Yes. Well."

He took a curve smoothly. "You were saying?"

She peered at him. "You can't be interested."

"I asked," he said.

He had. And they needed to find something in common besides Sara if they were to live together. So, she talked, first because she was nervous, then because he was listening. Her nervousness ebbed a little. She'd never realized what a good listener a quiet man could be. He had the funniest little quirk in the corner of his mouth. Not a smile, exactly. Just a...quirk. A sexy quirk.

Staring at that quirk rattled her again. "So this September the community theater's doing *Fiddler on the Roof*. Family entertainment. You should have heard the furor when some of the younger people wanted to do *Cats*. Tina was wild to do the costumes, but Mr. Murphy said he wasn't playing a tomcat, not in this stage of his so-called career. Anyway, I'm in the chorus this year, mostly because this is Sara's first time in an adult role and she could use moral support." Suddenly, she remembered all that financial information Nate had filled out for the court that first day, and her heart sank. He made huge charitable contributions to the arts. *Fiddler on the Roof?* He couldn't possibly be interested in either the play or the machinations of the committee members, all vying to be the biggest fish in a very small pond.

"Hey, look at that," Nate said then, and he made a quick, smooth brake and swung onto an access road that led to the water.

At the water's edge, there was a public boat launch and a long wooden dock, but today the place was deserted. Nate shut off the engine, got out. "Come on. Can you believe this?" His hand swept the lake.

Libby had lived in the area all her life, around the lake that was always changing, around the locals who never seemed to change, among the condominium resorts that were starting to sprinkle their way westward along the shoreline. So she didn't immediately see what Nate was referring to.

Then she looked out over the water and her breath caught. In the distance was a large island. The late-afternoon sun turned its distant line of beach to pure gold. Above it, in a still-blue sky, hung a full moon. She'd always thought there was something, well, magical about a moon that shone in the bright afternoon sky.

Nate walked to the water's edge, Libby beside him. "Will you look at that..." His voice drifted away, his gaze fixed on the horizon. He looked suddenly very young, almost vulnerable.

In that moment, Libby thought, *I could love him someday.* She knew Nate was a cynic. She never would have believed that he could love this, the simple gold of the sun...and the moon, shining in the afternoon.

He gathered her close, and she laid her head on his shoulder, her heart beating fast. He raised his left hand, his other went around her waist. "Dance with me," he whispered softly.

"We d-don't have any music." Her protest was shaky.

He started to move her to nothing but the breeze. "Sing for me." His voice was low, seductive.

"I couldn't do that."

There was a pause. Then, "Just sing something from *Oklahoma!*"

In that moment, she could refuse him nothing. So she sang in a whisper a rollicking song about western skies and cowboys. Nate moved her, turned her, rocked her to some other music entirely. She closed her eyes, and the golden light played against her eyelids. She laid her head on his warm chest, felt his arousal pressing into her belly, and knew that if he led her to the private, lee side of a dune and settled her in the rough grass, she would go.

Her song died away. Helplessly, she brought a palm up to his heart. "You do have one," she said, laying her cheek against her own hand.

He stopped. "Have one what?" He sounded gently amused.

"A heart." Against her, he went rigid, but she persisted, wanting him to acknowledge what she was sure he was feeling. "You love this, this quiet, out-of-the-way place."

"I've always liked the water," he said gruffly.

"But this place." Her voice rose in an effort to be understood. "If you like a place like this, then you must—"

"Don't read too much into it," he said harshly. "I also like Lake Michigan, especially the million-dollar coast, and electric lights that shine over the water whether or not there's a moon." He stepped back from her, but kept his hands on her shoulders. He looked her right in the eye.

"I'm no more than what you see on the surface. A millionaire from Chicago who wants his daughter because she's his." He paused, and slowly his grip relaxed.

She could not speak, so crushing was her disappointment.

He looked away, across the water. "I already destroyed one family, hurt one woman. I don't have what it takes to make a woman happy, Libby. I don't want to hurt you. I thought you understood, or I would never have proposed this, regardless of Sara. Our marriage will work if we just don't get too...involved."

"We're married, Nate. We're *involved.*"

"You know what I mean."

"And the dancing? The nuzzling? What's that? Just sex, I suppose," she said bitterly. "I'm not as good as you are at compartmentalizing. My life in Chicago. My life in the hick town. My visits with my daughter. My honeymoon with my wife, where I hold her and dance with her till she gets sand in her shoes and stars in her eyes, and then I remind her we don't get *involved.*"

He averted his eyes. "Chalk it up to the champagne in the punch at the reception." There hadn't been a whole bottle of champagne in the punch. In the depths of his eyes, there was genuine confusion. "The lure of the day, I guess. But it's just one day, Libby. Don't make too much of it."

She shook her head, tears blurring her eyes. What in hell had she gotten herself into today?

"I don't want you to get hurt," he repeated.

"Too late," she snapped. "But I'll get over it."

The ride to a simple lakeside motel was made in silence. Nate got two rooms. The next day they returned to Harborside, and the day after that, Nate went to Chicago for pressing business.

A WEEK LATER, Libby awoke to the sound of voices downstairs, a husky, familiar male sound and Sara's higher tone.

Nate was home. Her stomach gave a lurch. When she'd gone to bed last night, she'd half expected him, half not. And she didn't want to think about how long she'd lain awake, listening for his car. He'd said he'd be in late on Friday nights, taking the last commercial flight into Toledo.

The day before their wedding, she'd given him a key and shown him the bedroom down the hall. But after their harsh words out on the beach, she hadn't known what to expect.

All week she'd been on pins and needles, sure she had made a mistake, telling herself she'd be glad if the next weekend brought divorce papers instead of a husband. By Wednesday, she'd convinced herself he wasn't coming, so she'd made only a halfhearted attempt to clean out the craft supplies and Sara's clutter from "his" bedroom.

She'd be damned, though, if she'd ask his plans. The strain of the week had shown. Sara had inadvertently added to that strain, with a question or two about why Nate wasn't going to sleep in Libby's room. At the time, she'd been able to answer casually, explain that Nate would be coming in late on Friday nights and didn't want to disturb her. Sara had accepted her explanation. But a couple of days later, she had been sharp with Sara for no good reason, and Libby had also broken the stems of some very expensive hydrangeas when she'd been making an arrangement at the shop.

He'd called. Exactly twice, to talk to Sara.

But apparently their harsh words out by the lake hadn't changed his plans to be a weekend husband and father. She had underestimated his determination and commitment to Sara. That was good; Sara didn't need any more stress.

She was committed, too, she realized. For as long as their marriage lasted, she was a wife. She was committed for Sara's sake, but also for herself, because whatever her reasons, she'd married the man of her own free will.

Unable to lie in bed on that thought, she got up and put on a pair of shorts and a baggy T-shirt. Usually, she padded downstairs in a nightgown and slippers, not changing until the breakfast dishes were washed. Well, her nightgown was modest but its implication was not. She and Nate might be married, but there would be no such thing as casual intimacy.

Her T-shirt had dahlias on it, purple blooms the size of dinner plates. It was her biggest fashion mistake in a long series of them, but the T-shirt was perfect for the impression she wanted to convey this morning. Baggy and sexless. There would be no mixed messages from her.

She headed to the bathroom. In spite of her resolve not to primp, she couldn't resist spending a few moments trying to ease the tangles from her flyaway hair.

On the counter, she found Nate's shaving kit. A basket of potpourri had been pushed aside to accommodate his things. She picked up his still-wet razor. A man's razor, in her bathroom!

His towel was damp, but neatly folded on the towel rack. Her palm brushed it, and she felt the oddest tingle imagining him in her shower, wiping his bare body with a towel that had never known a man's skin. A very *neat* man, and she couldn't help a rueful, nervous-feeling smile as she cast a glance over the clutter of her skin creams and Sara's pale pink nail polish and puffy sponges.

This marriage was definitely going to take some getting used to, in the little things as well as the big. She and Nate had so many differences—big, basic differences. But it was the little things that felt so unsettling this morning. The shaving kit was a travel size, as though Harborside, her house—*their* house now—was a stopping-off place. Libby meant to give this marriage her best shot, but how in God's name could a person be a token weekend wife?

Her thoughts in turmoil, she headed down the stairs. She could hear Sara going on and on as though this were a normal Saturday morning. It was a deceptive normalcy, but strangely compelling. And, she told herself, she was glad that Sara was adjusting already.

"So, then Kathleen didn't turn stage *left* and she ran right into Samantha and knocked down those cardboard trees and Mr. Gerrard yelled, 'Stick with the script, go *on*.' So everybody cracked up because he got so red in the face and Kathleen was sitting on the tops of those trees."

"Must've been funny." Nate's back was turned to Libby, and for a second she watched him. In his too-new designer jeans and oversize Yale Rowing Team T-shirt, he looked good, lean and even more strikingly male than in his tailored suits.

In contrast to the bathroom, the kitchen was a wreck. Flour and sugar were drifts of white on the counter, and a streak of flour also whitened one cupboard door. Dishes were piled both in and next to the sink. A stray shell of an orange dripped juice onto the floor. Libby's mind's eye flashed to that neat shaving kit upstairs and couldn't believe what she was seeing.

Sara stood a careful few steps away from Nate and held

a bowl out him. "Think you should put these in yet?" She craned her neck to look around him. "Those look sort of done."

"Oh, shi—rats," Nate said. "I forgot."

"Hi," Libby said from the doorway.

Both of them, man and daughter, turned. There was a pause. "Hi," Nate finally said softly.

"When did you get in?"

"This morning." He paused. "I showered in your bathroom. I hope you don't mind."

Oh, so he hadn't spent the night. "Of course not. There's only one bathroom. One shower." She was blushing, she realized, and there was no reason to blush. Sara was watching them carefully; this was her first day living in the same household with her father. So Libby added briskly, "After all, this is your home." Of course it wasn't his home; the condo in Chicago was his home.

But he looked at her, then, really looked at her. And she was shocked to see longing sweep across his features at her words. The unexpected, utter yearning in his expression stunned her.

But it was over so fast she wondered if she'd imagined it. Even as she stood there, her heart squeezing painfully, he turned and busied himself at the stove.

There was an awkward pause. Finally Libby asked, "What are you making?"

Sara answered. "Blueberry pancakes. Only Nate forgot the blueberries."

"Here, I can handle this," Nate said firmly, taking the bowl of blueberries from his daughter. He proceeded to push them into each pancake one by one.

"That's not the way," Sara said.

"It'll work." Nate's tone was very grim.

Sara giggled. Libby's own mouth twitched as a few

minutes later Nate gave her a plate with some very brown, very pitted pancakes. Well, you had to give points for effort. "These look worse than my meat loaf," she couldn't help observing as she took them to the table.

"Well, you won't eat meat," Nate grumbled.

"You could maybe do a better job with bacon?" she retorted.

"You can do it in the microwave."

"Don't you cook?" Sara asked as they took their places around the table.

"Well, in Chicago I eat out a lot at my restaurants, or my housekeeper leaves me something to reheat later in the microwave."

"Oh." Sara managed to look both mystified and intrigued.

Nate smiled at his daughter.

"Well, no housekeeper does the dishes here," Libby warned, but she was smiling, too. She had imagined that powerful flash of feeling a few minutes earlier, she decided. But she genuinely liked this side of Nate, when he was trying so hard to be a father. This side of him was the reason she'd married him, this side was her only hope.

Nate worked his fork doggedly against the tough pancakes. "Delicious," he lied.

"Gross," Sara said, her mouth full.

A careful, tentative contentment started to steal over Libby. There was something very appealing about a messy, imperfect Nate.

"I thought we could go somewhere together today. A family kind of thing," Nate suggested.

The sense of contentment threatened to grow. "What did you have in mind?"

"A sail," Nate said immediately.

"Oh," Sara said. She had been chewing a mouthful of

pancakes very hard. Now she swallowed. She didn't take another bite, but instead looked at Libby, her eyes apprehensive.

Ah, Libby thought. For some reason, Sara didn't like sailing. Or she didn't like sailing with Nate. Sara had been quiet when Nate had brought her home from their one previous sailing outing. But Libby hadn't been able to get Sara to talk to her about it. Sara could swim, and Libby knew the water didn't frighten her. But although they'd both been out on powerboats, Sara had never sailed before.

"A nice, long sail to one of the islands." Nate downed his glass of orange juice in one long swallow.

Sara looked again at Libby, and her expression grew pleading.

"Well, Sara and I were going to..." Libby's voice trailed off. With a run-on mouth like hers, she ought to be able to think of something.

Nate, too, had stopped eating. "What were you going to do?"

"Well, Sara and I were going to scrub out the cooler at the shop," Libby improvised. "You know, tackle that mold with scrub brushes and bleach. With Tina holding down the fort, we won't have interruptions. And—" she was getting the hang of this now "—Tina and Trevor are coming for dinner tonight, and I have to cook." She made a mental note to actually call Tina and invite them.

"The *cooler?*" Sara's eyes now were accusing.

Well, I did the best I could, Libby thought.

"Oh, come on," Nate said, rising from the table. "Can't you clean the cooler some other time? We'll pick up something from the deli for later. I don't know about Tina, but I'll bet Trev won't mind skipping the couscous." He took his plate to the sink and started cleaning up, his back to

Libby and Sara. He mumbled something about her lack of a dishwasher, which Libby decided to ignore.

"That cooler's really dirty," Libby said lamely.

"I could hire somebody—"

"So could I, if I could afford to." Libby hoped her tone conveyed finality.

Nate turned on the water. "Sara, work some of that ten-year-old charm on Libby. It'll be fun. I'll give you another lesson."

He was really trying, Libby thought. Considering the way things had been left between them a week ago, could she do less? "Do you want to go, Sara?" she asked gently.

Sara bit her lip, then said, "Sure."

"Great." But Nate hadn't turned from the sink, and he couldn't see how unenthusiastic his daughter was.

They picked up cheese and fruit and headed over to Bittersweet Point, where Nate still docked his boat. The rented Catalina 34 had crisp white sails and an intricate web of roping. The boat itself was huge, but the cockpit had a tidy, miniature feel like a playhouse. Libby put down the bag of groceries and went out on deck, where Nate was using the inboard motor to clear the shallows.

Nate hoisted sail once they were out on the lake. Taking the wheel, he caught a decent westerly and they skimmed over the water. Wind whipped Libby's hair.

Saturday morning with her husband. Her millionaire, yachting husband. *Husband.* Maybe if she repeated that word, she could shake the sense of unreality she felt.

"Want to help me hoist more sail?" Nate gestured for Sara.

Sara had been sitting still and silent next to Libby but she stood at Nate's invitation.

"I don't think Sara wants to sail." Libby had to raise her voice to be heard.

"What?" Nate asked at the same time Sara stuck out her chin and said, "Sure I do."

Nate stood behind her, holding the line. "Now," Nate said to Sara, "you watch the sail till it luffs." He waited until the edge of the sail was flapping in the breeze. "Then you trim until the rippling stops." He pulled on a line. "Got it?"

Sara bit her lip and studied the sail.

"Now it's a steady wind," he said encouragingly. He waited a few moments, then let go and sat down on the seat beside Libby. Sara stood at attention, both hands still on the rope.

"We've got to talk," he said in a low voice only Libby could hear.

She nodded. "I know. We have to get some things straight." No more dances on the beach, she thought. No more singing. They'd just concentrate on what they came into this marriage for. Sara. Saturday mornings with Sara.

Maybe someday they could be friends. She'd never expected her and Nate to be friends, but heck, she'd never expected him to be her husband, either. Friends didn't sound too bad, she thought. She could handle friends.

"Later, on the island, we'll talk." He smiled faintly. "Neutral territory. With Sara around there's no hope of seduction."

She swallowed. "Sounds about right."

He nodded decisively, and glanced toward his daughter. "Sara's getting the hang of this. Before she knows it, she'll be crewing with me. There's a cup race on Lake Michigan I'm going to win with the *Melissa,* and it would be so great if she sailed with me." He paused. "Why did you think she didn't want to sail?"

"I thought something about it scared her."

"Sara wouldn't be scared." Nate looked mystified. "I'm here, and I know what I'm doing."

The man's confidence in his ability was reassuring to Libby, but she wasn't a ten-year-old girl. Since Nate had come into her life, Sara hadn't been sharing as much of her feelings with Libby. It was as though her time with Nate were something removed, something she held close to her heart.

Though Libby felt a sadness at being excluded, she understood Sara was growing up. Now that Libby and Nate were married and there was no immediate threat of losing Sara, Libby could allow herself to be pleased that Sara was coming to have feelings for Nate. Funny, though, they never touched each other. And Sara had yet to call him anything but Nate.

Looking at Sara now, Libby wondered if Sara wasn't getting the hang of sailing, after all. Sara wasn't smiling, hadn't relaxed her wide-legged stance, but she'd readily agreed to handle the sail. Sara was outspoken. If she was afraid, she'd tell Libby, wouldn't she?

"Is sailing dangerous?" Libby asked.

Nate looked up at the rigging. "Sure, it can be. But I minimize all the risks. For example, you wear your life jacket. You don't do stupid, daredevil things. If somebody goes overboard, you can't just stop dead in the water to pick them up."

"Did you tell Sara these things? About not being able to easily pick up someone who falls out?"

"Sure. I'm teaching her to sail. She needs to know the risks. The best way to minimize those risks is not to go overboard in the first place."

"But when you explained all this, did you reassure her that you're here and will help her anytime she needs it?"

He frowned. "Yes, I did." He paused. "Well, I thought I did."

Libby sighed. "Maybe you did. But when you reassured her, did you hug her or anything?" Libby already knew the answer. If Sara was still shy around her father, Nate was downright reticent. Maybe still scared of making a mistake. She could understand that. But it was a shame things had to be so hard for them both. How much easier it would be for Sara if Nate could make the first move—a quick hug, a pat on the back, a tug of a lock of hair. The spontaneous gestures of a caring father.

Nate had all the right moves when it came to grown women, she thought with a flash of bitterness. But he lacked the most basic instinct when it came to his daughter. How very ironic that was.

He flushed. "She doesn't want me to touch her." Swallowing, his eyes went to his daughter. "I tried once. She...flinched. Don't you remember how she was?"

"But that was early on. Before she had a chance to know you."

He acted as though he hadn't heard her. "I hated that she shrank from me."

Her heart went out to him. It was so easy to tell herself that he was an unfeeling man, but he kept giving her glimpses of a different person. A man she could come to care for.

"Try again," she urged softly.

He shook his head.

"Nate, you're the one who has to try again. Make the first move."

He glanced at Sara. "It didn't feel natural to touch her, and that's maybe what she was reacting to. No." He shook his head again, more decisively this time. "It's better this way. Give her time."

She swallowed down disappointment, then felt a surge of hope. Maybe with time... Maybe she could work with Nate, break down his barriers... For what? she thought, suddenly impatient with herself. So that she could spin fantasies of forever-after with a guy she hadn't even been certain would be home this morning?

No. But she did want this marriage to succeed because Sara, the child she loved, needed her father.

"She wants to please you with the sailing," Libby said softly.

"You think?" His eyes lit with a rare pleasure. "Well, she's doing very well."

"Tell her so."

"She must know."

Libby sighed. "Maybe she does, but it never hurts to praise someone."

"Right." Nate cast a more speculative glance at his daughter.

For the first time, Sara was smiling a little. The wind had picked up slightly, and her ponytail rode the wind like a jaunty banner.

Beside her, Nate seemed to relax infinitesimally.

"Do you mind that I asked Tina and Trevor over tonight?" Libby asked. She hadn't consulted him about her last-minute plans, and now it occurred to her that she probably ought to be checking with him, now that she was sure he'd be home for weekends.

"Do what you want." He gave her a half-formed, rather crooked smile. "After all, I think I've disrupted your life enough." When she didn't reply right away, he added, "Actually, I wouldn't mind seeing Trev."

"Really?"

"Of course, things could be awkward with Tina. Does she know I'm here?"

"I told her." Tina had nearly refused to come over, but Libby had heard Trevor in the background, urging his mom to accept.

"Well, wonder of wonders, after the way she turned up her nose at the wedding."

"Tina worries a lot." Suddenly, she wanted them to get along. She wanted her husband and her best friend to like each other. "Her husband hurt her, and she's afraid you'll hurt me."

As soon as the words were out of her mouth, she was sorry she'd said them. A person who wasn't involved couldn't be hurt. She needed to be as cool about this relationship as Nate.

His eyes were intent, his body still. A sudden gust of wind ruffled the hair across his forehead. Then he shook his head. "Libby, whatever you may believe, I don't intend to hurt you."

No danger of that. She had no intention of *letting* him hurt her.

Next to her, Nate was quiet. Then, as they came closer to the nearest in a tiny necklace of islands, he stood and shaded his eyes with his hand. "Let me maneuver this baby in close," he told Sara as he took the lines.

"Didn't I do okay?" Sara asked. She bit her lip.

He looked surprised. "Sure you did. I just want to finish up with the sails so I can take the wheel."

Sara flopped down next to Libby. "Nate said I did okay," she repeated earnestly.

"Of course you did. What did you expect?"

Her eyes clouded. "He wants me to be the best."

"But you don't get to be the best without practice. And besides, sweetheart, there are other things besides being the best."

"Like what?"

"Come on, like this perfect day." She was impatient, but not with Sara. With Nate, for not doing his job of reassuring his daughter, for leaving this part to her. "Did Nate tell you you should be the best?"

Sara nodded, looking down at her knees.

Libby looped her arm around Sara's shoulders and gave her a quick, tight squeeze. "Now listen to me," she said slowly and deliberately. "All I want from you is for you to be you. And whatever Nate said, don't take it too seriously. Nate talks a kind of way, but he doesn't exactly mean it. Besides, he wouldn't have tried so hard to find you if he didn't already think you were the best." She hoped so hard that it was true, that Nate really didn't expect his daughter to be the best at everything she tried.

"He wants me to win a sailing race with him that his yacht club puts on. It's really important." Sara sat with her knees pulled up to her chest, her arms folded over them.

Libby decided then and there that she would add another subject to her forthcoming talk with Nate. Her righteous indignation at the pressure Nate was putting on his daughter felt good.

And Sara was a safe topic.

CHAPTER EIGHT

WHEN THEY PULLED INTO the dock, there was only one other boat tied up. A family Libby didn't know was picnicking near the boat launch. Sara looked over the remaining picnic tables and asked if they could go somewhere and sit on the sand. So with Nate holding the bag of food, and Libby a tattered blanket, they walked behind Sara, uphill and down, in deep sand that tugged at their sneakers.

Libby was puffing from effort but she was having a good time. The breeze was warm, and chicory dotted the meadows with lavender blue. Finally they broke out onto a pretty stretch of beach. Libby shifted the blanket to her other hand and wiped her damp brow.

Sara gestured to them. "Let's go farther. There might be a better beach up ahead. More shells. Cooler rocks." She wasn't even breathing hard.

"No," Libby and Nate said at the same time, and she caught his eye and laughed. Mr. Perfect was winded, as damp and bedraggled-looking as she felt. "Kid, I'm too old to go any farther." When Sara took a couple more steps, Libby reached out, grabbed the end of her ponytail and held on.

"Hey, no fair," Sara said, reaching behind her and trying without success to dislodge Libby's hand. But she finally stopped.

"I'm going to die," Libby pronounced, flopping down

on the sand and using her forearm to take another swipe at her moist forehead.

"Come on," Sara said again, a whine creeping into her voice. "We've never been out here before. Don't you want to see what's up ahead?"

"How could it be better than this?" Libby smiled and shaded her eyes. The dunes rose steeply on one side, protecting the beach from the wind. The sand was hot under her thighs. It wasn't much different from a hundred beaches on what the tourists called the North Coast, but it had a stark, simple beauty.

Nate took the blanket from Libby and spread it on the sand.

"Well, I'm going ahead," Sara said stubbornly. When neither one of them spoke, she turned to Libby. "I can, can't I?"

"Just be careful, and check in." There was nothing to hurt Sara on the island, if she took a few simple precautions.

Sara took off at a near run and in seconds had disappeared around to the windward side of the dune. Nate walked on, more slowly, down to the edge of the water. Bending, he picked up a handful of pebbles and stood silhouetted against the sun, casting them over the water. The day had started out cloudless, but now, here and there was a feathery cloud that raced across the sky. The humidity was building; Libby's skin felt sticky. She scooted over to sit on the blanket and watched Nate.

He'd brought them out here, and one of the reasons was that he wanted to talk to her. She had a pretty good idea what he was going to say. She was his wife. He wanted her. Sex was pleasurable. She remembered sex that way, but she'd been in love with Brian when they'd slept together, had been certain he loved her. Over the years, she'd been occasionally attracted to various men. But she had never had sex with a man just because she wanted to.

And sex with Nate would be...

Judging from their kiss, he'd be an expert lover. Part of her hated that Nate was so good at...that. She wondered if his lack of tender feelings would mean he could be less involved, more distant, more able to judge her performance. She knew instinctively that his touch would burn her, drive her to lose herself in her feelings, and she hated the idea that he'd be assessing her.

She bit her lip. She'd waited so long to feel the touch of a man again. Maybe too long. Maybe her stubborn insistence on love was more than outdated.

And there were...variations. Heck, there were pretty tame positions she'd never even tried. With a husband, she might feel adventurous, but with Nate...

God. He *was* her husband.

"Nate!" she yelled, unable to bear her thoughts a second more.

He jerked, then turned and came toward her.

"You said we had to talk."

He sat down on the sand next to her, holding a little rose-colored pebble. "Right now?"

"Sure. Why not right now?"

"Oh, I don't know. Maybe because we just got here, we're not arguing, and maybe you'd like fifteen minutes to enjoy the day?"

She peered at him. He wasn't smiling. This was a new side of him. She hadn't expected sarcasm. "Sara could come back anytime, you know. And I suspect what you have to say wouldn't be suitable for your ten-year-old daughter to hear." Her cheeks felt warm and she reminded herself that he'd been photographed for the Chicago society pages with any number of women.

He rolled the pebble in his palm. "No, I don't suppose it would." He paused. "Okay. Just what exactly do you want out of this marriage?"

The question surprised her. She'd expected an intense effort to persuade her that, as a married woman, she had no reason not to sleep with her husband, a husband she clearly desired. "I don't know," she admitted slowly. "All I wanted was Sara. I had to take you as part of the package." She tried to smile to soften her words.

"Most women probably wouldn't find it that much of a sacrifice."

She stared at him, struck by his monumental ego.

He looked right back. "After all, I've got lots of money. And you know what? I've still got every one of my teeth."

To her utter surprise, she saw humor glinting in the depths of his eyes. Suddenly, things did seem a tad funny. "I'm pickier than that." But she was smiling. "Okay," she said after a minute. "I guess what I want is for us to be whatever kind of family we can for the time you're here. I don't want you to disappoint Sara or constantly push her, either."

"But what do *you* want?"

A husband who mows the grass. A husband who thinks I'm more than a convenient bed partner, a means to settle a legal dispute. A husband who gets up early and makes breakfast. Whoa. She started again.

I want a baby someday, fathered by a man who loves me. At that thought, she almost went from smiles to tears in one heartbeat. If their marriage failed, it would hurt Sara. If their marriage succeeded, Libby was shackled to this man for life. It was one thing to realize you would never have children because the right man hadn't come along. It was quite another to have a husband who didn't love you and was so focused on another woman's child that he'd never even mentioned the possibility of having a child with you.

"You were saying?" He had no way of reading her mind so he was still smiling teasingly.

He would never understand her. She took a deep, determined breath. She didn't remember her mother. Her father's parenting had been loving, but gruff and haphazard. Once, when she was a kid railing at the unfairness of life, he'd sat her down to a poker game. Then afterward he'd told her, "When things happen to you that aren't fair, you have to play the hand you're dealt." Other times, he'd told her of her mother's saying: When life hands you lemons, you make lemonade.

Simple homilies from simple people. "What I want," she said just as simply, "is for you to respect me and my feelings."

"Done." Now he wasn't smiling, but was staring down at her with sincerity.

"And that means?"

"We're doing it again, you know." His eyes never left her face. "Tiptoeing around our attraction. We're talking about sex. And I admit I want you. But I've never forced my attentions on a woman and I'm sure as hell not about to start forcing my own wife. You have a right to expect respect from your husband, and you'll get it."

She couldn't believe it. "You won't push me to have sex?"

"It's up to you. If. When. Where."

She couldn't believe it. It was more power than she'd ever expected Nate to give her. Tenderness welled in her. "But what will you do when you need—" She stopped, closing her eyes for a second. She didn't want to know.

Nate flipped the stone from one hand to another, his eyes on the shore.

There was a strained silence. Finally, she asked, "What do *you* want, Nate?" Such a simple question. One, she suspected, most married couples covered *before* the ceremony.

"It's not important."

"It is to me."

"Well, I haven't thought about it, I guess. I assume you mean besides sex." He gave her a flash of his charming smile. Libby was beginning to understand him, to realize that at times he used charm to cover his real feelings.

"Besides sex," she agreed.

"Well." Idly, he fingered the little stone, studied it. "I don't like yelling and I don't like fighting."

"I don't yell much."

"No, thank God, and with Sara's custody at risk, you've had plenty of opportunities. I wouldn't have married you if I hadn't thought you were sensible. Instead, I would have taken my chances with the judge."

How odd that he felt so strongly about such a simple thing. "Why don't you like yelling?" she asked softly. "Did you and Sara's mother have loud fights?"

"At the end we did, and it was hell. I used to think of Melissa—of Sara upstairs, listening, but we were so angry. Both of us. I'm not blaming Eve."

She sensed that he wasn't telling her the whole story. "And there's more?" she prompted. When he hesitated, she added, "You can tell me anything. I'm your wife." She realized that for once she actually felt like one.

He hesitated again, shrugged. "Hell, it's no secret." He tossed the pebble ahead of him. It landed with a little spit of sand. "Everyone in the neighborhood eventually knew what was going on. Some of the people I do business with in earlier years also did business with my father. You can't imagine how hard I had to work to persuade them that I wasn't like him.''

Libby put her hand on his arm. He didn't seem to feel it. His eyes were again on the horizon, his body curiously still. "He gambled."

Libby let out a breath she'd been holding. "Gambled, as in he couldn't stop?" Her mind scurried along, trying to recall everything she'd ever heard about gamblers, and it seemed as if she couldn't recall a thing.

"Sure. I've read all the books about it. We were a classic case. The thing is, my mother came from a wealthy family. Very concerned with appearances. For the longest time, we—my mom and I—tried to keep a lid on things. She'd juggle bills, pay the most pressing bill collector, play the dumb society wife, anything to put people off when they called about money we owed. She was so humiliated, and I just…hated that."

Libby squeezed his arm. She longed to do more, to bring him close to her the way she'd do for anyone who was hurting. But there was a proud, straight line to Nate's back, and she knew instinctively he wouldn't welcome her gesture. "Any kid would hate that kind of pressure. Kids need stability, a chance to be kids."

He nodded. "But in a way, my mom encouraged him. There was something frenetic in both of them when he was winning. Some years would be good, and I'd tell myself maybe his luck could hold. My mother would always say then that my father was going to make back enough money to pay off the bills, put some aside, then stop for good.

"But then it never turned out that way. He'd buy one new car, then another. A Ferrari, a Jag, both in the same year. Hell, both in the same *day*. Furs. Jewelry. My parents would whoop it up. At night from my own room, I'd hear them having—making love. When he was winning, they didn't hide anything at all. Didn't wait till I was asleep. They were so excited about everything, all the time. So noisy." He shook his head.

She hurt for him. "And when he lost?" she asked softly.

"When he lost, it was worse." His voice dropped. "They yelled when they were happy. My mom screamed when they lost. She stood on the front lawn when they took her mother's silver and she screamed like a banshee."

"Oh, Nate." Impulsively, she covered his hand with her own.

Gently, he disengaged her hand, set it back on her side of the blanket. "It was a long time ago."

"Not so long ago, I think."

"A *long* time ago." His voice was very certain. "When I first went to a banker for money, to buy an old building in the warehouse district, I went to the father of one of my childhood friends. He was president of a bank, and I needed cash and a big line of credit. He said, 'Why should I loan money to the kid of the son of a bitch who bilked me out of half a million dollars?' I looked the guy in the eye, and I told him I was no gambler."

"And he gave you the money?"

"No." For the first time he smiled a little. "He gave me a *little* money, and he rode me all the time for the payments. He treated me like hell because of who my father was, and he taught me how you can be a developer without taking all the risks."

They were both quiet for a moment. He had told her so much more than why he didn't like loud voices and fighting. She studied him. He was dry-eyed, watching the waves. He did that a lot, she was discovering. She was getting to know her husband.

And she wanted to do that. Suddenly, she wanted to know everything about him. The big events that had shaped his life and the smaller things—what he ate for breakfast when he wasn't burning the blueberry pancakes, what his favorite color was, his favorite old movie, what he'd been for Halloween as a kid, his...

And, well, whether he'd be rollicking and charming in bed, or whether he'd really share the experience with her, cover her body with his own and look at her with that intensity that darkened his eyes to navy, just before he put his mouth to her ear and groaned out his ecstasy...

It's up to you. If. When. Where...

She longed to touch him. Without a thought that he might misread the signals, she put her hand on his arm again, tugged when he didn't immediately respond. He turned.

"I want to..." Her voice trailed away before gaining strength. "Just hold you." She held out her arms, gathered him to her. Under the sky, she felt his hard, unyielding body against hers. His T-shirt was worn thin, his skin hot underneath, warmed by sun and the sand beneath them.

He wrapped his arms around her, fitted the top of her head under his chin. "I figured you'd be a sucker for a story about a sad little boy. You're so good with Sara, I just...knew."

Had he deliberately tried to manipulate her? She pushed the unwelcome thought away and touched the back of his neck.

"But make no mistake. I left that sad little boy behind long ago." His voice was rough as he drew back and tipped her head up. "That boy's a man."

His mouth came down hard, fastening unerringly to hers. His tongue touched her lips, probed, and she let him in.

The sun was strong; she felt weak, almost dizzy. How quickly comfort had turned to desire. She felt the back of his neck, sensed the breadth of his shoulders, felt the solidness of his chest. He thrust his hand into the mop of her hair and held her mouth more tightly to his.

A long whistle pierced the air. Both she and Nate jerked at the same time. He started to rise. "What was *that?*"

Libby fought her way back to the present. "Ah, Sara." Her voice was shaky.

"Sara?" He was on his feet in an instant. "Is she—"

"Checking in." Libby reached up and tugged at the denim at his calf to get his attention. She threw back her head, put two fingers in her mouth and blew a blast in response.

"God." Nate flopped down onto the blanket.

She managed a shaky grin. "It's easier than screaming my lungs out. Actually, Sara's whistle didn't sound as if it was coming from too far. It's just as well we didn't get too...carried away." She was unsettled. She'd had no intention of letting him kiss her like that again, especially after they'd reached an understanding about physical intimacy. She was as he said—a sucker for a story about a sad little boy.

Once again, the unwelcome thought that he had taken advantage of her surfaced. This time she didn't push it away. She had to remember that nobody got to the top without learning to read and manipulate others.

THEY'D STAYED at the beach too long. They were late, and a sailboat depended on the wind. At the rate they were traveling, there wouldn't be much time for Libby to prepare for Tina and Trevor's arrival. Libby liked to cook, but it looked as if they'd be ordering a pizza instead. She smiled. She'd call from the car. At least now she could use Nate's cellular phone so the pizza might beat them home.

Sara stood beside Nate. "Let me trim the sails."

Nate gazed at the sky, looking a bit concerned. "The weather's changing."

"I can do it," Sara insisted.

Nate looked off to the west. A few clouds had gathered and the water was rougher now. "No," he finally said.

"Come on, please," Sara begged. "You said you were teaching me—"

"Nate—" Libby started.

"I need to move us in quicker," Nate interrupted. "There's a squall coming. Fast."

Libby pushed down a flash of concern. The shallowest of the Great Lakes, Lake Erie was famous for fast-moving storms. But the sky was hardly dark. She'd lived on this water all her life, and she saw little to indicate a big storm was coming.

"I could help you," Sara said eagerly to her father.

Nate almost physically brushed her off. "Check the straps on your life jackets, make sure they're tight," he said curtly to Libby as he started to pull in sail.

Libby checked hers and then motioned for Sara. "Just a precaution," she said as she tightened the tapes that held the life jacket to Sara's small body.

"Everybody into harness," Nate said. "Right now."

Sara looked terrified.

"Nothing's going to happen," Libby said with false lightness, giving Sara's ponytail a quick tug. Nate could have spared a word of comfort for his daughter, but as soon as they'd all attached themselves to the harnesses that would keep them with the boat in case of accident, his attention was back on the sails. He was pulling in the mainsail.

Sara looked hurt, but better hurt feelings than alarm. Libby managed a smile for Sara's sake. "Now, help me fold this blanket. It's not a glamour job, baby, but it's better than being told by the captain to swash the decks.''

A tiny smile formed on Sara's face as she pulled a couple of corners of the blanket together. "*Swab* the decks."

"Whatever."

"And I do plenty of *that* at the shop."

Suddenly, the boat lurched, shuddered. A strong gust caught the sails and practically lifted the craft out of the water. Spray shot high over the bow. Libby dropped the blanket and grabbed Sara to steady her.

Sara looked scared.

The wind picked up, and in seconds, she and Sara were soaked from more spray. Libby pulled Sara against her. "There's nothing to worry about. Nate knows what to do."

"I *hate* sailing," Sara said with feeling.

Storm clouds were moving in, low and black. Nate was talking into the radio, but she couldn't hear what he was saying. So much for her lifelong experience of living next to the water. This was a different world, being *in* the lake.

She stepped over piles of line, some of it coiled, some of it not. "What can I do?" she asked as she got to Nate.

"If we were closer to the island, I'd try to duck behind it, out of the wind. But we're too far from safe harbor." His eyes were intent on hers. "We'll run with the storm, wait until it plays itself out or goes by us. It's all we can do now."

She nodded.

"Take Sara into the cockpit with you. Libby, you'll have to steer, and it's going to be a hell of a ride."

"I don't know how." She tried to keep panic from her voice.

He nodded. "You'll have to do your best. Keep her turned into the wind."

The concern in his eyes scared her. But his calm words helped. "That's all I have to do?"

"It's enough. I'm going to pull in sail as fast as I can."

Nate worked feverishly, but he couldn't get the sails in before the squall hit. The boat lurched.

"*Into* the wind!" Nate cried.

She could hardly hear him because the wind was howling. Icy rain came down in sheets, blown so hard that even the cockpit was soaking wet. Libby held on to the wheel, made adjustments. The boat jerked, caught the wind and moved.

A long streak of lightning thrust down from the clouds and found the water. In the sudden illumination, Sara's white face appeared. Sara jumped at the loud boom that followed. She clung to the boat, her elbows braced.

Nate lashed the lines for the sail, then he was everywhere, working against the storm. The wheel slipped in Libby's wet, cold hands. She'd never been so scared in her life. The big boat seemed tiny now, like a toy bobbing in an ocean.

"We're in the height of it," Nate called once. "The wind's seventy. It won't get worse."

Did he mean *seventy miles an hour?* Libby squeezed her eyes shut against the stinging spray and grasped the wheel for dear life.

"You're doing fine," Nate yelled at her.

Libby didn't know if that was true. There was only a terrifying, endless wash of gray-black water, spray and rain, clouds of vapor so thick it was like sailing into a blank wall.

Nate yelled instructions; she tried hard to comply. The wheel jerked in her hands; the boat shuddered again. Gear was everywhere, thrown about. Lines snapped. Metal shrieked. Wood groaned. The wind roared.

Sara's safety depended on her and Nate, and together they fought the storm. Most of the time, she couldn't see Nate, the rain came down so hard. Sometimes he appeared as a larger-than-life apparition, like a sailor of old, taking the boat through the storm.

After a very long time, the storm died down. Still, Nate didn't relax his tight composure as he started for the dock at Bittersweet Point. The storm had blown them badly off course. The rain still fell, now a dispiriting drizzle, as he took the wheel and maneuvered in the rough water. Libby sat next to him. The cockpit was so small, all three pairs of knees touched. Libby pulled Sara to her. Sara hiccuped and Libby held her tighter. "You're okay," she whispered. "Nate brought us in."

In truth, Nate had saved them. He'd done what needed to be done, made sure she knew what to do, had confidence that gave her confidence. He hadn't panicked, had given little sign that they were in grave danger. But Libby was no fool. She knew they could have lost their lives.

Nate slid alongside the dock. Shaking off Libby's arm, Sara got up and made her way to the side of the boat. She caught the pier and started to wrap a rope around it to secure the boat. Her shoulders were shaking.

Libby went toward Sara.

Docking wasn't easy, and the boat was rocking so hard in the rough water that they had to scramble out. On the dock, Nate grabbed Sara's arm. "Are you okay?"

Sara shook him off, too. "I didn't do anything," she said in a small voice. "I knew how to sail, and I just...sat there." Snatching her arm away, she started to cry.

Nate looked helplessly at Libby. She pulled Sara to her. "You've only had two lessons. Storms happen on this lake, and Nate knew what to do."

Sara coughed, swallowed, stood there stiffly in Libby's

arms. Libby found herself blinking back tears. She knew how hard Sara was fighting them, because what she wanted right now was to go somewhere warm with Sara and have a good cry. Her legs felt like jelly; her hands and arms ached from grasping the wheel. She wanted Nate to hold them, too. Surely, he would hug them, remind them he was the experienced sailor, that this storm wasn't really that bad.

"There's nothing you could have done, Sara," Nate said, standing apart. "The mistake was mine. I let us stay at the beach too long."

Tears ran down Sara's face.

Belatedly, his hand reached for hers, but Sara kept her own firmly on Libby's waist. He dropped his hand immediately.

Sara spoke. "But...I needed to learn. You needed me to crew the boat with you."

"Not through a storm. And we can still crew together if you want. Someday."

"I never—" her lip trembled "—want to sail, ever again."

Libby squeezed harder. "We'll talk later. Now it's time to get dry. Right, Nate?"

He looked completely out of his depth. The man who'd hauled sails and lashed rigging on a heaving deck in seventy-mile-an-hour winds looked overwhelmed by the challenge of soothing his daughter.

Nate gave them both one long look, then turned and headed for the car.

CHAPTER NINE

NATE LEFT the others in the kitchen and slipped out onto the sunporch. He reached into the battered refrigerator Libby kept out there for a beer. But he really just needed a few minutes alone. When they'd got home, there had been no time to talk things over, even if he'd known what to say.

Tina and Trevor had been waiting. You'd have thought that when Tina saw how bedraggled and shaken they were, she would have done the decent thing and gone home. Instead, when she'd heard their story, she'd given Nate a tight-lipped look of disapproval.

Sara had dried her tears and told about their near accident not at all the way it had really happened. The acting she and Libby did had apparently given his daughter a streak of the dramatic. She'd made it sound as if he was some kind of...hell, some kind of hero.

Tina wasn't fooled. She knew how close he'd come to blowing it, maybe even how shook he was inside. She'd glared at him and got as protective as a mother hen, sending Libby and Sara up to bathe, calling for a pizza. Then she'd got out plates and silverware, snapping everything down on the table to let him know what she thought of him.

Tina knew where every item in the kitchen was, whereas that morning Nate had to open every cupboard door to make a batch of pancakes. Tina obviously felt comfortable in Libby's house. Everyone did, apparently. Everyone but him.

Night had fallen. Through the old glass of Libby's porch, he could see the cove, then the white condominium on Bittersweet Point. The rain had stopped, but the waves were still crashing in. He was still shaking inside, remembering. If Libby hadn't had the guts to steer that boat, he honestly didn't know if they would have stayed afloat. He'd discovered something about his wife. She had courage.

He hadn't been on full alert, and a good sailor was always on full alert. Instead of keeping an eye on the weather, he'd had a good time at the beach, enjoyed his daughter, kissed his wife. He hadn't wanted to leave, to face all the problems that awaited him on shore. Once on the lake, if he hadn't been watching Libby, admiring the way the sun made her skin glow and brought out all the coppery highlights in her hair, he might have been watching the horizon instead. He'd have seen the telltale signs of a quick-brewing storm.

For him to put Sara at risk… That was unthinkable.

He'd known he wasn't husband material, but in those eight years when Sara was gone, he'd been so certain he could be a good father.

Hell.

"Nate?"

Trevor was silhouetted between the French doors.

"Trev," he acknowledged quietly.

"Don't mind Mom acting all bossy. She's really okay. Just worried about a lot of things." In the dim light, Nate could see the kid grin. "You know women."

Nate looked out at the water, letting out a long breath. "No. I don't know women." Libby, for example. She ought to be giving him hell for making a mistake. Instead, when they'd arrived at her house, she'd thanked him. Thanked him!

"I hear no man will ever understand women. You know, there's only a couple of steps down to this porch. If you could steady my chair, I could come down." Trevor hesitated. "If you want guy company."

Guy company didn't sound all that bad right now. He steadied Trevor's chair. Trevor pushed and maneuvered himself down the steps.

Trevor put his finger to his lips, warning Nate to be quiet. With a dramatic gesture, he cocked his head, listening. "Super. Mom's so busy fussing over Sara she didn't even hear me."

Right then, Nate realized how much he had missed this kid since moving to Libby's. He felt protective toward him, fatherly in a way he couldn't be with Sara, given that the stakes were so high with his daughter. In Chicago, he'd thought about Trev, about things in Harborside way more than he'd ever thought he would.

He admired the kid. How could he handle being in this wheelchair so well? Nate knew for a fact that the loss of mobility, and therefore the loss of control, would drive *him* to a bitterness that would be bone-deep.

"Anything but beer in the fridge?" Trevor pushed his wheelchair closer, maneuvered until he could pull open the door. Nate resisted the urge to do it for him. Trevor rummaged around. "Nada. Just the good stuff. I don't suppose, since there's no cola in here or anything, you could leave off being the responsible adult this once and let me have a beer."

Nate hesitated. "How old are you, anyway?"

"Fifteen," Trevor said hopefully. When Nate didn't immediately say anything, he added, "It's only six years to twenty-one." He sighed. "Forget it." He shut the door hard.

"Trevor? What do you need?" From the kitchen, where Sara, Libby and Tina were playing Monopoly, he could hear lots of chatter, then Tina's voice raised in concern.

"Just getting a beer," Trevor called back cheerfully. He said to Nate, "Now listen."

"A beer? You're not going to have a beer! We've discussed..." Her voice came nearer.

"Cola! A cola, Mom! Now, give a guy a minute alone, you hear? Go tell Libby how to run *her* life."

She laughed, with a warmth in her voice Nate had never heard before. "Don't take too long out there, or I'm coming to check," she warned, but her voice was not at all stern. Then her footsteps receded.

"I don't think she remembers there are steps here, or she would have come down to see what was going on, out here in the dark." Trevor rolled nearer to Nate.

Nate set his beer bottle down and then settled into a seat so that he was on a level with the kid.

Trevor shifted. "I wanted to talk to you. I got something on my mind. Had it on my mind a while." His voice was earnest, nothing at all like the teasing tone he'd taken with his mother. He turned his chair to face the water when he spoke, in a gesture that seemed eerily familiar to Nate.

Trevor cleared his throat. "The thing is, I don't want anybody to know I'm talking to you about this. My mom wouldn't like it. She won't talk about him, ever. But I think about him, all the time now."

Nate waited.

"I guess you know my dad left us."

Nate nodded.

"He left a few months after I ended up in the chair, four years ago."

Nate sucked in a breath. Lord. People in Chicago thought *he* was a tough bastard. But he had nothing on a man who walked out on an eleven-year-old kid who'd just been confined to a wheelchair.

"Don't feel sorry for me!" Trevor said in a low, fierce voice, and then he swore under his breath.

Nate knew he'd made a mistake. But the kid had picked a hell of a confidant. He was no good with kids, he was discovering. "Okay," he said quietly. "I'll try not to feel sorry for you."

"Good. My dad was there, you know, when I got checked in this hockey game and went into the wall. I think maybe Mom blamed him but it wasn't his fault, so maybe she didn't blame him. I couldn't tell because they fought so much." The words had come out in a rush.

The conversation had become very painful for Nate, as visions of himself as a kid welled, listening to the fights from upstairs, then thinking about his own battles with Eve, knowing his two-year-old daughter could hear them.

"The thing is, I never see him. I don't even know where he is."

Nate was stunned. "You don't visit?"

"Never."

"Trev—"

The kid put up a hand. "I warned you. No saying you're sorry."

"Okay," Nate said quickly, feeling completely at sea.

"Look, before my mom comes back, I want you to know some things, so listen." His eyes went back to the dark horizon. "I don't know if you've ever thought about what I can do. My mom says I can take driver's ed when I'm sixteen and the school will rent a handicapped van so I can learn. Of course we can't afford a car like that. Anyway. I can beat anyone in Super Nintendo and I was in a wheelchair-basketball tournament and I was *good*. Do you believe I was good?''

"Sure I do." The kid had a keen intelligence and a steely determination that Nate both recognized and respected.

"And...the thing is..." His voice dropped. "Well, there's this girl at school. She's not big in the chest or anything, but she's pretty and kind of fun." His voice picked up speed. "I kissed her some, and touched her chest, outside her clothes one night. And I got real...hard."

If Nate had been holding his beer, he would have dropped it. Why was Trev telling him this? If he needed to talk to somebody about his feelings for this girl, why not his mother, or Libby? Libby was great with kids.

Trevor never took his eyes from the horizon. "I get hard a lot. So I know when the time comes, I...can. I think about doing it, you know, all the time. The girl would have to...help some, but it would...work."

Nate almost choked. Sure, ask the kid to tell Libby about getting a hard-on for a pretty girl. Nate had once been fifteen, and he understood. God, yes. Lately, he'd been feeling like a kid himself, aching with longing, with an untouchable, pretty girl tantalizing him, just out of reach. A girl who was all woman, a woman he wanted to touch, to stroke, to taste, to take. A woman who was his wife in name only.

"So, what do you think?"

Nate needed his beer for real now. Trevor was looking at him earnestly. It struck him that the boy probably had nobody to talk to about this. Of course the kid needed to know what he should do about what he was feeling. And Nate had just been drafted for the job of telling him.

"Well," he started, feeling for the right words, "you've got to decide when you're ready. Your body is ready, but you've got to decide if you're ready for all the things that can come after. Pregnancy."

"Rubbers," Trevor countered. "I know all about them."

Nate cleared his throat. "Right. And you've got to use them every single time. But that's only part of what I'm saying. The time needs to be right." He held up his hand as Trevor started to protest. "You asked me, okay? You're too young. You're not ready and the girl won't be ready." In the face of the kid's curiosity, Nate felt old, jaded. Sex had once been so important. Now the men and women in his circle treated it as something casual, indulged in anytime there was attraction. The only one who felt differently was Libby.

He, too, looked out toward the horizon. "You respect the girl's feelings. You don't push her into anything. Also, Trev, you don't tell other guys how you scored or got lucky. It's private, always."

Trevor thought about that. "I wouldn't want her to feel bad. You know, after." He sighed. "It's not going to happen. Not with Ann, anyway. She slapped my hand when all I was going to do was open a few buttons."

The disgust in his voice made Nate smile a little. Maybe he hadn't done too badly with the kid, after all. He twisted off the top of his beer. He felt the oddest sense of... Belonging, maybe. All of a sudden, the sunporch felt warmer. Kind of comfortable.

"Ah, Nate?"

"Yeah?"

"Do you think, well, you came back for Sara. So I thought maybe you'd know... I figure, my dad left because of me being in the chair. Now, don't say he didn't because I *know*. But I was thinking if my father knew I could do stuff, drive a car...be a man with a girl, then maybe he'd want to see me."

Right in that moment, Nate wanted to track down this kid's father and strangle the life out of him.

Trevor spun his wheelchair to face Nate. "My mom says you can do anything, that you've got money and lawyers. So what I want you to do is...find my father."

Nate had no idea how to respond, no idea whether Trevor ought to see his father or not. He did know that Tina Samms wouldn't like his interference. He was silent for a moment. Suddenly, this decision seemed every bit as difficult as any business decision he'd ever had to make.

Trevor waited. Nate could see the tension in his still profile as he pretended to watch the horizon. He knew then, absolutely knew, that Trevor had every intention of finding his father whether Nate helped him or not.

Abruptly, the light snapped on. Tina Samms stood in the doorway. "Trevor—" She stopped as she caught sight of Nate, and her lips pursed in disapproval. "What were you doing out here in the dark?" She cast her eyes about as if her son and Nate could be up to something on Libby's sunporch.

"Talking to Nate." Trevor's customary cheer was entirely absent. He cast a quick glance at Nate with warning in his eyes.

"About what?"

Libby appeared behind Tina, her flyaway hair glowing in the yellow light. Libby touched Tina's arm lightly. "Come on, Tina." To Nate she said, "I sent Sara up to bed. It's been a long day for her, and she kept yawning over the game."

"It's been a long day for everybody," Nate agreed carefully. He saw the protectiveness of Libby's gesture toward Tina.

Tina came onto the porch. "Trevor, I'll help you with the steps."

Nate stepped forward. "I'll do it. He's heavy."

Tina's shoulders straightened. "I've been doing it fine for four years."

Libby shot Nate a look that warned him not to interfere. Nate stood back and watched Tina struggle with the heavy wheelchair, grunting with the effort. In Nate's world, he closed a woman's car door, put a light hand on the small of her back to guide her up a flight of stairs. Polite gestures for women who expected them. He hated to watch Tina struggle, but he didn't have clue what to say. What to do. About anything.

He looked again at Libby. She was frowning at him. God, what a day this had been, really the first day they'd spent together as husband and wife. Tomorrow he had to get the crews moving at Bittersweet Point in preparation for building. There were calls from Jeff in Chicago; his answering machine was full. He and Libby had to talk about some things, things they hadn't seemed to have time for up until now. They'd yet to discuss the bills. Even the food he ate, the beer bottle in his hands, was hers.

With his mother's help, Trevor had negotiated the steps. Tina planted a quick kiss on the top of his head. Libby had already gone down the hall ahead of him, and Tina and Trevor turned their backs, closed the circle, leaving him alone on the porch.

He gave a harsh chuckle. It was hard to believe he'd had that fleeting sense of belonging. He was a weekend husband by choice. His wife didn't sleep with him by choice. His daughter apparently thought she'd failed him, out on the lake, and he *knew* he'd failed her. His wife's best friend hated him.

He couldn't wait to get back to Chicago.

"THEY WANT YOU this time, Nate. I've done my best, but they won't settle for hearing from the second-in-command any longer." Nate's assistant, Jeff, sat next to him at the conference table, across from his general contractor.

As contractors went, Jim Fioli was one of the best—tough, a guy who knew how to brazen it out with the workers. He was a good man to have with you in a pinch, and Nate was definitely feeling pinched.

Fioli grunted, pushing a stack of papers aside. "The carpenters are talking about walking out in sympathy with the plumbers."

The plumbers had no problem with Nate; they were in a contract dispute with another firm. But labor unrest had a ripple effect, touching every building project in the city. Right now the last thing Nate needed was a ripple effect.

The Iris Complex was in trouble. Buried in the paperwork he'd read on his way back to Chicago, this time Nate could see the seeds of his own downfall. He fought down a flash of panic. He'd been in tight situations before. He'd be in them again. So far, he had more reserves than any developer in the city.

He'd been up all night, crunching numbers, then all morning he'd been checking them against figures Jeff kept. Jeff's numbers were surprisingly accurate; the kid was doing a hell of a job. Now, if Nate could get the project back on schedule, he'd be okay. He couldn't afford any fines caused by delays in construction. He had an ironclad contract with Fioli; Marta had seen to that. The contractor would be the first to have to pay any fines. But Fioli flew without a net. If he folded, Nate could be next. The development business was like that. Bankruptcies had a domino effect.

Thank God there were no hitches at Bittersweet Point. He and the banker, Kevin Smithson, were seeing eye to eye on everything from the financing to the plans for an ultra-luxury resort, complete with indoor tennis courts, a lap pool, boathouses and hot tubs.

Nate decided to meet with the Iris workers at their union meeting on Friday night. He was reasonably confident he could handle them, but he wasn't looking forward to the task. Once, he'd relished the challenge. Where had all that fierce drive gone? He could still function as if he gave a damn, but nowadays everything seemed so...difficult. The air-conditioning hummed, but he was hot. He drained a cup of coffee anyway. He needed the energy.

He'd gone to Harborside the last three weekends, though this week he'd had to leave on Sunday morning in order to get back to business in Chicago. Funny how he'd resented coming back early. Libby baked bread on Sunday afternoons. Yesterday and today, he'd often found himself thinking of a shabby house on a cove, his mind conjuring curtains flapping in the open windows, a dark-haired girl chattering, a woman baking bread. A woman baking *bread*, for God's sake, and the image was earthy, sexy.

Nate looked down at a column of figures. But his mind wandered. Last weekend had been rainy, and Libby and Sara had been playing Monopoly again. For a while, he'd stood in the doorway, watching.

Then Sara had asked him to join them, so he'd sat with legs crossed on the braided rug in the living room and re-learned a game he hadn't played in twenty-five years. Libby had been lying on her stomach, intent on the game, but once or twice she'd teased him about the irony of a guy like him playing Monopoly. He told himself that he wanted to play only because he wanted to do things with Sara. He told himself he couldn't possibly be attracted to a woman who whooped when he was sent to jail, or landed on her hotel.

He'd won, of course. Then afterward, he'd wondered if

he should have let Sara win. But she was laughing over something with Libby as she put the game pieces away, so he'd decided he'd done okay.

Suddenly, he was smitten with the idea of asking Libby to move to Chicago. Why not have Sara and Libby here? He had everything they needed and more. A state-of-the-art kitchen, a housekeeper to cook in it, a pretty bedroom and matching bath for Sara, a balcony that overlooked the glittering lakeshore.

Libby could have a shop downtown. She was talented, and the naturalness of her designs would be in demand. She'd make a killing. He had contacts; they could invest in some big-time advertising. And she'd be home every night.

How would she react to the idea? She showed no inclination to move. In fact, she never even asked him how things in Chicago were going. She must not care. Well, he'd married her precisely because she didn't care, because they could have a marriage for Sara and he'd be able to keep his distance.

Hell. Nate abruptly shoved aside the stack of papers. What difference did it make, anyway? He lived in Chicago, and even *he* wasn't home every night. Last night he'd spent at the office, and the night before that, he'd been to a fancy charity auction for abused kids that had run on for hours.

He was lucky he could reserve weekends for Sara. This Friday night was Sara's play. She'd been talking about that play all week, every time he called. He'd meet with the workers at dinnertime on Friday, then he'd have just enough time to take the last commercial flight to Toledo and still make the opening curtain. He'd make everything work out.

Fioli mopped his forehead. "Damn building computers that tell you what temperature you oughta like. It's so flaming hot in here." He glanced over at the huge window, but it couldn't be opened. "Nate, I'm relieved about Iris. But I wonder how you let this labor unrest get out of hand. Not like you to let Jeff handle things like that." He shot Jeff a look. "Nothing personal, kid. It's just that some problems need the boss's touch."

Fioli stood and crumpled a piece of paper, his attention back on Nate. "Something distracting you, pal? If there is, you'd better tell me. I've got my new summerhouse in Door County riding on this deal."

With his thumb, Nate absently twisted the wedding band on his hand. "Nothing's distracting me. I've just been commuting a lot, from Ohio, where I've got another project in the works. It's been hard for me to give Iris time." Iris was a jealous mistress, he'd discovered. She seemed to resent every moment he spent in Harborside.

But Fioli wasn't listening. Instead, his eyes widening, his gaze was drawn to Nate's left hand. "Nate. Did you get *married?*"

Nate hadn't told anyone of his marriage, but he hadn't made a secret of it, either. He was wearing a wedding ring, after all. "Yes. Quietly. To an out-of-town woman. You don't know her," he added quickly, feeling oddly protective of Libby. Fioli was a good guy for business, but he was crude in his talk about women. And Fioli and his wife had an "understanding" that Libby wouldn't be able to fathom in a million years.

Fioli looked stunned. "Married. I can't believe it. You had it made for so long." He paused, thinking. "Is she knocked up or something?"

Nate started to rise, swept with an overwhelming rage. His fists balled.

Jeff put out a restraining hand, gripped Nate's arm hard and held on. Nate looked down, vaguely surprised that Jeff had the guts to rein him in. But the gesture gave him a second's pause, enough that he could answer with a controlled reply. "As a matter of fact, my wife is not pregnant. But if she were, it would be a private matter."

"Sure, sure," Fioli said quickly. "I just meant you'd do the right thing by her, you know? All that damned honor and everything. No insult intended."

Nate gave him a cool nod. He was boiling inside. It was shocking just how furious he was; he hadn't felt that way since the night the government had absconded with his only child. *Careful,* he thought. Get a grip.

Fioli gave him a grin, placating and knowing. "It's not the end of the world. As long as your wife isn't one of those romantic women, the kind who want you to spill your guts all the time and be home every night." He laughed. "As if you'd marry a woman like that. It'll work out. Men like us…"

"Jim," Nate interrupted in a deceptively low tone.

"Yeah?"

"Shut up."

Fioli flushed dark red. "Okay."

CHAPTER TEN

LIBBY HELD ON TO her program with one hand and twisted in her seat to look again for Nate. The school gymnasium was buzzing, two hundred folding chairs filled with the good folk of Harborside. On her other side, Tina was talking with Bart Portnek about costumes for the upcoming production of *Fiddler on the Roof*. All the community-theater people were here, because any occasion celebrating the arts—even a school play—brought them out. After all, there wasn't a symphony, ballet or even a professional theater troupe nearby.

"Psst! Libby! Come here!" Sara, in costume, was standing in the aisle and motioning to get Libby's attention. Libby climbed over feet and apologized about a dozen times, making a couple of promises to talk later about flowers for a wedding and the garden club picnic.

"What's up?" she asked with a bright smile as she came up to Sara. "Have you got stage fright?" That was intended to be a joke, because Sara had never had stage fright in her life.

"Naw." Sara screwed up her face. "Oh, you're teasing. Real funny." She stuck out her tongue. "I just wanted to know if you'd seen Nate yet."

Libby had been holding the seat beside her for half an hour. "He said he'd be here," she assured Sara with more confidence than she felt. This time, she'd been so sure of him. He knew how important this play was to Sara. But as the minutes dragged by and he hadn't appeared, she'd be-gun to wonder.

She was angry, and getting more furious by the minute, because Sara aside, Libby had been stupid, stupid, *stupid.* She'd gone to a department store in Toledo and bought a dark green dress. Flowing—but at least a solid color. And she'd splurged on a designer scent that smelled of sophis-tication and sandalwood, and put pearl studs in her ears. She felt prettier than usual, but oddly out of place, quivery with anticipation. As if she were a girl on a date with the handsomest boy in town.

Why had she bothered? Why had she spent one minute of her life trying to look attractive for a man like Nate?

The lights in the gymnasium dimmed suddenly, then went down jerkily. Jenna Baker's boy was spending his first semester as a stagehand. "You'd better get back," she whispered to Sara.

Sara was still looking hopefully toward the open door by the refreshment table. "Do you see him? You're bigger than me. See if you can see him."

Libby looked, but he wasn't there. "Maybe after the first act," she said, still hoping herself. "But *I'm* here." In her greasy stage makeup and garish costume, Sara looked like a little girl playing dress-up. How she would have liked to have shared this moment with Nate, asked him to pose for a picture with Sara for the camera she had in her purse. But she wouldn't admit to any disappointment right before Sara went onstage. "Go. Shoo!" She made her tone as light as possible. "And Sara, break a leg!"

Sara grinned at her words. She loved the expression, al-ways said it felt like "real" theater when people used it.

Libby turned from the stage. Instead of returning to her seat, she stood for a few moments. From this vantage point, she could see the open doorway more clearly.

"Psst!" Sara again, and Libby dutifully turned around. The red velvet curtain billowed, and she could see only one bare arm, frantically gesturing her to come onstage.

There was a lot of giggling going on backstage. Sara poked her head out. "Mr. Gerrard said I could talk to you for a minute. I just went back to the dressing room, and guess what was there. From Nate. Red roses, a whole dozen! Everybody was wondering who they were for and I nearly died of embarrassment because they were for me." Yet her eyes sparkled with pleasure. "Do you know what they *cost?*" She paused for the barest second. "Well, of course you do. Did you know before about my red roses?"

"Not a thing," Libby said truthfully.

"And there was a card." She pushed a card out from behind the curtain.

The card said only, "Break a leg, Sara. All my love, Nate." But from the starry look in Sara's eyes, Libby knew it was enough.

That is, it would be enough—more than enough—if he managed to put in an appearance.

The curtain billowed again, sending up a cloud of dust. "Only stars of shows get red roses. And how did Nate know a real theater expression and everything? Wow, wow, wow, this is so very cool." Someone called for her, and she said, "Gotta go."

Sara disappeared behind the curtain and Libby retook her seat.

"No Nate?" Tina asked as a tape played the opening music.

Libby shook her head.

Tina made a sound of disgust. Remembering the roses, Libby felt a sudden urge to defend him. "Maybe his plane was late," she whispered.

"But he didn't bother to call you on that little toy phone

of his, did he?'' Tina squeezed Libby's hand. ''Listen, don't worry about this. You'll have a good time and Sara will be great. You don't need him.''

She sighed. ''Tina, he's my husband.''

''Don't remind me.''

''And he's Sara's father. He bought her roses today, and had them delivered backstage.''

That gave Tina just a moment's pause. ''But where *is* he? Look. The guy wants his daughter like some kind of trophy. And now that he's got her and has you to take care of her, he takes off for his big-time life in Chicago.''

Her voice had risen, and she looked around and dropped it. ''Sorry.''

Libby nodded and faced forward. The director was announcing the start of the play. Her stomach felt sour, unsettled. She could certainly see how Tina had come to her conclusions. But Tina hadn't seen him so intent and determined at the first custody hearing, hadn't seen him swallow and look away when she'd given him his first picture of Sara, hadn't seen him making pancakes with Sara, trying so hard to fit in to somebody else's life and she hadn't seen him immediately after the storm, his face wet and gray with worry about his daughter. Oh, heck, maybe Libby was reading too much into Nate's behavior. Maybe it was all wishful thinking.

She felt very alone, too, because she didn't dare admit to her best friend that she'd missed Nate this last week, that she'd looked forward to having him home, burning breakfast and making plans. And she knew what Tina would say if she confessed to the dreams she was having, hot, hot dreams of black hair and blue eyes and aristocratic features taut with desire, dreams that caused her to wake up with the sheets twisted under her.

But by the end of the play, Nate had still failed to appear

and—roses or not—Libby was furious. Sara had come out for a glass of punch, and the girl had watched and waited until Libby couldn't stand it. When the director had called the cast backstage for some instructions about tomorrow night's show, Libby was relieved.

Libby and Tina were talking to Barb Fielding at the refreshment table when Kevin Smithson came up. "Where's your famous hubby?" he asked Libby.

She flushed, and he chuckled. Barb was giving her a knowing smile, too, doubtless thinking her high color was from all the implications of being a newlywed. As if either one of them had a clue what her life was like.

"Still in Chicago, I guess," she said, and the words didn't sound as offhand as she'd intended.

"Why would he be interested in a kid's play, anyway?" Tina added.

Libby saw the looks Kevin and Barb shot one another. "He wanted to be here." No way would she have the gossip mill buzzing about a rift between her and her new husband. "And he had roses delivered backstage for Sara."

Kevin nodded. "I figured he'd want to come. The guy has a real thing for that girl of his." His eyes crinkled with good humor.

"I knew that, right away," Barb added. "Remember at the courthouse that day, Libby? He wanted Sara so bad, everybody was talking about it. Wow, he was gorgeous. And when I saw him, I knew he'd be right for you. You always did have an eye for line and form." She laughed, then did a big, fake sigh of envy for Kevin's benefit. She held out a tray of cookies to Libby.

For diplomacy's sake, Libby selected a cookie made by one of the other women, but also chose one of her own. She bit into her own cookie, made with honey and organic flour. Barb and Kevin had engaged Tina in conversation.

Libby was only half listening but heard Kevin mention Bittersweet Point.

Nate had spent a lot of time poring over documents related to Bittersweet Point. It was the biggest building project to hit Harborside. Libby had thought she had a good idea what Nate's business was like. After all, she ran a business of her own, and coped with defective inventory, taxes, fussy customers. But Nate dealt with all these things and more on a scale that boggled the mind.

"So what are your plans, anyway?" Kevin asked casually.

Tina's face had gone white. "I don't know," she finally whispered. "I thought I had more time."

"Well, you've got no lease. You must have known this was going to happen."

"But I didn't realize he was going to *tear it down.*" Her voice rose in alarm. "I thought he'd add others to it. And Trevor and I could stay until he found buyers or tenants for it."

The alarm finally penetrated Libby's fog of misery. "What's the matter, Tina?"

"Bittersweet Point," she snapped. "My home. Didn't you hear Kevin? Our banker and your *husband* plan to tear down the condominium. Put us on the street."

A bit of cookie turned to sawdust in Libby's mouth. "No, Nate's going to add to what's there."

"Kevin says he and Nate are tearing down the building."

Libby glanced at Kevin. Tina had to have misunderstood.

A slight flush darkened his cheekbones. "The style's not right. Surely you know that. On the outside, the place is ugly—"

"It's my home." A couple of people had stopped chatting and were listening.

"Nate wouldn't run you out of your home." Libby

touched Tina's hand. It was cold under her fingers. "He'd never do something like that to anybody, and especially not to Trevor."

Libby's thoughts raced. To Tina, the condominium she rented was much more than a place to live. She had her son to think about. The area was not known for choice in real estate, and most of the housing—the lower-priced housing for sure—was old. Old houses had narrow hallways and steep stairs, and light fixtures and cabinets placed high on walls. The houses Tina could afford wouldn't accommodate Trevor.

But Nate wasn't some wicked landlord. He was just a businessman...

Oh, God. She remembered some things. Some talking on the telephone she'd paid little attention to, about scheduling and groundbreaking and some kind of trouble.

Kevin looked very awkward but determinedly logical. "Even if we added on, do you know what those condos are going to cost? We're going for the upscale market—"

"That kid needs a place to live." Kurt Flanders, a beefy man with a baritone voice that carried, weighed in. "We didn't know you and Perry were planning to evict that handicapped kid."

"Challenged," Tina corrected dully. "He's not handicapped. He's challenged."

Kevin's upper lip had begun to sweat. "Nate's plans have been on the front page of the *Harborside Herald*, Tina. You *knew* what was happening."

"Yes, I knew we'd have to go *someday*, that we'd just got lucky with the rent." Her knuckles were white around her glass of punch. "We'd have to move when the other units were built and sold. But I thought I had lots of time. Just when is the wrecking ball coming, anyway?"

Libby put out a hand again. "I'll talk to him."

"And say what? He doesn't give a damn."

"He does." Her voice sounded very sure.

But did he? she couldn't help wondering. Surely he did. But heck, if he gave a damn, he'd be here now, ready to assure her best friend that she'd have a home for her son.

People she'd known all her life were muttering, the news flashing through the crowd. Most of the townspeople had supported the Point redevelopment, glad to see the mess the old developer had made being cleared up, glad to have somebody of Nate's stature taking over the job. Just last week Margaret Matwing had said how nice it would be to have something done with the crumbling break wall over at Bittersweet Point.

The lights flashed, a sign that the janitors wanted to close the gymnasium. But nobody made a move to depart.

"Bittersweet Point is bringing a hundred jobs to this town," Kevin said firmly. Slowly, the people around Libby quieted, each obviously thinking. The shop owners had been pleased about the venture, anticipating more money that would be spent downtown. The town needed the jobs, and needed the money the project would generate.

Kevin pressed his advantage. "Tina, if you'd made a move to collect all that money in child support Jonathan's been racking up all these years, maybe..."

"Leave Jonathan out of this!" Tina's voice rose again. "Trevor and I will be fine. We're always fine. No thanks to the *men* in this town."

Barb had been silent up to this time. Now she rounded on Kevin. "That was a low blow to bring up that jerk," she said with vehemence.

Libby knew she had to do something. She had to reassure her friend. She had to stick up for Nate. She had to have faith that her husband would do the right thing. She drew a deep breath.

"Nate Perry is an honorable man," she said in a loud, clear voice that commanded attention. "He doesn't realize Tina's not able to make plans right now. He'd never put her out. In fact, I promise he won't."

Near her, people nodded, then whispered. Husbands and wives turned to each other and took her statement with faith and relief. Nate Perry wouldn't do such a thing. His wife had promised. And his wife was Libby Jamieson Perry.

"It's a misunderstanding," the kindergarten teacher said to her date, and Libby could hear the word *misunderstanding* passed along from group to group. Libby says it's just a misunderstanding...a misunderstanding...yes, a...

Lord, what had she done? She'd managed to douse the flame of gossip before it had gotten completely out of control. But she'd put her reputation on the line for Nate. The reputation she'd spent a lifetime earning. If she was wrong about Nate, her place in the town was in jeopardy.

But Nate was her husband. Could she do less for her husband?

And she really *was* sure Nate had no intention of seeing Tina and Trevor forced to rent some cramped space where Trevor couldn't use his wheelchair. She had to be right, because she couldn't bear it if the man she'd agreed to share her life with could be that callous.

Married people were a twosome who took on the world as one. No matter how she'd planned things going into this marriage, somehow Nate's fate had become hers. She hoped with all her heart that she was right about his plans. And his motives.

LIBBY WASN'T SLEEPY. She'd taken off her stockings, but she was still in her new dress. She tucked her bare feet under the flowing skirt. Its long sleeves felt good in the cooler air of the sunporch. Sitting alone in the dark, she brooded.

Nate loved Sara. That much she was sure of. But it was precious little to build a life on.

Libby wrapped her arms around her calves. Was Tina right? Was the sum of Nate Perry really only the cold, hard face he presented to the world?

A key turned in the front door. Nate. Safe. Relief, totally unexpected relief, went through her. She heard his tread in the hallway. Slow, heavy. Weary-sounding.

Quickly, she got up and flicked on the light. "Nate. Can you come here?" she called before he could make a get-away upstairs.

He came, and she was waiting for him.

"Where were you?" she demanded without preamble, knowing she sounded shrill and not caring. She'd had hours to run various scenarios over and over in her mind. And each one sounded worse than the last. She wasn't just angry anymore. She'd been worried. That almost made her angrier.

He straightened at her tone. "In Chicago. Where else would I be?"

"It's a big city. Where in Chicago?"

His eyes narrowed. "In a meeting. You've never asked me before where I've been. So far, you haven't been all that interested in how I'm spending my time."

"Well, I'm your wife." Her voice was still raised.

At the word *wife* something in Nate's eyes flickered briefly. Vulnerability? Hope? Before she could tell, his expression hardened; his mouth tightened. He shoved his hands in his pockets and said coolly, "Then from now on I'll give you a schedule when I leave on Sunday nights. I'll fax you any revisions during the week. Sometimes my plans change come Wednesday."

"That's not what I mean." She bit her lip. In actual fact, she *did* wonder what he did in Chicago all week. He conducted business, she reminded herself. But she knew he socialized, too. He had a whole life there that didn't include either her or Sara. "I don't give a damn what you do on Wednesdays." That was a lie, but she felt pushed into it. "What I give a damn about is Fridays. Specifically *this* Friday. You missed Sara's play!"

Abruptly, his cool facade vanished. He leaned his head back against the wall and closed his eyes for a second. "I was in a meeting, and I missed my flight. I tried to call. Several times, in fact. But your line was busy and then just rang and rang. If you had an answering machine like the rest of the world—" He cut himself off. "My car was in Toledo at the airport, so I rented a car in Chicago. I drove."

"It's six hours by car from Chicago. Surely you knew you wouldn't make it."

"Yes," he said quietly. "I knew."

He knew. And he looked so sad.

She wouldn't allow herself to react to that sadness. This time, they were going to have a real discussion. "What are you going to do about it?"

"I'll talk to her."

"And tell her what? That you were too busy to bother?"

"Libby," he said quietly.

"She wanted you here. Instead of visiting with her friends, she spent most of the time before the opening curtain looking for you. Even afterward, during refreshments, she was still hoping. You spoiled the play for her."

Her mind's eye flashed to the roses that were in a vase in Sara's bedroom. But she wouldn't take back her words. Not even when his shoulders slumped.

Libby steeled her heart against his distress. "If you'd had your priorities straight, you'd have been here."

"Priorities according to who? *You?* I'm trying to make a living for Sara, for you and this family—" He stopped abruptly, looking suddenly confused.

Sensing that he was thinking about what he'd just said, Libby looked him straight in the eye. "Since when did Sara ask you to work eighty hours a week and make millions of dollars for her? Since when did I? You do all that just for yourself, because you're…" She stopped.

"Please." That tight line to his mouth was back. "Say what's on your mind."

You do all that because of your father, she'd been about to say. She'd heard the shame in Nate's voice when he'd talked about his insecure childhood, the note of pride that he'd been able to forge a different kind of life. Now she couldn't use something he'd told her in confidence to wound him.

She cared too much, damn it.

That thought pushed her over the edge. "We have different values in this house. Those values say that we're here for each other. We don't have much, but we share what we have. We do things together. We touch each other. What do you have in Chicago? Lots of money and all the people who want it."

"How would you know? You've never been to Chicago. How do you know what my life there is like?"

He had her there. She didn't know anything about his life, but that was by choice. "I know enough. I know that wheeling and dealing have made you an unfeeling man!"

He looked as if she'd struck him. "You're yelling," he finally said.

"You're right! I'm yelling. And do you know how I know you're an unfeeling man? Not just because you've failed your daughter, not because you've failed…" She hesitated, then said it, "Not because you've failed me, but because you're going to run a kid in a wheelchair out of his home!''

"*What?*"

"Trevor Samms. And Tina. I had to stand there and hear that you're going to run them out. Oh, yes, that's what was said about you in that auditorium tonight. I told this whole town that you're not going to do it, and do you know what?'' Her voice dropped but it was trembling uncontrollably. "I realized you share so little of yourself that I wasn't sure *what* you were planning. I defended you, but in my heart I wondered if my husband was going to put my best friend and her boy on the street!''

He stared at her, and she was vaguely surprised that he continued to listen. What was he still doing here, listening to her yell? He hated yelling.

To her astonishment he touched her, something he'd not done since the day they'd picnicked on the island. He reached out, touched her arm, then grabbed and held on when she tried to jerk away. His eyes were an intent, blazing blue. "What am I supposed to be planning for Trevor? Tell me what in hell you heard."

"You and Kevin Smithson have plans to tear down the condo. Is that true?''

He looked utterly nonplussed, and relaxed his grip on her arm slightly. "Well, sure. You knew that I was redeveloping the Point.''

"We thought you were going to add more condos to Tina's. That it would take a year or more to build them all. That Tina could stay in her home until then.''

"We're tearing them down.''

At his words, shock and hurt lanced through her in equal measure. It was true, then. She had actually married a man who was everything Tina had said. What in God's name had she done? Slowly, she looked down to where his hand still gripped her forearm. A masculine hand. A hand wearing the wedding band she'd put on his finger. A hand she'd wanted on her skin. "You bastard. You really are going to put them out."

"No. Of course we're not going to do that. She'll have time to find something…"

She jerked, and her arm came free. Unable to keep back the tears, she swiped her arm across her eyes and stumbled toward the door. She pushed out into the cool dark and headed toward the water, moving fast.

If only he didn't follow. If only he responded to this messy scene by doing what he did best—withdrawing. He could head out in his rented car and be back in Chicago by dawn.

Nate followed. He didn't know what to do, what to say. Libby was far ahead. Even in the slight moonlight, she was surefooted, knowing the path to the water from a lifetime of treading it.

His strides were longer, and eventually he caught up to her. As he'd expected, she was crying.

Eve had cried when she was upset with him, and he'd never known the right thing to say to her, either. But where Libby had left the room, he'd had to listen to Eve for hours, crying, curled next to him in bed. He'd ached all over then, his eyes had burned, and he'd felt utterly helpless. He remembered the feeling well, and this time he felt the same, only more intensely. How was that possible? He'd been so careful to shield his heart. He didn't even share a bed with this woman.

For the first time, he was glad they didn't share a bed. How could she honestly believe he'd deliberately hurt a woman and her disabled kid? Well, he'd be damned if he'd let her see how she'd hurt *him*, believing he was a cold-hearted bastard. He'd expended more emotion on Libby and this family than he'd done in years. If she didn't know him by now... Damn her, anyway. She gave acceptance so unstintingly. To everyone but him.

Now Libby stood on the edge of the little ribbon of natural sand that divided the rough grass of the backyard from the lake. He stood as close to her as possible, but he resisted the urge to touch her. She'd only push him away again. "We have to talk," he said, and he hated how rough his voice sounded.

"There's nothing to talk about." In the moonlight he could see her chin come up.

"There is. What is the problem with Tina?" When she didn't immediately reply, he added, "To solve problems, I've got to know what they are."

"Sure. Ever reasonable," she retorted bitterly. "I'm worried about my friend, and you're calling it a *problem*."

He hated it when women got irrational. "Clearly, it's a problem."

She sighed finally, and he could tell she was blinking away tears. His stomach clenched.

"We all thought you were just going to add on to the condominiums, and until they were sold, Tina and Trevor could live there."

"So I gather. But my plans were never a secret. Go on."

She sighed again, but she sounded calmer now. "I think we believed that because we wanted to. Nate, that's the only place Tina can afford. She works as a seamstress, helps me in the shop, but she barely gets by."

He was astonished, and the tight knot of anger in his stomach loosened. He'd figured, with Tina and Trevor living in the luxury of Bittersweet Point, that Tina was well-off. "What about her ex-husband? Doesn't he help?" But he remembered the conversation with Trevor and already knew the answer.

"She doesn't even know where he is, but she doesn't make any move to find out, either. She's proud of making it on her own."

Nate understood pride. But it seemed that for her son's sake, Tina needed to let go of some. "The guy fathered a kid. He ought to pay to support him."

"I agree," she said unexpectedly. Okay, Nate thought. Some common ground. He wondered if Libby knew how much Trevor thought about his father.

Libby pushed a few strands of hair out of her eyes. The wind had picked up. Against her hand, the aquamarine in her engagement ring glinted. He had the strongest urge to soothe her, to pull her to him the way she did with Sara, to stroke the hair away from her eyes. To gain comfort in return.

He put his hands in his pockets.

She spoke. "Pretty soon Tina and Trevor will have more...*basic* concerns than covering old ground with Jonathan."

"They won't have to live in a rattrap." He kept his voice carefully controlled so she wouldn't know how much her assumptions had hurt him. "Look, you think I'm a selfish bastard, but in actual fact I give quite a bit to charity."

"I know," she said.

"Oh." Now he remembered all those forms he'd filed with the court. And of course there'd been full disclosure of all his assets and liabilities on the prenuptial agreement Marta had had her sign.

"So that's your solution, Nate? You'll throw her out, then give her money, like she's a charity case."

He hadn't meant it that way.

"You do that, you know." She turned to gaze at him in the cool, silvery dark. "You give to charities, but globally. Big charities, the impersonal ones. You help all kinds of people from a distance. Now Trevor will be the Disabled Kid charity, won't he? And you won't think about allowing Tina any dignity. Take the money or move into some crummy joint where Trevor can't get down the hall to a bedroom. But you've written a check. Your conscience is clear."

She was right. Damn her, she was. But she was wrong, too. He did care about Trevor. Much more than globally. He'd no more deliberately hurt Trevor than he'd hurt Sara.

Or Libby. He had a vision of her in the kitchen, her hands in bread dough. It was an earthy image, with her pale, curving bare legs in cutoff jeans, and her hair sparkling in the light of the window.

He wanted people to care for. It was a stunning thought. For so many years, he'd thought if he only had Sara, his life would be perfect. But now this town—he cared about it somehow—in some rusty, fumbling, scary way he cared. He wanted to show his love for Sara. For Libby, he wanted to…

He cut off the thought. He was crazy to hope. He didn't even know what to hope *for*. He knew exactly why she'd married him. She'd made it clear in a thousand ways that he wasn't her idea of a husband. "What am I supposed to do about Tina?"

"Do you have to tear down the building?"

"Yes, I do." With the Iris Complex in jeopardy, it was more important than ever that Bittersweet Point stay on schedule.

"If I…" she hesitated. "If I asked you not to?"

He hesitated, too, suddenly wishing more than anything that he could do as she asked.

"As a favor to me?" she asked.

"I can't," he said finally.

"Why? Because you'll lose some money?"

If she only knew, he thought. "Yes. Because this time I can't lose money." Thank God she didn't know how tricky things were getting financially. She thought he was a failure with Sara. He knew he'd blown it tonight with his little girl. In fact, Libby had made it clear she didn't think much of him on any front. He clung to his material success, grabbed for his pride and held on with both hands.

In the dim light of the moon, he couldn't see her expression clearly. But he could tell she was studying him.

"Would you do it if I were really your wife?"

He stared at her, not sure for a second what she meant.

"You know what I mean!" She sounded impatient, disgusted with his slowness. "Will you help Tina if I agree to have sex with you?"

At her words, the anger he'd held in check flooded through him, at the same time pure lust shot through his groin.

Libby clapped a hand over her mouth, aghast at what she'd said. She had been so angry, so intent on making a point. Sensible, Nate had called her once. Sensible, she would have called herself. Sensible! How did this man bring out so much emotion? Embarrassment heated her cheeks until she figured they must be glowing in the night.

He moved a step closer. She came face-to-face with his broad chest. His voice was a tight whisper. "So you want to be a wife, do you? A tad late, but an offer, just the same."

She held her ground. Her toes dug into wet sand. The tension was unbearable. She licked her lips.

She was close enough to hear him take a breath before his hand tilted her face up. At the same time his lips came down, his other hand came around to the small of her back. He kissed her so fiercely, with such raw, aching, angry passion, that she felt herself bend backward.

So this is what it means to be swept off your feet, she thought as he lifted her to meet his mouth. His thighs molded to her legs, his arousal, hard and demanding, pressed forcefully into her belly. His breathing was uneven; she heard a low sound deep in his throat and couldn't help an answering one of her own.

She was excited, deeply excited, aroused to a fever pitch. Not only by this moment, but by the things that had gone before. The days—the nights—he'd spent in the room down the hall, the mornings when she'd spy the rumpled sheets of his bed from the doorway. The bathroom, with its lingering scent of a man and in the mornings its mirror fogged with steam. The tender way he looked at his daughter. The vulnerable, somehow yearning way he occasionally looked at *her,* and now, the hard, commanding feel of his mouth and his hips pushing against her own. All blended into splendid desire.

"So you want to be a wife?" he whispered again, this time his voice harsh with thinly suppressed desire.

"Yes," she struggled to whisper back.

"For Tina. For your friend. Because you need a favor from your husband."

No. Yes. Her mind was foggy with desire. "Yes, I—"

Abruptly, so abruptly she almost fell, he released her.

"No thanks." His voice was as cold as ice.

She stared at him, conscious of the loss of his body against hers. Her lips felt tender, her body chilled.

He turned and left her on the beach.

CHAPTER ELEVEN

LIBBY COULDN'T STAY out on the beach all night, though she was tempted. She'd sat on a creaky lawn chair and watched the waves over the water until she was as cold and miserable on the outside as she was on the inside.

The offer she'd made was so out of character that she was stunned at her own behavior.

And Nate had punished her for making it. His kiss had been calculated, she thought now, to show her that she did feel desire for him, that if he'd made love to her on the beach it would have been because she'd wanted to. Not as a sacrifice for a friend, but as a woman taking something for herself.

And he'd made no promises about Bittersweet Point.

She hadn't heard his car start around front, so she knew he was still in the house. Her house. *Their* house. It was dark. He must have gone to bed.

She dragged herself to the house. Tomorrow, she'd have to apologize for insulting him.

Of all the stupid things to say, offering herself up like some maiden chained to a rock for his enjoyment. Nate brought out her worst qualities.

She couldn't forget his promise. She was to decide about intimacy. If. When. Where. He'd been an honorable man, and she had not been an honorable woman. She'd been dishonest, because in offering herself, she hadn't really been thinking of Tina. Libby was used to thinking of herself as right and him as wrong. It was hard to believe that she had tried to manipulate Nate.

The hallway light was on. Sara's door was ajar, but the door to Nate's bedroom was firmly closed. She hesitated outside that closed door, then moved on, uncomfortable in her own home. Once in her bedroom, she took off her fancy dress and her pearl studs and put on her sunflower-patterned nightgown. Her breasts felt heavy and tender from the excitement of Nate's kiss.

She had barely gotten into bed and had not yet shut off the light when there was a quick knock on her door. Before she could even reply, Nate swung open the door.

He stood in the doorway, still in the pants from his suit, his white cotton shirt half-unbuttoned, his cuffs open.

Libby grabbed for the sheet. If he'd knocked a minute before, he would have seen her naked. Now, in her modest nightgown, she felt ridiculously exposed. Exposed as a small-town hick woman who'd tried for sophistication and made a fool of herself.

"What do you want?" There was a quaver in her voice that she hated.

"Don't worry, I haven't come to take you up on your delightful offer." He rapped a fist on the door frame. "Hell, that's not what I came to say."

Before he could say whatever he had intended, she blurted out, "I'm sorry."

He nodded, his eyes fixed not on her face, but on the big sunflower splashed across her breasts. "Are you?"

"Yes."

He glanced into her eyes, briefly, his expression unreadable. "All right."

"You see—" she started at the same time he said, "What I want to say—"

He nodded to her to go ahead.

"This isn't working," she said miserably. "Our marriage. Our motives were good, but it's just not working."

His body went curiously still. There was a beat of silence, then two. When he spoke, his voice sounded flat, too. "Are you saying you want to end it?"

Did she want to end her marriage? The reason she'd married was still valid. Sara, asleep down the hall.

But if she ended this charade of a marriage, her house would be her own again. Not that Nate had changed anything. Her art, her threadbare quilts thrown over everything, her mom's wicker rockers—nothing had been touched. It was only his suitcase in his room, his shaving kit in the bathroom. Not really much at all.

Only his presence everywhere.

If she ended it now, there'd be no more waiting for Friday nights, telling herself she *wasn't* waiting.

No more tension with Tina.

She would explain to Sara. Libby would help her adjust. And there would be no chance of any further disappointments.

Everything could be as it was. Secure. Unchanging. Ordinary. Pleasant.

"No," she said. "I don't want to end it." Then she had a sudden, scary thought. "Do you?"

"No." He wasn't smiling, but his body seemed somehow to relax infinitesimally. "I'd only end it if I felt our marriage wasn't good for Sara."

In the end, it was all about Sara. That thought should have pleased her.

He hesitated. "Did I really spoil the play for Sara?"

"No. She wanted you there, but she had a good time. She loved the roses."

Amazingly, he cracked a smile. "Good. I'll talk to her

tomorrow. I'll tell her that no matter what, I won't miss at least my weekends with her."

"Don't make promises you can't keep," she warned quickly. "Say you'll do your best if you can't be sure you can keep your promises."

His face tightened. "I always keep my promises."

Lord, they'd been making peace, and she'd managed to offend him again. "I don't suppose," she said slowly, "that you could give her more time? Spend more time here, or invite her to Chicago."

There was a very long pause. Libby pleated the sheet she still held between her fingers like some shy virgin.

"I'd thought about inviting you both to Chicago, but this isn't a good time," Nate said finally. "And I can't spend more time here. Not now."

Her disappointment was keen. "Oh, I see." But she didn't, not really.

"Things will work out. I can make them work out." He turned to go. "By the way," he added almost casually, "I'll think of something for Tina and Trevor. Something besides writing them a check."

Her heart leaped. "What will you do?"

He smiled faintly. "I don't know. Yet. But you can tell Tina they've got time before they have to move, and even then things will work out."

Okay. All *right*. This time, not for a moment did she doubt he meant to keep his promise. Warmth shot through her. She smiled, too.

There didn't seem to be much left to say, yet he lingered in the doorway. The fingers of one hand tapped a restless beat on the door frame. Finally, Libby relinquished her sheet, smoothed it in her lap, tried to forget that she and Nate had had a rousing fight and she had been very *un*sensible. She tried to be casual about Nate in the doorway.

Casual about being in bed, in a silly, unsexy sunflower nightgown with nothing on underneath.

Finally he spoke. "The thing is, I remembered something you said. Before. Tonight, did you really defend me to everyone who thought I was going to put Tina and Trevor out?"

She nodded.

There was a long pause. "Thank you," he said softly, and then he turned away. A moment later, she heard his bedroom door closing.

"MARTA WAINWRIGHT."

Nate had bypassed the secretary and gone straight to Marta's private line. "It's Nate," he said.

"Nate. How are you? More to the point, what can I do for you? Iris throwing a tantrum again?"

He passed a weary hand over one brow, then looked out his window, over the tops of the skyscrapers. "Always. But that's not why I called." He paused. "How easy would it be to find someone who disappeared?"

"Disappeared? How?"

"I don't know. I have his real name, age, description, social security number. I assume he'd be working as a pilot." Trevor had written Nate a letter, delivered to his Chicago address, with all that information. Nate hadn't made the kid any promises, because he still wasn't sure he should.

"If he's a pilot, he'd be easy to find. Licenses, flight plans, all that. Why?"

Nate saw by the lights on his own phone that he had two incoming calls. He let the outer office field them. He said, "Well, then, maybe he's not a pilot. I don't know how hard he's trying not to be found. The guy owes quite a bit in back child support, but I don't believe the woman's been seriously looking for him."

There was silence on the other line. "No problem," Marta finally said. The consummate attorney, she didn't ask why Nate wanted her to find a man who owed back child support. "While I'm at it, do you want me to find out where he keeps his money? Assuming he has any, that is?"

Nate smiled. "Yes. But Marta, keep this on the q.t., okay? I'm not sure what I'm going to do once this guy's found."

Again, she didn't ask any questions. "Sure."

"Good. Marta, did I ever tell you what an excellent attorney you are?"

"Every month with my retainer check." Then she laughed, an attractive, husky sound. "We do understand each other." Her voice went low, suggestive. "Anytime you want to find out how good perfect understanding can make you feel…"

"I'm married now."

She laughed again. "I prepared your prenup, remember? I know exactly why you're married, and I don't remember any old-fashioned promises of faithfulness in that document."

He was silent. He'd known an offer like this would be presented to him sometime, despite the wedding ring on his finger. Libby hadn't asked for faithfulness. Marta was right; theirs wasn't that kind of marriage. On the sexual front, at least, he didn't owe her a thing. Lately, his body had been on fire at the slightest provocation from Libby—when she passed him in the narrow hallway or the door to the bathroom, when she handed him a glass of wine and their fingers touched accidentally.

"You're almost too beautiful to resist," he said in his

best charmer's voice, but his heart wasn't in the compliment. "But, no thanks."

There was a long pause, then Marta sucked in a suddenly harsh breath. "You care for her. My God, you really do. Now listen," she added quickly. "I like you. Not just as a client, and not just as a potential bed partner. So this is both legal advice and friendly advice. Don't let this marriage thing get out of hand. That woman is not our kind."

Marta was right. He knew that. Hell, he'd come to the same conclusion countless times. But almost without his knowing it, the knowledge had lost some of its punch, even some of its certainty. "Just find Jonathan Samms," he said. "And do your best to keep Iris off my back."

NATE KEPT his promises. All of them.

The workers had started on Bittersweet Point, and the one white condominium stood in the middle of a sea of tread marks on the moist earth. The condominium was in the way. What the builders would do when they had to start construction on the sleekly rustic replacement condos, Libby didn't know. She didn't ask. And Tina didn't, either, only grudgingly acknowledged that Nate kept his promise.

Nate kept his promise to Sara, too. He was home every weekend, taking the last flight out of Chicago.

Now Libby checked the clock over the kitchen sink. Nate was due in about twenty minutes. She stuck the rest of a block of cheese into the refrigerator.

At long last, Nate and she were working some things out. Getting down to a routine of sorts. Libby cooked dinner on Friday nights. Nate cooked breakfast on Saturdays, an overcooked meal that also broke Libby's rules about a healthy breakfast. Chewy waffles. Scorch-bottom blueberry muffins spread half an inch thick with butter.

She sighed. At least Nate's concoctions were made with

organic flour. She knew, because she did the shopping, one week using her own money, the next Nate's, which he deposited in a checking account on a regular basis. It was ridiculous, he'd told her more than once, that either one of them had to cook, or that she had to clean. She cleaned during the week, while he was in Chicago, both to forestall argument and to remind herself that nothing much had really changed.

She wondered what she was trying to prove. She worked hard in the shop. Nate acknowledged that fact. He didn't want to do anything but ease things for her.

But there was no reason to get too used to what Nate's wealth would provide. Without love between them, she couldn't help wondering how long her marriage could last.

And besides, fixing up her house, cleaning it, were part of her, part of her life. She had the feeling if she gave in to Nate on these issues, she'd be giving in on more.

Would that be so bad?

She hadn't been listening for his car, she told herself. But her heartbeat picked up of its own accord when she heard the well-toned hum of his Jag. A few moments later, Nate opened the screen door of the kitchen. Over these last months, at some point that she hadn't noticed at the time, he'd got into the habit of coming around back.

"Hi," she said, looking up from the cutting board, where she was starting to chop a tomato.

"Hi," he said from across the room. He did that every Friday night, came in the kitchen door and paused there. It could be damn awkward, the way he always just stood there.

Today, he had his garment bag slung over one shoulder, a thin designer briefcase in his other hand. His hair fell onto his forehead. The sleeves of his blue broadcloth shirt were rolled up over forearms tanned from days on the water. He wore no tie any longer and his shirt was opened a button or two, showing the barest gleam of shiny, coarse dark chest hair. He'd already started to shed his Chicago clothes like an outgrown skin.

And even in dishevelment, he was perfect. How did he manage to look charming and sexy on a hot evening after a day's work and a wait at O'Hare, a drive from Toledo?

Neither one of them had ever mentioned her offer of sex or that hot kiss on the water's edge. The day after Nate went back to Chicago, Libby had put the sunflower night-gown in the dresser drawer and bought herself a new one in town. Not a sexy nightgown, just a soft-green one minus sunflowers. Maybe a tad more sheer, with a bit of lace. Looking at Nate, she felt herself blush for no reason at all.

Quickly she pulled the terry-cloth towel from the vee of her neck, where she'd put it to cover her puff-sleeved, red polka-dot blouse from spatters. She felt suddenly flushed, conscious of how carefully she'd dressed. And how silly she looked. Because with the red blouse, she wore a white skirt with so much eyelet lace that she felt awash in it. Why had she let Tina pick red, with her red hair? "A square-dancing outfit," she said lamely, indicating her clothes.

He hadn't taken his eyes off her. "I figured. Even you wouldn't wear that getup any other place." But he was smiling a little. In confusion, she looked away.

Before either of them could say more, Libby heard a familiar pounding on the stairs. "Nate!" Sara called. "I saw you drive in."

Nate took a few steps into the kitchen. Out of the corner of her eye, Libby saw his face split into a grin so wide and genuine that she suddenly wished he would smile at her that way. "Kiddo, you look great."

"I look cool," Sara corrected. Her dress was a satin-and-glitter concoction that Tina had made for her. The silver lamé sneakers from her first shopping trip with her father adorned her feet as she twirled around the kitchen, bumping Libby's elbow and sending up a splash of tomato juice. "Whoops, sorry," she exclaimed, then did a do-si-do around Nate. "What do you think?"

"Pretty." Nate cleared his throat. "As always, Sara. Very pretty." He nodded toward Libby with this last, and for a breathless minute she actually thought he might be complimenting her. But she knew better. He couldn't possibly like red polka dots and eyelet.

"Dinner will be ready soon," she said quickly.

"Have I got time for a shower?"

"Sure. Are you coming with us tonight?"

"I'd like to. I don't square-dance, though."

"It's easy!" Sara exclaimed. "I'm doing the do-si-do." She demonstrated again, folding her arms across her chest and doing a proud marching step around Nate. "Don't you dance?"

"Ah, ballroom stuff." He clarified when she frowned. "You know, like the waltz."

"Oh, the waltz. Like they do in Cinderella on Ice."

Libby caught the pained expression on Nate's face and burst out laughing.

"Do you do line dancing or even rock or *anything* cool?" Sara asked.

His voice was grave, but his eyes had an unexpected twinkle. "Sara, I just don't do cool."

Sara laughed, too. "Well, I used to think you were awesomely cool, but now I know you're just a fath—" Abruptly, she cut herself off and looked away.

Just a what? Libby's hands gripped the dishtowel, and her eyes met Nate's. He had gone still. What had Sara been about to say? That Nate was just a father?

In so many ways, he was a father. He'd looked over

Sara's report card and told her he was proud of her grades. He worried about her when she was up on that horse he'd rented for her. He wanted her to share his interest in sailing, but since the storm, he hadn't pushed her. He'd been sensitive to her fear. Like a caring father.

And in so many ways, he wasn't a father. He never disciplined her. He wasn't here often enough to have to. He never hugged her. He was so very...careful.

There was a yearning in his eyes, in his expression. Sara was still turned from him, her hands plucking a bit of glitter on her skirt.

Make the first move, Nate. Take a chance.

"I gotta call Kathleen," Sara said abruptly, and turning, rushed from the room.

He'd had his chance, and he'd blown it. "Look, Nate—"

"I need that shower," he cut in, and then, following Sara, he left the room.

NATE COULDN'T BELIEVE how crowded the gymnasium was for this evening of square dancing. Libby said it wasn't as crowded as it would be later in the year when the cast of *Fiddler on the Roof,* which included Libby and his daughter, would cap the season with three performances.

The amazing thing was that he knew so many people here. He'd figured he wouldn't know a soul. Trevor was with two younger boys, showing them how he popped wheelies with his wheelchair. Now Nate recognized a carpenter from the job site at Bittersweet Point, and the heavy-equipment operator, Bart Portnek, and he even recognized the guy's wife, from the time Bart had forgotten his lunch and she'd brought some sandwiches to the job site. He recognized others. That woman who worked in the courthouse—what was her name?—and Kevin Smithson and his young wife. Amazing.

Various people spoke to him and Libby as if the two of them had been married twenty years instead of two months. A couple of people talked about the Point. Mostly they talked about the weather and if out on the lake the perch were biting.

Libby hung around until she saw he was in the middle of a group of men and then with a little wave, she took off. Sara stood off to one side with Kathleen and a group of girls. A much smaller group of boys stood in their own knot, a good distance from the girls. Each group looked at the other, tossed heads and pretended they weren't looking at all.

Nate excused himself and went over to the refreshment table. The casserole Libby had served for dinner had been some weird bean concoction. He'd never tell her, but he always ate on the plane beforehand. Kevin Smithson joined him and chose a can of cola.

"Ready for the dance?" Kevin asked.

"I guess so. Sara is excited about it."

"Are you an expert?"

Nate smiled self-consciously. "Never did it in my life. In fact, I was thinking I'd just watch."

Kevin grinned. "You want to live in Harborside, it helps if you like powerboating, acting and square dancing."

Nate liked none of those things. He didn't live in Harborside. *And* if he was learning a new skill, he learned it in private.

The lights went down and the caller took his place. A boom box played a country song. Various groups began to form squares. Most of the dancers wore jeans or denim skirts; few were as tricked out as Libby and Sara. He couldn't help a smile. Libby was unique, even in a town like Harborside.

Libby was speaking to the caller. Then she looked

around, saw Nate, headed toward him. Out of the corner of his eye, he caught sight of Sara. Suddenly, his daughter seemed to be standing alone, her group of friends hovering behind her like the chorus in a Greek tragedy.

In the kitchen earlier, had Sara really almost said she saw him as a father? After the storm on the lake, he'd almost been afraid to hope. She seemed to like him, but it wasn't enough. He wanted what Sara and Libby shared, but he didn't know exactly how to go about achieving it. He couldn't do it the way Libby did, with hugs and the right words all the time. He'd be so awkward that Sara would be embarrassed, would surely withdraw. He had to get there in his own way.

As he and Kevin watched, the group of boys huddled, talked, shifted. One boy approached his daughter.

"I think Sara's got a boy interested in a dance," Kevin said.

The boy said something, hung his head shyly. Sara flipped her hair over one shoulder, rubbed at the gym floor with the toe of her silver sneaker. Then she nodded. Careful not to touch each other, Sara and the boy got into a square made up of six other kids their age.

Watching, Nate got a lump in his throat. He couldn't blow his chance with his daughter. More than anything, he wanted to be around to see her grow into womanhood.

Libby was hurrying toward him now. "Tina's saving us a place."

Tina was saving something for him, even a spot in a square? "I'm sitting this one out."

She smiled at him. "Come on. It's not hard."

"Do it." Kevin gave him a little clap on the shoulder. "One thing I've learned, guy. If your wife wants to dance, life is a hell of a lot easier if you dance."

Near him, Trevor was making up a square with a slight blond girl as a partner.

Libby's eyes sparkled.

Nate knew he'd look foolish. But if Trevor could square-dance in a wheelchair, Nate could certainly do it.

"Okay," he said, and was rewarded with a smile from Libby that was downright incandescent. Something very tight in his chest loosened then. What the hell. She wanted him to dance, and he suddenly wanted to please her.

A guy with an electric violin had joined the caller.

"All right!" the caller shouted, clapping his hands for silence. "Everybody ready?"

There was a chorus of hoots and yells.

"Now, we've got a special treat tonight. I mean, besides John here on the 'lectric fiddle." John bowed to a smattering of whistles and applause.

"The treat I've got is a little secret I learned from a pretty redheaded gal. Seems we've got a beginner in our midst."

Nate shot Libby a glance and got a very bad feeling.

"Who?" somebody called.

"Handsome feller from the big city. I guess they don't do much square dancing in the big city." He shook his head. "So anyway, we've got a feller to teach our country ways to." John played a few bars of doomsday music on the fiddle. Everyone laughed. All of a sudden, a spotlight came on, lurched, sought, found Nate.

"I didn't think he'd make fun of you," Libby whispered back. "I just asked him to start with an easy dance."

"The lovebirds are whispering," the caller noted for the crowd. Nate had the fleeting satisfaction to see that in the harsh light of the spotlight Libby's cheeks bloomed. Around him, the laughter had an easy sound.

"Now, we're going to start with something simple.

Honor your partner.'' All around him the men bowed, the women curtsied. Libby went into a deep curtsy almost to his feet, her skirts pushing out around her like a parachute.

He bowed, feeling very awkward.

She put her hand in his. It was hot, a little damp.

For Nate's benefit, the caller put them through a few simple moves without music. A do-si-do like the one Sara had done. An allemande left, in which Nate forgot to do a full rotation and almost ran into Tina as a result. She gave him a tight-lipped smile, but everyone else laughed with good humor.

Then they tried it to music. The caller called out the steps a split second before the dancers were expected to perform the maneuver. It was harder than it looked. But kind of fun in its way. Swinging. Nate felt himself unexpectedly caught up in the music, the simple, insistent rhythm of the calls.

Flashing hands, a sashay of hips, then a prance back to Libby.

"Now back to kiss your pard-ner," the caller chanted. A peck to his wife's cheek, a fleeting touch of her hand. All around him, couples were whirling.

"Gents to the cen-ter."

A beat late, Nate joined three other men in the center of the square. Some guy he didn't know clapped him on the shoulder and gave him a thumbs-up sign.

The fiddle slowed.

"Your sweetheart's a cryin'." The fiddle turned a tad sultry.

Then the music stopped. "She's got a look in her eye, boys." The caller's voice had gone low, husky. "Wants that spoonin' real, real bad. What're you gents gonna do?"

"Kiss her!" the gents cried.

The music resumed. "Back to your squares, then, and do it," the caller chanted at last.

All around him, men whooped, kissed their partners exuberantly, pulling them off their feet, giving them a twirl. He looked down into Libby's eyes. Hers were shy, her lips parted. He had never been spontaneous, given to public displays of affection.

But suddenly, he ached to kiss his wife, with her perfect skin and red polka-dot blouse over breasts that were rising and falling with the effort of the dance.

He bent to her, kissed her lightly, when what he longed to do was grab her like the other husbands and act like a caveman staking a claim.

He wasn't really her husband, though. Did she want a kiss like that? She kept her hands firmly against her sides, and the moment passed. The caller sent them into a final allemande left, a swing, and then the dance was over. Everyone clapped. Nate felt so damned...disappointed somehow.

The caller blew into the microphone, and the hiss stopped everyone short. "Now, listen up, everyone. Our city feller did pretty good for his first dance, though once he did sorta step on Tina's foot, and once he was all by his lonesome tail in the middle of an empty square." The crowd laughed in appreciation.

Suddenly, Nate didn't care. They weren't laughing at him. They seemed to be laughing as though he was included. As though he was one of them.

"But he did do something very wrong."

A man from the next square called out, "What?"

"When I told the fellers to kiss their ladies, he didn't kiss his lady. Only a little peck. I think that redheaded gal deserves more than that, don't you? I mean, her just gettin' hitched." He paused. "Go ahead, son. Kiss your wife. Show us what she means to you. We'll wait."

There was laughter, a whoop or two. The spotlight, which had lost track of Nate during the dance, crept closer.

The crowd was clapping in rhythm, like at a football game. Nate was trapped. The caller couldn't possibly know that he'd touched Libby more times during the dance than at any time in the last two months of married life. Libby's eyes were wide and apprehensive, as though she expected him to turn away from her, embarrass her in front of everyone.

Show her what she means to you.

What the hell. He'd wanted to kiss her even before he'd walked into the doorway of the kitchen tonight. He'd wanted to kiss her since the day he'd *met* her.

So he did. And whatever Nathan Perry did, he did to the best of his ability. He swept a surprised Libby off her feet and into his arms like a bride crossing the threshold.

She was solid and surprisingly heavy; he had to brace his thighs to hold her. A hush fell over the crowd. The spotlight was in his eyes before he closed them. He dipped his head and captured her mouth. As her arms went around his neck, the crowd applauded.

He kissed her and kissed her, suddenly intent on proving to everyone that she was his wife. His pretty, redheaded gal.

CHAPTER TWELVE

A HALF HOUR LATER Tina Samms caught up with him. Nate was thirsty from all the dancing, and had come to the refreshment table to get a can of soda while Libby was in the ladies' room.

He hadn't had a chance to talk to Libby at all. They'd danced several more dances, joining Sara's square. In the short breaks in between dances, people kept coming up, talking.

Libby was always at the center of things, and she, well, she *sparkled*. For the first time, he truly understood why she didn't want to leave Harborside. Her roots in this town gave her life a sense of purpose, belonging. And of course she wanted those same things for Sara. Also for the first time, Nate wondered if he could give Sara those things in Chicago.

Nate himself belonged in Chicago. The feeling of purpose Libby got from this little lakeside town, he got from his business, from the steel and glass of the towers he built by the water.

Only lately, those things just seemed like...things.

Things with problems.

"Nate?"

He turned in surprise to see Tina standing next to him in a cowgirl outfit with white fringe.

"Tina," he said warily.

"Can we talk?"

"Sure." From the force of long habit, he silently offered her refreshments, and refrained from sipping his own soda until she'd popped the top on hers.

Behind him, the music was starting again, insistent, echoey-loud in the vast space. Tina headed for the door of the gym and he held it for her.

Outside on the blacktopped parking lot, he waited. For some reason, he was tense. He stood up to contractors, plumbers, bankers, politicians. But he felt so uncertain around Libby's friend. Trev's mother.

"Look," she finally said. "I just wanted to say thank you for leaving the condominium where it is for now."

He could see the words were difficult for her to say. He nodded in acknowledgment.

She took a determined breath. "I know it's hard for the workers to go around the condo all the time. It must be costing you money to leave the building up."

It was. And it was no small thing to have cost overruns at Bittersweet Point, given what he continued to lose on the Iris Complex. He pushed down the familiar tight feeling in his gut.

"I don't know what Libby said to persuade you."

If you only knew, he thought. "I didn't understand your situation," he said, his voice more curt than he intended.

"I'm not a charity case. I pay my rent every month on time." She sighed then, frowning. "I don't know why I'm defending myself. I've acted like a horse's ass."

"No, you haven't," he murmured automatically, uncomfortable with the sheen of tears in her eyes.

"I have." She studied her soda can. "I've interfered in your marriage." Her voice picked up speed. "I've said things about you to Libby, that she shouldn't trust you."

Oh, God. He'd known Tina didn't like him. He should have known she was keeping the waters churned. As if he and Libby didn't have enough problems on their own. "What did you say?" he asked.

She hesitated. Finally, she said, "I told her you were a handsome charmer like my ex-husband and that if she was foolish enough to care for you, you'd hurt her." She paused again. "I thought I was being a good, caring friend."

Nate thought about her words and felt a grudging respect. The woman had guts to face him, and she was obviously a loyal friend to Libby. "You don't even know me." Then he wondered why he was defending himself. He wanted nothing from this woman.

"Right. I don't know you, and I was wrong in at least one of my assumptions. I still wonder sometimes if you'll hurt Libby in the end, but..." She changed the can to her other hand, her head down. "Anyway, I assume you kept the condo for my son. For that, I thank you from the bottom of my heart." She swiped away the tears that had formed in the corners of her eyes and gave him a smile that was more form than real.

Nate shoved his hands in his pockets. "Tina, I'm going to have to do something about that condo someday soon. I have no choice."

She nodded. "I know."

"If you need a loan—"

"No!"

"Not a gift, a loan."

"No." This time the word came out softer. "I'll figure out something."

"I'm sure you will."

She turned away then and started back toward the gym door. He breathed a sigh of relief, glad she was gone.

She was almost at the door. He'd never understand the impulse that prompted him to speak. "Tina."

She turned.

"You need to talk to Trevor." He hesitated. "He tells me things you need to know."

She went still. "What things?"

"He'll tell you. Just talk to him, Tina," he urged. *While you still can. While you have a relationship that's sure and warm, before you're afraid to reach out to your own child.*

SARA TALKED NONSTOP from the back seat in the car going home. It was just as well, because Libby was unsettled, nervous around Nate. How could he have kissed her like that, in front of half the town? She thought back to the closed, contained man he'd been when they'd first met and couldn't believe it.

You'd think, after all this time of living—at least on weekends—in the same house, Libby would be comfortable around him. Not so. So now it was a blessing that Sara was chattering.

"Do you know they *dared* Josh to ask me to dance?" Sara said indignantly.

"Do you like him?" Libby was prepared to offer sympathy.

"He has a big nose. Though my nose is kind of big, too."

"Your nose is not big," Nate said firmly. It was the first time he'd spoken since they'd pulled out of the parking lot. Libby shot him a glance. He seemed intent on his driving.

"Josh is okay."

"The dare didn't hurt your feelings?" Libby probed again.

"Well, kind of. But then I thought, well, my friends dared *me* and that's why I danced with *him*. I have to be fair and everything."

From the front seat, Libby could smile without hurting

Sara's feelings, and she did. Nate was frowning as he smoothly executed a curve.

"It was when we were playing Truth or Dare," Sara explained.

"Truth or Dare?" Nate repeated.

"Sure. When it's your turn, you have to decide which it is, Truth or Dare, and if it's Dare you have to do anything the other players decide and if it's Truth you have to answer any question they ask about your sex life."

Nate made a peculiar choking sound in his throat.

"So you picked Dare," Libby said. After all, there'd be no guilty thrill in Truth, since Sara could have no "sex life." In the dark, she Dared herself to reach out and pat the top of Nate's thigh, reassuring him of Sara's essential innocence. The moment she felt denim over taut male muscle, she was reminded of their kiss. Lord.

"It's easy," Sara went on. "Like if you picked Truth, Lib, you'd have to answer a question."

Truth. About her nonexistent sex life! She didn't dare look at Nate.

"Like..." Libby heard genuine hesitation in Sara's voice before she rushed on. "I've been thinking, you and Nate are married and I kind of know that means you do it to have babies, and that's called sex." She took a quick breath. "I didn't think anything about you two, you know, except that Kathleen's mother is going to have a baby and I've seen her mom and dad's bedroom and there's only one bed in it. Kathleen says you do it in a bed. And at our house, you know, Nate has his own bed."

There was silence in the car. Libby smoothed down her dress with suddenly damp hands. Finally, she said gently, "Do you have some questions about sex that I can answer, honey?"

Beside her, Nate cleared his throat.

"Well, I know how people do it," Sara said. "And it sounds disgusting."

"Sara," Nate finally said. "Maybe you'd feel more comfortable talking about this with Libby alone."

There was no doubt who of the three of them was the most uncomfortable. Libby felt a ridiculous urge to giggle at her suddenly old-fashioned husband, and to kiss the man silly and strip the jeans from his body as she envisioned bedrooms and making babies.

In the back seat, Sara shifted. "Well, I can understand why you two wouldn't want to do anything so weird. I was just kind of thinking, you know?"

They pulled into Libby's driveway. Nate put the car into park and was out of there like a shot.

SARA HAD BEEN overexcited by the dance and hard to settle down. But when Libby checked a half hour later, the girl had finally fallen asleep, one arm slung palm up over her forehead, as though she was having dramatic dreams.

Now Libby sat in cutoff jeans and a T-shirt, on a wicker rocker in her living room. The windows were open, and she listened to the hum of insects outside the screen and tried to relax.

Her reading light was on. She held a *Victoria* magazine in her lap, telling herself that a featured bouquet in an antique silver holder would be perfect for a gazebo wedding she had contracted. But it was difficult to concentrate on much of anything except what she'd been thinking about ever since Nate had kissed her so thoroughly in the school gym. Sex. Sex and Nate. Images. Black hair, strong and silken between her fingers. Moving bodies, silvery in the night. Nate. Nate and sex.

Cripes.

Resolutely she picked up her magazine. *Old-fashioned garden flowers work best for the look,* she read.

"Hi." Nate came downstairs and passed her on the way to the kitchen. He'd rolled up the sleeves of his chambray shirt in deference to the warmth of the night, she noted, but he hadn't changed into pajamas or whatever he wore to bed.

What did he wear to bed, anyway? She'd bet...nothing but his skin. Maybe a pair of briefs in case Sara ever came through the closed door to his room. Libby had never seen a pair of pajamas in his suitcase.

Sex. Nate.

Cripes.

Choose accent flowers in the creamy tones of old lace, unbleached muslin...

He was back with a glass of iced herbal tea in each hand.

"Thirsty?" he asked, holding one frosty glass out to her.

Sure. Thirsty. *Hungry...*

He handed her the glass and took a seat on the sofa across from her. Her nerves took another jump. He didn't sit with her in the evenings. Always, after Sara went to bed, he excused himself, and hours afterward, passing his closed door on the way to bed, she'd still hear the hum of his computer, the sound of his fax, sometimes even his beeper.

No wonder she couldn't get interested in antiques or old-fashioned flowers tonight. There was no way she could do that with her husband sitting across from her on the sofa.

Nate. Who'd kissed her tonight as though he meant it. Who'd kissed her...

As though he'd changed?

"I hope you're not upset about Sara," she said abruptly. "You know how kids talk, but I'm sure she doesn't know anything about sex beyond the basics."

"I figured that. After I'd had a chance to think about what she said."

"And I don't think we owe her any explanation about how we live. After all, she's the kid, and we're the parents, right?" She waved her magazine for emphasis.

He was looking straight at her, studying her with an intensity that was definitely unsettling. "Right."

"Just think," she rattled on brightly. "A few months ago, you might have accused me of telling her too much, being in the wrong, and you'd have used that information in the custody hearing."

His smile faded, and she was sorry she'd been blurting things out without thinking again. "Well, wouldn't you have?" she challenged.

He passed a weary hand over his forehead. "I'd have told Marta about it."

"And she would have gone from there. Morals charges." Of course, Libby thought, she herself would have made the same charges against Nate. All those women he'd been seen with around Chicago, before their marriage. The knowledge of how different she was from Nate's usual choice in women still hurt.

Nate studied his glass. "That's all past, isn't it?" When he looked up, she saw that rare vulnerability in his eyes, the expression he tried so hard to mask.

Her heart squeezed. "We have a strange arrangement. But in many ways, I guess it works."

He nodded, drained his glass. Libby tried not to examine her feelings too closely. Their marriage was nothing like what she'd contemplated a marriage to be. In many ways, it disappointed her still. Nate's continuing inability to really connect with Sara. Her own needs for real intimacy. But she and Nate got along better than she'd ever imagined. "Are you pleased with things exactly as they are?"

He gazed at her, his expression closed. "It was what I asked for, wasn't it?" There was a long pause. "Ah, are you? Pleased with how things are going?"

"Sure." What a lie, a whopper so big Libby would have disciplined Sara for telling one like it. But how could she say she wasn't satisfied, when Nate had given her everything he'd promised? Over the past few weekends, she'd dared to dream. Tonight, she'd dared... Oh, heck. Disappointed, Libby opened her magazine again, pretended to read. Nate picked up a copy of the local paper, the *Harborside Herald, Serving the Lake and the World*. The headline read, Water Commission All Wet on Drains Issue. In a minute, Nate appeared to be engrossed in the story.

Somewhere in the house, a clock ticked. Outside, there was the rhythmic whisper of waves on the beach.

"Tina and I had a talk," he finally said quietly.

"Tonight? About what?"

"The Point. Trevor. Among other things."

She nodded. "Tina said she was going to thank you. But I wondered if she really would."

"I respect the woman. I know the things she's been saying about me. She actually admitted it. Gutsy."

"Oh." Absently she fingered the magazine on her lap. Did Nate believe Libby thought those things, that she'd talked with Tina about Nate, criticized Nate? Well, she had, and suddenly some of the things she'd said seemed somehow disloyal. Some things between a husband and wife needed to stay at home, between them. That is, if he were a real husband, and she were a real wife. Confused, she shut her magazine.

He put down the newspaper. "Anyway. There's something I've wanted to talk to you about for a while. I don't want to break Trev's confidences, but I really could use some advice."

She felt herself begin to warm from the inside out. Her feelings for Nate might be confused, but this was cozy, to be sitting here talking with him like this, and the sensation was mixed with that lingering sense of anticipation from the square dance. "Okay. I won't tell him."

"Trevor wants me to find his father."

"Oh, no. Nate, you don't understand—"

"He thinks his father left because Trevor ended up in a wheelchair, and supposedly wouldn't be able to drive or have a normal relationship with a woman."

"But Trevor's doctor told Tina he can function..." She stopped as she felt the heat on her cheeks.

"I know. He told me. In some detail, as a matter of fact."

"Trevor told you all that?"

He ignored her astonishment, intent on what he was saying. "Do you think Trevor's right about why Jonathan Samms left?"

She didn't have to think about it. "I'm pretty sure that's what happened. Jonathan was very into sports and being what he called a 'real man.' He had affairs, and in a little town like Harborside, it was incredibly humiliating to Tina. But Trevor's injury, I think, was the clincher." She took a thoughtful sip of tea.

"Trevor wants to find him," Nate repeated.

"But why?"

"I'm not exactly sure. I think to tell his father that he *can* do all those things, in the hopes that he can have some kind of relationship with his old man. The thing is..." Nate stopped and looked away as though he was suddenly self-conscious, then, "Trev keeps talking about how I came back for Sara. That seems to have given him some impetus to find his own father."

"You couldn't have foreseen that."

He gave her a crooked smile. "I couldn't foresee a lot of things in this crazy town. What I'm concerned about is this. If Jonathan Samms is the bastard I think he is, how will Trev handle a rejection?"

She shook her head. "I don't know." She thought for a moment. "Maybe it's just as well that Jonathan's not been found."

Her words hung in the air for a moment. Then Nate said very quietly, "But he has."

"Oh, God. You found him?"

"Marta found him. He calls himself Jonathan Sinclair, and though he's never paid a dime of child support, he owns a charter flight service and a condo in Lake Tahoe. He also has a nineteen-year-old wife."

"Oh, God," Libby said again. "Does Trevor know you found him?"

"No. But when I saw him tonight, I almost told him. Libby, Trev is going to find his father. Maybe not this year. But eventually he'll find him, because he's determined. I know. Even when I was his age, if I'd wanted something as badly as he does, I'd have found a way." He leaned forward as he spoke.

Libby had no doubt of it. "But what will Trevor do if his father blows him off? How could he handle something like that? He's probably thinking about only one outcome."

Nate got up and went to the window. She could see his broad shoulders, then the reflection of his face in the blackness of the glass as he gazed at nothing. "I don't know a damn thing about kids. But, I've been thinking, my own father and I left so much unfinished business. He died at the track, did I ever tell you that?" He shoved his hands in his pockets. "Isn't that just like some damn soap opera, that my father died at the track of a heart attack just after he'd taken every last cent from his pocket and put it on a horse that didn't even place?''

Quietly, Libby got up and went to him. Without touching him, she stood next to him. Watching his reflection.

He spoke again quietly. ''For years, I've thought of all the things I wanted to say to him. Things like, I did okay, I made it, I'll never be like you.'' He hesitated. ''And the things for years I didn't think I'd ever want to say, because I didn't think I *felt* them. Somehow, this summer, I've been thinking about some of the stuff we did together. He's the one who first taught me to sail. He liked the water.''

''You like the water, too.''

''Yes.''

Very deliberately, she pulled his hand out of his pocket. Amazingly, he offered no resistance when she slipped her hand in his. The touch of palms—his hard, flat, hers callused—sent a wash of longing through her.

He lifted his other hand, absently made a trail in the faint dust of the sill. ''What I've been wondering, is whether Trevor doesn't have the right to *know*. Good or bad, so that he can get on with his life.''

She shook her head, sighed. ''I just don't know, Nate.''

He turned to her with a little smile. ''I thought when it came to kids, you had all the answers.''

''Maybe I've been willing to ask the questions, that's all. If I'm so great with kids, how come Trevor didn't come to me? How come he came to you?''

''Because I have money and lawyers, he said.''

''Come on.'' She squeezed his hand. ''That's not really why. He chose to talk to you. You're better with kids—people—than you give yourself credit for, Nate. I wish…'' She stopped. Quite suddenly, still conscious of his big hand linked with hers, she didn't feel like talking.

There was something about his vulnerability, his sharing,

his willingness to become involved, that did for Libby what all his money and class and perfection of form could not. She was suddenly full to the brim in feelings as heady and sweet as any she'd ever experienced.

She looked up at him and found him studying her. His eyes were fixed on her mouth, his lids half-closed.

Normally she would have looked down in confusion, in shyness. She almost did. But instead, she raised a finger and touched it to his lips. He sucked in a quick breath, but he didn't move. She'd always accused Nate of playing it safe with Sara. Of not believing in love.

But hadn't she been doing the same thing? Playing it so very, very safe? So afraid he would hurt her. Maybe he would. But how would she ever find out if she didn't take a chance?

After all, she had fallen in love with her husband.

A tad uncertainly, she traced his eyebrows with her finger. His cheek was freshly shaved, the skin satiny if she stroked downward, faintly scratchy if she brought her finger up. Through it all, he was still, and Libby almost forgot to breathe.

"Don't," he finally whispered harshly.

"Why not?" she whispered back.

His hands fisted by his sides. "I'm trying to be a gentleman here. You're making it—" he sucked in a breath as she traced the line of his lips "—damn hard."

She felt his breath against the pads of the two fingers she put across his lips to shush him. "I don't want you to be a gentleman."

As if in slow motion, he brought his hand up and covered hers. "I thought you didn't believe in it this way."

This way? Oh, *this* way. Sex without love? Was that what he was trying to say, that he didn't love her?

She knew that. All at once, she thought she knew exactly

what Nate was trying to tell her, that he always needed distance. But hadn't he shown her that he'd changed?

And did it matter? She'd be making love with Nate because *she* was in love. "Aren't you the one who told me that sex was pleasurable, natural between husband and wife?" She refused to look down, though her cheeks felt very hot.

There was silence, a long beat of silence.

Finally, he reached up to capture a lock of her hair, to run it between his fingers. "Do you know," he said in a husky whisper, "how soft this is? No hair spray, no styling gel."

"It flies all over. It's that awful red—"

He crushed a handful in his fist. "I like it."

How thrilling to hear him say so. Emboldened by the compliment, she put her hands on his shoulders and kissed him on the mouth, an openmouthed kiss that coaxed his lips to open under hers.

He gave a groan as he felt her tongue, and suddenly he was very involved, his hands stroking, then clutching her hips, pressing them intimately to his, rubbing her slowly over his arousal. Pleasure started where he was pressing, spread, returned to concentrate and grow deep within her. "You don't have to do this," he whispered finally.

"No," she said softly, "I don't. And if you're trying to say making love won't change anything between us, I know that."

There was confusion in his eyes before he closed them and kissed her again, kissed her so thoroughly that she could barely breathe.

Against her mouth, he said, "I...care about you. That's all I can say, but—"

"Stop." Before she surrendered fully to the curious combination of weakness and strength his kisses where conjuring, she had to say it. "I'm not asking for anything. You were the one who said we could...make love without becoming involved. That sex was just sex. Didn't you say that in so many words?"

He held her tightly to him as if he was afraid she'd pull away, but he looked down, straight into her eyes. "Yes. That's what I said."

The tiniest flash of disappointment went through her, because even now, she was fantasizing. But love was a gift, not something a person gave with expectations attached. "You said it was up to me. If. When. Where." She drew another deep breath. "So I'm saying yes. Now. In my bed."

Without another word, he swept her up in his arms and crossed to the hallway door. There he paused.

For the first time since her marriage, Libby felt like a bride. She felt small against his frame, tight with anticipation, very, very shy. The bare skin of her thighs touched the bare skin of his forearms. It was warm where their skin met. It was warm against his chest, where the worn chambray hid a wall of taut muscle. His heart thudded in rapid quickstep against her ear.

"Damn these small doorways," he whispered finally.

Belatedly, she looked up. Her house had a lot of narrow twists and turns. Against him, she smiled at Mr. Perfect, who was trying to do the right thing and carry her to bed but was foiled by her small, old house. "I can walk, you know."

"Right." He kissed her hard, then set her down in front of him. As she climbed the stairs, she had the sensation that he was watching her, her hips and her legs. Nate. Her husband. Tonight for the first time, he'd sleep in her bed.

She went into her room, but didn't turn on the light. In the living room, she'd been as aggressive as she'd ever been in her life. Now she needed the darkness. It had been so long.

"So very long," he whispered, his hand finding her breast, caressing. For the barest second she thought he could read her thoughts, and they were so carnal, she blushed. Then she wondered. A long time for him, too? What a fanciful notion.

But then she couldn't think at all as his hands did slow, wonderful things. In the dark, she saw the gleam of his wedding band as his hands pulled up her T-shirt. He unclasped her bra, and her breasts were in his hands, then. Her breath quickened, and she started to sway toward him.

"Sara's asleep?" He whispered the question.

She whispered, "Yes."

"I'll go close her door."

Oh. Good idea. She grabbed for the edges of her T-shirt, suddenly shy again.

He paused in the doorway. "You've got a choice. You can wait for me to undress you. Or you can get naked while I'm gone."

She didn't have the nerve to take off her clothes while he was gone. So she stood there, the edges of her T-shirt still in her hands, her bare toes digging into the worn braided rug.

When he returned, he closed and locked the door. Hearing the rusty scrape of the lock, Libby felt a moment's panic. Lord, after all this time, just after they'd reached an understanding of sorts about how they were going to live together, their relationship was about to change irrevocably.

He seemed to have no such last-minute panic. "Now, where were we?" He caught her around the waist, bent her to his powerful body and kissed her.

Over on the bed, there was a square of light from the window, but here by the door it was dark. The darkness was curiously safe and dangerous at the same time. Safe because her imperfect body was hidden from his experienced eye, dangerous because in the dark he was mysterious, larger than life. He groaned when she opened the buttons on his shirt and pushed her hands inside. Her palms were on his warm flesh.

He slipped her T-shirt over her head. "Now," he said, and he pulled her to him, rubbing her against his body so that her nipples became exquisitely stimulated by the hair of his chest. She moaned, too.

It had been so long. She'd waited so long. She'd spent so much time with him near and untouchable that she felt drawn tight, captured and tumbled by something as powerful as the storm on the lake. She started to tremble. Nate. *Husband.* Lover.

If. Where. When. *Now.* Without shyness any longer, she slipped out of her cutoff jeans and underwear and stood naked before him.

He took off his own jeans. She heard the rustle, felt his body bend, straighten, and then she was aloft again, carried and gently set down on the center of the square of light, right in the middle of her own bed.

Looming over her, he blocked the light, held her with hands on both cheeks and kissed her hard. With thoroughness and care and passion. His skin was like a blanket on the beach, warmed by the sun.

As he kissed her neck, emotion welled in her. Happiness that she'd waited for this man to come into her life. As he nipped her shoulder, happiness that he was her husband, the man who'd come back for his child. As he trailed his open mouth along the inside of her arm, she cried out at the wave of sensation that rushed through her.

Then, overwhelmed with love and sensation, she grabbed at his shoulders, swung her body and rolled on top of him.

She kissed him, touched his ear with her tongue, took a tiny nip at his neck. Then, emboldened by his harsh breath and hoarse murmurs, she closed her eyes and moved lower. Chest. Broad, hairy, male. His flat stomach.

Her chin brushed his erection, and he almost leaped off the bed. Grabbing a fistful of quilt, he groaned. Libby opened her eyes. Oh my. He was so very…aroused. Slowly, she lifted her head.

In his passion, his head had come off the bed, and now she looked into his shadowed face. The light from outdoors had washed and cleaned his features so that he was all angles and planes, a perfect melding of male form and function.

"Come here," he said in a raspy whisper, and he pulled her to him, up along his body, until when she reached him she was gasping. He rolled her to her side, facing her, and touched her between her thighs. Intimately. She gasped again. She leaned in to kiss his shoulder, to have something to press against as this incredible sensation got bigger and bigger. Without thinking, she bit down.

He jerked, moaned.

"Oh, I'm sorry!" She tried to sit up, but he grabbed her arm.

"No," he said thickly. "No sorry. Do what you want. Just…" He stopped as if there were no words.

So she lay back and let him touch her. This time, she turned her cheek to the quilt, feeling the seams of the old fabric, the valleys of tiny stitches against her face.

And when she was oh, so close, when her lips pressed so very tightly against the bedding, he pulled her hips to his. Taking her hand, he guided it to his arousal. "When you're ready," he said, and his voice sounded strained and gritty.

She was momentarily confused. They were on their

sides, facing each other, and she had expected him to come over her, take her, press against her with his power. But, no. They would share this moment, side by side. She'd never been so ready for anything in her life. She took his hard length in her hands and slipped it inside.

His breath whooshed out but he didn't move. It took her a second to realize that he wanted her to move her hips, to fill herself with him. She inched down and against him, his thighs tangled with hers, his chest pressed hard against her breasts, his arm looping around her neck as if he meant to hold on to every last inch of her. It had been a long time, but this felt right. So very right that she couldn't believe she'd shared a house with this man yet resisted him so long.

She opened her eyes, gazed into his. They were open, a shadowy gleam. "Hi," he said softly. "Hi," she said back. It was the greeting he gave her every Friday night. It was too dark to read his expression, but the one syllable now sounded as if he was greeting her for the first time ever.

Libby hadn't wanted to love this man, but she did. So she showed him love, holding back nothing. With her hands, with her mouth, with her entire being, she gave herself to him.

He had started out slowly, tenderly. But soon, inevitably, he demanded. And she was glad, for as he thrust into her, she felt her desire grow and quicken.

He groaned again at the end, harsh and fierce, and the knowledge that she pleased him fired her own passion. She saw a field of orange—poppies, daylilies, laid out under yellow sunshine so bright and hot it hurt her eyes. She shuddered in climax and held Nate tight so he could see it, too.

CHAPTER THIRTEEN

NATE WOKE to a breeze stirring the sheer curtain at the window. The night had been warm, and they'd kicked off the quilt and sheets. Now Libby lay asleep next to him, her hair damp with perspiration.

He picked up a lock of red hair that had fallen across the bridge of her nose, smoothed it back across her neck, not wanting to wake her. Not wanting to wake *his wife*.

If she awoke, this would have to end. It would have to end all too soon, anyway. After all, Sara would be up soon; his daughter was an early riser. And she'd asked those questions last night—had it only been last night? Yes. He had no idea where he and Libby went from here, and he couldn't confuse Sara further just now.

How foolish he'd been to assume he and Libby could be intimate and have it be just physical. He'd already known, bone deep, that Libby was like no other woman he'd ever met, so how could he have imagined he could have physical release without involvement?

She rolled on her back and snored a little, a tiny, ordinary-sounding, unladylike snore. He couldn't help smiling. This woman gave so much, turned a simple act like lovemaking into something fine and special.

He didn't deserve that. He didn't deserve *her*. He'd never been good at sharing feelings.

He let out a breath, planted a whisper-soft kiss on her shoulder and got out of bed. He might not deserve her, but he had her, and she had him. Stuck with each other. Different as night and day. And coming together with such sparks.

He picked up his discarded jeans and, forgoing his briefs, started to slide them on. Well, he and Libby were married, and they'd made love, but even in the flush of wonderment, he wasn't naive enough to think that one night of lovemaking—no matter how profound—could make up for their differences.

But it did change things. She'd been right. It did change things. She was creeping into his heart.

Did he dare let her in?

After all, he was no gambler.

Nate finished putting on his jeans, then opened the door and peered out. No Sara. Holding his shirt, underwear and sneakers, he headed down the hall to his room.

NATE HADN'T REALLY looked at her all day. Right now he was showing Sara some stupendously wonderful computer game that would only work on his supermegabyted machine. He'd brought the whole works downstairs and had set it out on the dining-room table.

Sara was thrilled with the new toy, the kind of toy that had never come into her life before Nate. Yet, in unguarded moments, her face was quiet, more content. Today, she didn't seem as careful to keep a little distance between her body and Nate's. Libby was glad of that, too. Maybe Sara, who'd gone through so much with her stepfather, was finally coming to trust Nate. Maybe Nate would somehow pick up on the change...

And maybe pigs would fly. A favorite saying of her father's, and never one to fail.

After all, Libby should know. After their night together, after they'd been as intimate as two people could be, he'd hardly looked at her. It wasn't that she'd expected hearts and flowers, but couldn't the man *look* at her?

Suddenly, as if feeling her eyes on him, he glanced up. She met his eyes. Over the blip of computer death and oblivion, they stared at each other.

His jaw tightened, his eyes stayed locked on hers. Then, as if unbidden, he smiled, a tiny smile so warm with shared secrets that she almost stopped breathing. And she knew in that moment that whatever Nate wanted to pretend, last night had meant something to him. Maybe something bigger than he knew.

His pager went off and the moment was lost. But she would never forget that look in his eyes, would hug it to herself at night when he was in Chicago and she couldn't sleep for wondering what he was doing there.

Nate pushed the button to silence the pager and stood up. "I'll use the kitchen phone."

Libby wandered into the living room. Outside, the day was brilliant. When she could pry Sara away from the keyboard, she'd suggest a swim.

She didn't intend to listen, but she overheard snatches of conversation. Nate raised his voice at one point. "Well, then for God's sake, tell them!" Finally, he said, "Yes, I get it—" and then "—all right."

A couple of minutes later he came into the living room, where she was refolding a quilt. "I've got to go back to Chicago."

"When?" She kept her voice carefully bright.

He raked a hand through his hair. "Right now."

Disappointment stabbed her. "Oh, Nate, you just got here." The memory of last night lingered. She'd been hoping for tonight... "Sara will be disappointed. I was going to suggest we have a swim and roast hot dogs after. I bought marshmallows. I actually gave in to nitrates and wall-to-wall sugar.'' Oh boy, she thought. Roasting wieners and toasting marshmallows. Just the thing to tempt Nate to stay.

"Sounds like fun." Was she imagining the wistfulness in his voice?

"Stay," she said softly.

There was a long silence. "I can't," he said finally. "Something's come up in Chicago."

There had been casual references to problems in Chicago before. Libby had ignored them, sure that Nate was in total control. Those problems had not seemed vital, anyway, not compared to whatever was going on in Sara's life, or in Tina's, not as elemental as too many bills at the end of the month. Now, maybe because she felt so in tune with him, she picked up on things. The tension in his shoulders, the tight set of his jaw.

"Problems? Real problems, I mean?" she asked with genuine sympathy.

He looked at her for another long moment. "Real problems," he agreed.

"Tell me."

"You don't want to know." He sounded offhand, but was there a note of hurt in his voice?

"Tell me," she urged again.

"I can handle it."

"Nate. I'm your wife, remember?"

It was a reminder of a hot night behind a closed door. Husband. Wife. Still, he hesitated. Finally, he said, "Walk with me?"

"Sure." He must be impatient to be off, yet he was willing to take at least some time for her. Libby called to Sara that they were going for a walk, and received only a one-syllable sound of acknowledgment.

Nate motioned for her to go ahead of him through the

sunporch door to the yard. They walked along the narrow beach, passing the boundary of her property. Next door, the Matwings, husband and wife, were deadheading the climbing roses. Libby had a quick wish that Nate liked chores. She quickly suppressed the thought, as though it was faintly disloyal.

"Funny," Nate said finally. "Nobody seems to care if people trespass."

"Nope," she agreed. "The lake's big enough for us all." But she knew what he meant. Out East, where she'd gone to school, large stretches of ocean were patrolled on behalf of owners who thought a stray jogger posed a threat. "Now," she said gently, "you have to go, and I'd like to hear about your problems."

He stopped. "Why now? Because of last night?"

Because I love you, and now I want to be your life partner, in every way possible, to share your burdens, to bring you joy. "Yes," she said, "because of last night."

He gave a harsh chuckle. "I must have been better than I thought."

"You were great," she said.

"You were…" He stopped and looked away.

She wished she knew what he was going to say. "Are you angry that I haven't paid attention to your business before?"

After a second, he started walking again. "I guess so," he admitted, sounding surprised. "I guess because it was important to me, I wanted it to be important to you."

"It is," she said, and she spontaneously took his hand. "Everything you do is important to me. But you're right. I've been so sure everything in Harborside is so superior, I've just…let you handle things."

"I *can* handle things. But my workers have finally

walked off the job at the Iris Complex. An honest-to-God wildcat.''

Libby knew that was bad.

He turned to face the water, toward Bittersweet Point, and used a hand to shade his eyes. ''I'm going to go over the time limit in my contract. That means I pay fines. Fines for every day I'm late.''

Every *day?* ''Do these fines amount to a lot of money?'' He shrugged, but she could read a wealth of worry into the one gesture. ''Do you have enough to ride things out, Nate?'' she asked very, very quietly.

His voice was just as quiet. ''How would you feel if I didn't?''

God, was he saying he didn't have the money? She couldn't believe it, but that's what he was implying. Of course, if it was a lot of money...and it surely was. Well, she was in love with the man, and that emotion had never had anything to do with the amount of money he had. In fact, that money had been a barrier, something that made him seem not quite real, and certainly it was a barrier to him being willing to share her simple life-style in Harborside.

He waited. She felt a flash of pure elation. Maybe this was the best thing that could happen.

No.

She couldn't be that selfish. Success in business was important to Nate. She couldn't wish him ill, even if she'd spent sleepless nights cursing his money and his lawyer and all the power that the money brought.

She must have taken too long to reply because he brought his hand down and turned toward the direction they'd come. ''That's what I thought.''

''Oh, Nate. For Heaven's sake. *Look* at me,'' she finally said sharply, and gave a yank on his arm for good measure.

He looked, and in his eyes she saw the end of a dream. "Nate, I don't give a damn about the money, do you hear me? I never gave a damn, and I've said so often enough that you ought to believe it. What I give a damn about is you. You're my husband. My partner."

He gave a mirthless chuckle. "A partner who's about to become worth considerably less."

"Never. You could never be less to me, unless you stop trying, unless you become that closed-up man I first met. Do you know how much you've changed? You're... softer." He gave her a funny look. "Okay, bad choice of words." She tried a laugh, but it came out sounding tinny and false. She had an overriding sense that her next words were important, and a scary feeling that she wasn't up to the task of choosing them.

"You try, Nate. You're not so sure you have all the answers anymore." She thought, went on. "You're involved. You make breakfast for us all, drive Sara to her horseback-riding lessons, go along with whatever she and I have planned for the evenings. You're doing something for Trevor. Before, would you have even known he needed you? And you keep trying with Sara, even though I know she hurts you sometimes."

Too close to shore, a powerboat came speeding by. The wake sent in a few waves, bigger than before. One wet Libby's worn sneakers. She took a quick step back. "I'm proud you're my husband," she said to his back.

He took a backhanded swipe at his eyes. "Sweat," he said quickly. "It's hot."

"Right," she said, aghast that her powerful husband would shed a tear at her words, words that hadn't begun to convey her feelings.

Finally, he let out a long breath and turned. "We need to head back," he said quietly. "Iris won't stand delay."

"What will you do?"

"I'll get them back to work eventually. Then I'll assess the damage. Round up some financing. Jeff heard about a guy who's formed a new investment group. They're looking for some high-return investments, and they're willing to take high risks." His smile was undeniably bitter. "In other words, they're willing to gamble on Nate Perry and his reputation for pulling off a project in the end. Now I've got to do a bit of wooing."

"You'll do fine."

He smiled finally. "You sound confident. Got some spare cash, too?"

She took her cue from Nate, made sure her tone was light. "I'll take a hammer to Sara's piggy bank."

The tension eased somewhat. Libby was right about how he was changing. For so long, she'd denied to herself that he was changing because she was afraid she'd fall for him. But he was a good man, an honorable man.

He was the man of her heart.

They were almost back home when he spoke again. "Bittersweet Point is what screwed me up. I was cash poor when I got involved."

"Bittersweet Point? Then why *did* you get involved?"

"For Sara," he said simply. "Kevin Smithson convinced me that if I had a stake in the town, I'd get more sympathy from the judge."

Never would she have imagined that he'd knowingly make a bad business decision because of his daughter. So his motives had been right, all along, even if trying to curry favor with the judge was the wrong way to go about things. Realization of how harshly she'd judged him, realization that she loved him, twined through her. The words she longed to say, the I-love-yous, remained unsaid. She'd wait. He had business to conduct, some storms to ride out. When she said she loved him, she wanted him ready to hear it, with his heart open and free. She only hoped that day would finally come.

He stopped on the middle of her beach. Over at Bittersweet Point, the one condominium still stood, stark and ugly.

A thought struck her. She didn't know a thing about Nate's business, but... "Is there something you could do to reduce your costs on Bittersweet Point? I've seen the *Herald* articles on the Point. You've got so much going on over there. Docks, a marina, restaurants, indoor tennis courts—just so much."

"The kind of buyers we want to attract demand those amenities. I'm known for offering that type of environment. An upscale playground, my literature always says."

"Well, how about a downscale playground? A *middle-scale* playground." Suddenly excited, she gripped his arm. "How about something for families? Look at how limited the housing is around here. People rent the cottages, but some of them are so shabby and inadequate. Wouldn't they buy something if they could afford it? Not something fancy, but something new and pleasant?"

He shook his head, and in spite of the problems he had, there was a spark of genuine amusement in his eyes. "Always thinking of family, Libby. Now don't get your back up," he said quickly. "I wasn't making fun of you, just...smiling a little. Okay?"

"Okay."

"Listen, I've got to go." He leaned forward and kissed her lightly on the mouth. "I really need you pulling for me this time."

"What can I do?"

"Just stand there a minute. I want to remember you like

you are today, real and genuine. Barefoot, in a yellow romper, with the wind in your hair.''

AFTER NATE LEFT, Libby and Sara got out the old charcoal grill. Sara was pleased at the idea of junk food, and she ate way too many gooey, blackened marshmallows. Libby even tried one herself. It stuck to her lips. She shuddered and Sara laughed.

But the day seemed hollow without Nate. That was a frightening feeling, because it would always be like this. She would be alone much of the time, seeing him off, waiting for him to return, building her life around two days at the end of the workweek.

Now, without him, the sun going down behind Bittersweet Point didn't seem as brilliant, the pink sky wasn't as vivid, and she didn't get that familiar pleasure when she spotted the blue heron fishing off her dock.

Sara, too, seemed quieter than usual. When Libby asked her what she was thinking about, Sara said, ''Nothing.'' When she suggested Sara try the computer game again, she said she was waiting for Nate, because they had a tournament going and it wouldn't be fair to practice too much in between. When Libby suggested a walk, Sara claimed her stomach hurt from too many marshmallows.

So Sara sat on an old wedding-ring quilt in the yard and listlessly picked a grass blade to chew.

Libby chewed over issues instead. She wanted to help. Nate had dismissed her suggestion that the Point be turned over to families. Libby knew she was no asset to Nate in business. But the man she loved was in trouble. It didn't sit well that she was in Harborside waiting for the grill to cool down so she could scrub it, and he was in Chicago fighting for his professional life.

Bittersweet Point. She couldn't get it out of her mind.

For one thing, she knew that Nate had left Tina's condominium standing at some cost to himself. It needed to be torn down so building could begin. In fact, some of the foundations had already been dug. The sugar cube stood smack in the middle of the work.

A thought struck her. She could do something. Maybe it was more symbolic than real, but it would help. Not just Nate, either. Maybe she had a real chance to put some things right. She shot to her feet. "Come on, Sara. Let's take a little drive."

A FEW MINUTES LATER, Libby stood in the huge, hospital-white kitchen at Bittersweet Point. Tina was furious.

"How dare Nate Perry interfere with my life?" Tina's eyes were snapping. "How dare he go looking for Jonathan without even talking to me about it? And all along, he's been talking to Trevor behind my back! Trevor's *my* son."

Libby winced, but she spoke calmly. "I told you, Trevor doesn't know. Without your permission, Nate won't tell him Jonathan's been found."

During their discussion, Tina had been stamping around the island in the kitchen. Outside, Trevor and Sara shot hoops, and there was the rhythmic *thunk* of the ball bouncing off the garage doors.

Now Libby struggled with some anger of her own at the rigid way Tina looked at the world, her willingness to believe the worst of Nate.

Tina slapped her palm on the countertop. "It's not like the guy has done so great with his own kid!"

"That's not fair, Tina. Nate has tried very hard with Sara, under tough circumstances. It's okay to be angry, but it's not okay anymore to take potshots at Nate."

"Give me a break."

"He's my husband," Libby said quietly, but with a new conviction. "My first loyalty will always be to him."

"We've been friends for twenty-five years!"

Impulsively, Libby got up and looped her arm around Tina's shoulders. "You'll always have my friendship. You and Trevor are among the most important people in my life."

"But you'll choose *him* over me?"

She took a deep breath. It was hard to say her next words. "If it's necessary, yes."

"God." Tina sank into a chair. When she looked up, her eyes were wet with tears. "I never thought you'd say that."

"Who's the most important person in your life?"

She took a swipe at her eyes. "Tough question. You know who."

"Then talk to Trevor. You have to take chances, even with the people you hold most dear." She gave Tina's tight shoulder a squeeze. "Nate hasn't done anything more than talk to your son. All these months you've had misgivings about whether Trevor's really happy. You know that despite all those jokes he makes, he can't sleep. You know he sits on that deck and broods. You know what he wants and you can support that decision or you can see him grow more and more distant from you."

Tina was rigid for a second more, and then her shoulders slumped and she sobbed. Libby knelt and gathered her friend close, the way she'd do with Sara. The sobs came and came. "I just…Jonathan hurt Trevor so…he hurt me…I didn't dare…and if I admitted I needed him, even financially, then I wouldn't be standing on my own…"

"He owes this family," Libby said firmly, her heart squeezing in sympathy for Tina and outrage at what Jonathan had put her friend through. "That you need him financially doesn't say a thing about your independence.

Like Nate says, he fathered a kid and now he doesn't want to take any responsibility. So, you force him to take responsibility. With him contributing his fair share, you can afford the kind of place your son deserves. And Trevor gets what he needs emotionally.''

Tina blew her nose. "What exactly *is* that? What could Trevor possibly need from a father he hasn't seen in four years?"

Libby shared Nate's thoughts about Trevor needing to see Jonathan, to get some perspective on his father as Trevor was coming into manhood himself.

"I don't know," Tina finally said, calmer now. "I know Nate isn't the bastard I thought he was. I think I knew that long ago, just because Trevor knew, and Trevor is the most perceptive kid sometimes..." She got up, went to the sink and filled the teakettle.

"If you thought that, why didn't you stick up for Nate, instead of warning me against him?"

Hesitating, Tina finally said, "I've been so jealous of you."

"Of me?" Libby was astonished.

Tina put down the kettle and stood at the counter, her hands gripping the edge. "Even before Nate. You had your shop. I could cope with that, even though my business was less...tangible. When Julia died, we got even closer. You had Sara and we were both single moms. And then Nate came. I thought he might hurt you. But in a way..." Libby had to strain to hear her next words. "In a way I was afraid. I wanted him to be a jerk because then he'd go, or you'd send him away and things would be like they used to be. You and me." She turned and gave Libby a watery smile. "Two independent broads who take on the world from a little out-of-the-way place called Harborside."

"Oh, Tina." Libby swallowed. "I listened to you about

Nate." How could she not have seen this side of her friend? After all, before Sara came, she herself had envied her friend her son.

Tina's head was down. "Can you forgive me?"

Libby thought, but not for very long. Tina's words against Nate had been motivated by fear and by anger at men in general, but also by a genuine concern for Libby. Libby had felt that concern in a thousand ways, when Tina had taken over the shop when Libby was down with the flu, when Tina had gone with Libby to the emergency room that time Sara fell off her bike, when Tina had opened her home to her all those Christmases when Libby was alone, before she had Sara and Nate.

"There's nothing to forgive." She rose and held out her arms. "You're stuck with me. Friends. Buddies. Comrades-in—" The last word was lost in a poof of breath as Tina flew across the kitchen and hugged her. They clung together for a moment before Tina pulled away. "If Nate is the man you want, I'll do anything to support you. I'll even give the guy a fair shot."

Libby smiled and spoke the words in her heart. "I haven't said anything yet. Lord only knows if I'll scare the man to death when I finally do say it. But I love him."

Tina said, "Then I wish you all the happiness in the world. And the luck." To her credit, she didn't add that Libby would need it. There was a pause, then Tina spoke again. "I guess I'd better get Trevor. It's time we had an honest discussion about his feelings for Jonathan."

DEAR DAD,

I suppose you know by now that Mom found you, since you must have gotten your papers from the court about a hearing on the child support. So you'll be here on August fifteenth. Mom really, really needs the money. She does okay with her sewing, better than before the—

Trevor paused and bit his pencil eraser, not wanting to have to say the word *divorce* or remind his father of all the fights between his parents.

…better than before. She wouldn't ask you, except we have to move. So if you could be okay about it, that would be cool.

Anyway, I want to see you. I've wanted to for a long time. I figure we can shoot hoops. I can do lots of sports, you know.

Trevor crossed out the "you know" part. This letter was much harder to write than he'd thought it would be. He got a sicko kind of pinch right in his gut every time he thought about seeing his dad.

For a moment he turned to his list, which had columns of all the stuff he could do. He'd put it in his computer so he could add stuff as he thought of it. Even using the smallest type, the list had grown to more than a page. He'd planned to include the list with the letter, but now he thought maybe he should wait. Like when he saw his dad, he could maybe *show* his dad the coolest things.

Maybe when they met, his dad would say something, do something that would make it easy for them to hug and stuff. His mother hugged him, and now that Trevor was pretty much grown-up, he didn't mind, as long as his mom only did it in private.

Will you call me when you get to town? I'll talk to Mom so you won't feel weird or anything when you call.

Trevor read what he'd written and frowned. The letter sounded like something a little kid would write. So he added some stuff about sports and complicated statistics about the baseball pennant race. That way his father would know Trevor wasn't going to act like a baby when they met again. After all, his father probably thought he was helpless, and he most definitely wasn't.

Trevor flexed his muscles, admiring the good big bulge of his biceps. His legs might be wasted but his arms were totally awesome.

He picked up his pencil. Now how to end this thing. Your son, Trevor? Sincerely, Trevor? Yeah, right. How dopey could you get? Yours truly, Trevor? Double barf.

Love, Trev.

CHAPTER FOURTEEN

"IT'S A GREAT IDEA," Nate said. He was sitting across from Kevin Smithson at Harborside Savings and Loan. On the mahogany conference table between them were a new set of blueprints and piles of paper, all covered with numbers. Nate had just driven in from Chicago; in fact his luggage was still in the trunk of the Jag.

"On paper your plan looks profitable. But why do you want to change the whole concept of the Point midstream?" Kevin played with his pipe. He was so young he looked rather silly sporting a pipe, especially because he'd tamped tobacco into it repeatedly but never made a move to actually light the thing.

But Nate didn't smile. "It's something Libby suggested."

Kevin raised his eyebrows, but Nate resisted the urge to defend himself. A good businessman listened to everybody, then made his decisions.

"Libby knows this area," Nate told the banker. "She said there was a shortage of vacation housing for families. So my assistant and I checked it out. She's right. Over nearer Cleveland, they're glutted with upscale developments right now. Even here, there's pressure. Look at our projected first-year vacancy statistics." Nate shoved a paper under Kevin's nose.

Kevin pushed it around with the mouthpiece of his pipe,

thinking. "But you've only got one consumer poll telling us how a family-type thing would sell."

"I don't have hard figures," Nate said, trying to contain his impatience. "That's because nobody does this kind of thing around here. Yet." It was a hell of a gamble, no doubt about it, to build a resort for people who weren't in the habit of thinking they could afford anything like a vacation condo. "Look at the numbers, Kevin. Not putting in all the add-ons means we could sell these things very reasonably. I have super marketing people in Chicago who would do up a concept when the time came to sell them. Doing it this way gives us a lot more wiggle room."

"But you still want the same amount of financial backing from the bank, even though these will cost less to build."

"Yes."

Kevin put down the pipe and leaned forward. "What is Harborside Savings and Loan subsidizing for you?"

The guy got right to the point. Nate had had several strategies figured out for handling this meeting, but at the last second he settled for the simplest: honesty. "The Iris Complex. I've got the numbers on that in my briefcase."

"Why would a little bank like ours want in on something as big as Iris?"

"Because you stand to make money."

"Make money or lose money?" Kevin countered.

"Look, you either believe in me or you don't. The time is long past since I've gone begging."

Kevin looked at him for a long moment. "You have my respect. In the end, all someone really has is his belief in a man's integrity and grit. Isn't that true?"

"Yes."

Kevin waved the pipe. "This'll have to clear the loan committee."

"Kevin, your father-in-law is president of the bank. I'm sure his floor limit is high."

Kevin was grinning now. "It does help to be a big fish in a small pond, doesn't it? Okay, friend. Let's go get a piece of cherry pie at the Shoreline and celebrate the family-condo concept."

THAT NIGHT, Nate stood in the hallway holding his garment bag and briefcase, and agreed to drive Sara to rehearsal for *Fiddler on the Roof.* Libby could pick Sara up after rehearsal, but she couldn't take Sara there because she'd promised the garden club she'd make a sunflower centerpiece for the head table at the High Summer Luncheon. Libby's part wasn't being rehearsed that night anyway.

"I'm sorry, I know you just got home," Libby said apologetically as she rushed barefoot through the house in her cutoff jeans and a faded purple T-shirt advertising floral preservative. "Sara, come on now, you're going to be late and I know Nate must want a shower after that drive in. Sara! Where are you? Now, drat that blue pitcher. I can't do van Gogh and the darn sunflowers without my blue pitcher. *Where* did I put it?"

Nate walked into the kitchen and rummaged around in the cabinet under the sink, where he'd seen Libby put the pitcher the week before. He held it up. "This?"

"Yes. Oh, how do you *do* that?" At his frown of puzzlement, she wiped the back of her hand over her sweaty upper lip. "You know, look all pulled together and perfect all the time."

Because he did all his worrying on the inside, Nate thought. He paused, then took Libby's arm and used his other hand to deliberately smooth her hair away from her hot forehead. She caught her breath at the gesture; she smelled like sun and greens. "Hi," he said softly.

"Oh. Hi." She shook her head quickly and looked up at him with a tiny, secret smile.

How he'd missed her!

"Later?" she whispered.

"Later," he confirmed, thrilled at her eagerness, the way she seemed to hunger for him the way he desperately wanted her.

Now more than ever he needed to be successful. He wanted her to be proud. He wanted to give her and Sara the security he'd lacked. He wanted his money and he wanted his family. In short, he wanted it all.

"I hate for you to have to hit the road again so soon after you got home," she said.

"I don't mind." It was the polite, charming thing one said automatically when asked for a favor. But the funny thing was, he *didn't* mind. He felt he belonged on the rare occasions Libby asked him to do something for her. Usually, everything was clean and dusted and ready on Friday nights, as though he were a guest in her house.

He frowned with a sudden thought. Libby had said this was *home*. Home. For him, too? What a warm thought. What a frightening thought, because he was dangerously close to letting her into all those places inside him that had been closed and locked for so many years he'd never thought he'd open them again.

"Sara!" she called again.

Sara came pounding down the stairs. "I'm ready." She skidded to a stop in the doorway of the kitchen and then she noticed Nate. "Oh, hi."

"Hi." As always, he got this funny lump in his throat when he saw Sara. After these months of getting to know her, it was easier to believe she was ten years old, but somehow the reality was always a tad shocking. He pulled his keys from his pocket.

"You don't have to stay at the rehearsal," Libby said as he held the door open for Sara. "I'll be done at the Legion Hall in plenty of time to pick her up."

But Nate stayed. He didn't mind sitting in the darkened auditorium on one of the bleachers, watching Sara run through a couple of songs. Several other parents were there, and they were joined by some of the adult cast. There was a low hum of whispering, as a dozen unrelated conversations went on around him. Onstage, a group was finishing "Sunrise, Sunset," a bittersweet song about time passing that made Nate shift uncomfortably. He remembered the song.

But now Sara was singing a happier tune about a matchmaker, and she and a couple of other girls came right to the edge of the stage and belted it out. Sara was the prettiest of the three, and the most talented. She definitely had a flair for the dramatic, throwing her arms out in an exuberant, totally unselfconscious way.

Hey, his kid was great. Nate was a good judge of these things. He had season tickets to both the experimental and the conventional theater in Chicago. His daughter was every bit as good—for her age—as any actress he'd seen.

He smiled as Sara hit two false notes in a row.

"Ouch," the mother next to him said under her breath.

"She's good, don't you think?" Nate asked her eagerly. "That's my daughter."

The mother smiled at him in the dark. "Sara Perry. I know who she is."

Nate nodded, unaccountably pleased that this woman— who was a stranger to him—knew his daughter, used her new last name freely. Who wouldn't love this child? This talkative, gifted child who, without even trying, could steal your heart? Who wouldn't want to throw their arms around her and...

His mind turned quickly from the thought, then came back of its own accord. With all the worries about Iris, he ought to just let his relationship with Sara ride a while.

But that was getting harder to do. As he felt his old world narrowing, pinching, he wanted to come into the new world, to be spontaneous. To hug his little girl.

But she made sure he didn't. They spent time together; she seemed happy to see him on Friday nights. But she never got really close to him. She never said she loved him. She never called him anything but Nate.

"Nate!" Sara was standing on the edge of the stage, calling him.

He walked to the bottom of the stage. Sara leaned over. "Mr. Greenfield says I can do my lines with my father. My big scene." Nate was confused. With him? "Except Mr. Murphy isn't here. Mr. Murphy is Tevye," she added by way of explanation.

Oh, the father in the *play*. Now he understood. He'd last seen *Fiddler* at a posh dinner theater in Chicago years ago, in those early days when losing his daughter had been a constant raw wound inside him. The story of a father trying to cling to tradition, yet deal with modern daughters, had been hard for a man in his circumstances to watch.

"Come on, Nate." Sara's voice was a little whiny. "I need someone to play Tevye. Mr. Greenfield will give you a script." Nate looked up to see that Mr. Greenfield was indeed going to the edge of the stage, where a long table held coffee and scripts.

Nate was no actor. The idea of strutting around the stage reading a bunch of lines was completely foreign, a public display of strong emotion—even if acting a part—uncomfortable.

"Maybe one of the other parents, or one of the boys..."

"A *boy?*" Sara was definitely whiny. "The *boys* are

shorter than me, and I have to look *up* to do this scene right.''

Mr. Greenfield came over to Sara and looked down at Nate, too. ''Mr. Perry, all you have to do is read with a little inflection to give Sara something to bounce off. Start out pushing that milk cart and then get up and walk around when your daughter makes you angry.'' He chuckled. ''I'm sure you have some experience in that area.''

Not exactly. Sara was on her best behavior on weekends. Over the phone during the week, he could sense sometimes that Libby and Sara had had a rocky day, but they didn't share it with him. It was that guest thing that they both kept up. At first, he'd liked things that way. Neat. Quiet. Contained. But now, he wished....

''Go ahead,'' one of the fathers called. ''We'll watch— and critique.'' A couple of people clapped.

Self-consciously, Nate mounted the steps to the stage. He was used to being in the public eye. But that was on his own turf. Now this stage felt too high, well-lit, exposed. He took the script and walked over to the cart, the old wooden floorboards creaking loudly. He began the scene with other characters.

Sara entered stage left and began her lines. She was Chava, the third daughter. Even so, the part was for a teenager, and Nate felt a rush of pride that the director had thought Sara good enough.

Sara/Chava leaned forward earnestly and read one of the lines that begged for her father's understanding.

Tevye was a warm, caring man, but Nate read the lines woodenly. Sara forged on. Finally, she said, ''Come on, Nate. You're ruining my ability to *conjure emotion* here.''

Nate would have laughed if he weren't so conscious of everyone watching him. He took a breath and put more emotion into his part. In fact, he strode about for emphasis, though he felt ridiculous when he did so.

"Very good, Tevye," Mr. Greenfield said genially. "I guess I won't have to make you sing 'If I Were a Rich Man' to get you in the mood, after all."

Sara strolled around the stage, in her element, although she wore a jean skirt and silver lamé sneakers instead of the peasant garb that would presumably be her costume on opening night. She talked about marrying a young man, being desperate for her father's approval. With only occasional instructions from the director, she floated around, sometimes looking earnestly at Tevye, sometimes playing for the tiny audience of parents.

And Tevye wanted to give his approval. Nate felt Tevye's love for his daughter, yet his resistance to her choice of husband. Tevye spoke to Nate's own uncertainties, his fear of his daughter withholding her love, his fears for Sara's happiness. His wishes, his dreams.

Tevye pointed out the importance of tradition.

Nate thought of how he'd maintained the status quo with Sara all this time.

Tevye reflected on his daughter's happiness as she spoke of her young man. Happiness that would be complete if her father gave his blessing. If he took a chance.

Was it time for Nate to take a chance? Could a gambler's son who hated to gamble take the risk that Sara would reject him?

Vaguely surprised at his own actions, Nate flung out his arm with a flourish as he acted the part. Tevye almost did it, almost welcomed a man into the family who went against everything he believed in.

In the end, though, Tevye stuck with tradition. Even though Nate knew the play, and therefore the outcome of this scene, he felt the agony of unshed tears in his own throat. Tevye knew his decision meant he'd never see his daughter again.

Chava's face crumpled; her body slumped. She started to back away slowly. Tevye clutched his script to his chest, then, in a last, futile gesture, held out his hand to his retreating daughter.

Chava exited stage left.

Tevye looked to the rafters and silently asked God why in a loving family, things had to be so very, very hard.

The crack of applause startled Nate. Quickly, he reoriented himself. He was in a high-school gym in the Midwest and Tevye was a figment of some writer's imagination. He felt himself flush as the applause went on.

Sara came running back out and took a deep, stagey bow. A couple of the fathers whistled. Sara turned to Nate and beamed. She grabbed his hand, held it aloft. Then she swung into another bow, this time taking Nate with her. She waved as though she were on Broadway.

And then it happened. Right there under the stage lighting, Sara threw her arms around him and said, "Wow, *gosh,* you were so terrific, Dad."

Dad. Dad! *Dad.* Nate's arms closed around her and the lump in his throat practically choked him.

And near the doorway of the auditorium, Libby stood clutching her car keys in suddenly limp fingers, not knowing whether to laugh or shout like Sara or quietly shed a tear. Or maybe she'd do all three. After all, how many times in this life did a dream come true?

TREVOR'S FATHER never called. Now Nate and Trevor were standing outside the motel where Jonathan Samms was staying while he was in town for the court hearing. Evening was falling, and hopefully Samms would be back soon. If not, Nate and Trev would be here tomorrow. Trev was determined to see his father before Samms returned to California.

It had taken Tina a long time to finally give her consent for Trevor to do this. Her stipulation was that an adult had to be with him. She probably had hoped Libby would accompany her son.

But it was inevitable, Nate thought as they waited, that Trevor had picked him. In fact, it seemed that every conversation with the kid, from those late-night talks on their respective decks at Bittersweet Point, to the one they'd had at midnight over the phone just last night, had been leading to this moment. Yet Nate still had no real idea how or why Trevor had come to attach himself to him.

Or how he'd come to care for Trev.

He shifted, incredibly uncomfortable as he anticipated the meeting to come. Whatever the outcome, it was sure to be emotional. Trevor was quiet for once, lost in thought, pushing his wheelchair forward slowly, back slowly.

Say something to ease things, Nate thought. Okay. "You can see by this place that Libby was right about her idea of a family resort." His hand swept the shabby, pink facade, where in summer the rooms of the beachfront motel were also let by the week to vacationing families. Several of those families were playing on the beach right now, and the cheerful sounds they made were starting to grate on the two on the porch. "Families would surely buy or rent something more pleasant if it was available." *Good move, Perry. This kid is waiting to see his father for the first time in four years and you're talking business.*

But what was he supposed to say? He'd already cautioned Trev about expecting too much from this meeting. *Oh, and you'd be any different? If you could have your old man back, you wouldn't be nervous? You wouldn't hope? After all, you waited eight years to see your daughter and then just assumed she'd love you.* Hell. Maybe he was an idealist, after all.

Trevor was on a forward push.

"It was Libby's idea, this family-resort concept," Nate tried again. He wished he had Libby with him. She'd know what to say, what to do.

Trevor came inching back. "Great idea," he said with no enthusiasm. Then he perked up. "Do you want to see my list?"

"Your list?"

"I've been making a list of all the things I can do." The kid's grin was back, slightly off kilter but still broad. He pulled a folded paper from the pocket of his T-shirt. Unfolding it, he said, "I've been adding stuff as I go. If when I see my dad I'm excited and forget things, I can show him."

Nate took the list. There were three columns, in very fine print. He scanned the list. *Cooking,* Trev had written, and then under that: *Sandwiches, burritos, pizza bagels. Dishes, dishwasher and by hand. Laundry—know not to put the red shirt in with anything white* and then a hand-written exclamation mark. Even here, even now, Trev could make Nate's heart lighter. He looked at the second column. *Basketball. Eighty percent free throws from the foul line. Starter on special league.*

He swallowed, hesitated and then just did what he wanted to do. Nate reached out and rumpled the kid's hair, then gave him a friendly punch on the shoulder. Trev feigned a dramatic death, then shadow punched.

"Hey," Nate finally said quietly, ending the battle by handing back the list. "Whatever happens, we'll deal with it, okay?" Trevor faced him, and it suddenly struck Nate how incredibly brave the kid was. He had no reason to believe his father had any feelings for him, but he was going to find out. To offer his love.

"He's here," Trevor said breathlessly as a sleek black rental pulled into the parking lot, crunching gravel under expensive tires. Behind the tinted-glass windshield, Nate got the impression of a large man, and next to him, a young woman. The car stopped and the driver's door started to open.

Suddenly, Nate had a premonition.

He was down the step and had his hand on the door handle just as the door slammed shut and the engine started again. Before Jonathan Samms could shift into reverse, Nate pulled the door open. He reached in and hauled a very surprised Samms to his feet.

"Stay a while," Nate said with deceptive calm. "Your son wants to see you."

Maybe because he was surprised, Samms took a step forward. Nate took advantage of the opportunity to shut the car door behind him.

Father and son looked at each other. Samms had the dark oak complexion that suggested a permanent tan. His shirt-front was open three buttons, exposing his chest hair. A huge gold arrowhead on a chain around his neck caught the light.

Trevor bumped easily down the one step, got closer to his father. Samms's eyes flickered over his son, taking in his wheelchair.

Finally, Trevor said, "Hello, Dad." A flash of a smile, quickly dying. Trev held out a hand as if to shake, then seemed to think better of it and put it on the arm of his chair.

Samms spread his legs slightly apart in an aggressive stance. "Trevor."

Pretty sure now that Samms was not going to bolt, Nate

went around to Trevor's side and put a hand on the kid's shoulder. Trev felt strong. Under Nate's hand, there were hard muscles and thick bone. Touching still didn't come easy to Nate, but he knew Trevor could use the support.

"I wanted to see you," Trevor said to his father. "I wrote you that letter. Did you get it?"

"How did your mom find me?"

"I found you. I mean, I started it because I wanted to see you."

Under Trevor's gaze, Samms's eyes shifted.

The passenger door opened, and a young woman got out. She held a bottle wrapped in brown paper. "Jonathan, what is it?" she asked in a half-vexed, half-anxious tone that told Nate that she knew very well what "it" was. Nate took in the woman's waist-length black hair, huge sunglasses, the tight tank top covering very ample breasts, and knew he was looking at Jonathan Samms's trophy wife.

Samms ignored her. "You picked a helluva time to see me, boy," he said in a hearty tone, with a big smile. "After all, your mother just spent the afternoon picking my bones in that courtroom."

Nate saw Trev's chin go up. "You owed her."

Samms shrugged. "So she says. So the judge says. But I never have paid much attention to what goes on in this one-horse town. Out-of-towners never got any justice here. In a few years, you'll find out there's a big world out there."

Once Nate would have said the same. Now he thought of his family, and his wife's friends who had become his friends, too.

"Who're you, anyway?" Samms finally addressed Nate.

"Nate Perry. Friend of the family."

"Friend of Tina's, I'll bet."

Trev said, "Oh, Dad," but Nate cut in. "I'm married to

Libby Jamieson." Samms's eyes narrowed at the name. "Actually, I'm here to run interference for Trev, if he needs it. *Does* he need it?"

"From his old man? Naw." But Samms wouldn't look at either of them.

"Jonathan, come *on*," whined the woman.

"Well, the lady calls," Samms said with a broad wink at his son. "But we'll keep in touch, okay?" He started to turn.

"Dad! Wait!" Trevor whipped his wheels forward a foot or so, moving fast despite the coarse gravel. "I've got something I want you to see."

Looking pained, Samms stopped. Trevor fished out his list, held it out. Samms took it and read with a frown. "What's this?"

"All the stuff I can do," Trevor said eagerly. "I thought if you were staying a day or two we could shoot hoops, or the Mud Hens are playing in Toledo, I know that's minor league but I figured you wouldn't want to drive all the way to Detroit. Anyhow, you know I'm in the chair. You can see I didn't get up and walk like we thought I might at first. But it doesn't matter." Trevor's voice took on speed and vibrancy. "I can do anything, Dad. I'm getting good at guitar. I swim. When I'm sixteen, I'll be able to drive a car. The other day I went dancing."

His father's head shot up.

"I mean, I had to do it in the wheelchair but I danced with lots of girls. They don't mind the chair, Dad. None of my friends do. I don't. That's the thing. So I was kind of thinking—hoping—if you got to know me, you..." He took a visible breath. "You wouldn't mind, either."

There was a long pause. Nate tried to catch Trevor's eye, to somehow communicate his encouragement and pride in the kid.

"He can do every last thing he says, Samms," he finally said quietly. "He's also an honor student and a whiz on the computer and a fine kid. Any man would be proud to have a son like Trevor."

The late-afternoon sun beat down. Jonathan Samms wiped a bead of sweat from his upper lip. Trevor wrapped his hands around the rims of the wheels of his chair. The young woman put the bottle on the hood of the car and came to stand by Jonathan. She addressed Trevor for the first time.

"Uh, I'm Cindy."

"Hi," Trevor said.

Cindy pushed hair off her shoulders and gazed up at her husband.

Finally, Samms spoke. "Look, ah, Trevor. The thing is… Well, I live in California now, and my business is pretty busy. Flying charters in the mountains. It's rugged country, we have problems up there sometimes, and the business keeps me real, well, like I said. Real busy."

"I could come out there. To see you."

"Well, that wouldn't be a good idea. Nobody knows I have a son. That you're—" He cut himself off, then continued. "For one thing, I've got a lot of guys who work on the planes, and they're pretty macho…"

Nate got a tight feeling in the gut. He wanted so much to intervene, to save Trevor from what was coming.

Hell. What he really wanted was to punch Jonathan Samms in his tanned face, and see those perfect, upright legs crumple.

"*I'm* macho," Trevor said boldly. "As macho as I want to be."

Nate's heart swelled.

"But actually, I'm not into macho that much. Macho

guys think it's cool to hurt people." The faintest quaver crept into his voice. "Really, I think macho...sucks."

Samms fisted a hand, started to bring it down hard on the hood of the car, but at the last minute changed his mind and brought it down gently. Then rapped it once, twice. Cindy put her hand on his forearm. "Aw, God, Trevor," Samms said, and his voice had gone thick. "I didn't want it to be this way."

Hope started a faint beat in Nate's chest.

"I loved you. I did. When you were born, I must've passed out about a billion cigars. Remember how we used to toss the football? But I'm not into touchy-feely stuff. I mean, with grown-up girls I can, sure." He paused. "Oh, what the hell. What I mean is I'm no kind of father. You're old enough to have figured that out by yourself. So to ask me to get around the fact that you're crippled now—"

"I'm not," Trevor said at the same time Nate interjected, "He's not."

Trevor straightened his shoulders. "I'm not crippled. Not handicapped. Not whatever."

"I don't know the *politically correct* way to say it—"

"You don't have to know it. I'm not even a 'person with disabilities.' I'm just Trevor."

"Your dad didn't mean anything. He's not trying to hurt you," Cindy said with a kindness Nate had not expected from her.

Nate knew he had to end this fiasco of a meeting. "Trevor, let's leave and give your dad a chance to think things over." Without thinking, just wanting to get away, Nate grasped the handles of the wheelchair and started to turn Trevor away.

"No!" Trevor put his hands on the wheels and hung on tight. Nate stopped. He'd known what this meeting could bring, the heartbreak Trev could suffer. But he'd hoped against hope. And now his own heart was breaking as he saw Trev try to deal with the coldhearted man who was his father.

"Trev," Nate started.

"I said *no*. Stay out of this." He straightened his shoulders. "You said you loved me when I was born, Dad. When my legs worked. Do you love me now?" He was starting to cry, tracks of tears down a face that was whiskered with downy fuzz, the faintest beginnings of a grown man's beard.

Jonathan Samms hung his head. "Yeah."

"So," Trevor said, and his voice was high and tight with suppressed sobs. "Do you want to be my father? Do you want to do stuff together? Do you want to try again?"

Samms's other hand crumpled the paper Trevor had given him. "Like Cindy says, I don't want to hurt you. I know what I'm supposed to say." His voice went lower. "But I can't."

"Because I'm crippled."

Cindy said, "Jonathan, please," very softly.

Samms hung his head, whether in shame at himself or because of Trevor, Nate couldn't tell. "Yes. Because you're crippled. I'm sorry. Really sorry. But I can't deal with it." He spread his hands in a gesture of futility. "I never could. Everywhere we went, I knew people were looking at me because I had a crippled son."

"You bastard," Nate said, and he started to move forward. The urge that drove him was primitive, protective. So angry.

Samms quailed at Nate's advance.

With a swift move, Trevor got between them. "Give me my list." Samms looked confused. Trevor pounded on the handle of his wheelchair. "Give me back my damn *list*."

Samms looked mutely at the list he held, then he handed it back to his son. "I wish—"

"To hell with wishes." Trevor crushed the list into a ball in his fist. To Nate he said, "Let's get out of here. *Now*."

CHAPTER FIFTEEN

TREVOR BRUSHED OFF Nate's help and yanked on the door of the Jag. Trevor wished Nate would go over to the driver's side.

Trevor got the door open and hoisted himself out of his wheelchair. He bumped his elbow on the door frame getting in, something he never had a problem with. Pain shot through him, and he said, "Damn, damn, *damn,*" and finished with as many cusswords as he could think of, even the real bad ones he never used. Nate didn't correct him, and for that Trevor felt a rush of gratitude that mingled with his rage at his father.

Nate started to fold the wheelchair, but Trevor snatched it out of his hand and started folding it himself.

Thwack. Clunk. Snap.

Done. He had to let Nate load the chair into the back seat, which was something Trevor would have liked to do, but there wasn't room for him to maneuver.

Without a word, Nate got in the car. Actually, Trevor was glad Nate wasn't talking. He was very glad Nate wasn't feeling sorry for him. Yet Trevor had an urge to say the very worst things he possibly could to Nate, which wouldn't be right. But he just felt like doing something. Something like cussing out the whole damn world and then punching somebody's lights out.

Nate sat for a moment. Finally, he spoke, and when he did, he said the worst thing possible. "I'm sorry."

Trevor couldn't help it—he blew his stack. "No! Don't say you're sorry for me! Not after—after—not because—" Then to his utter horror, he burst into tears.

It wasn't a few drops of moisture coming down, like sometimes happened to guys in movies. These were sobs, terrible hoarse sobs that seemed to come from somewhere in his gut and spill out all over. "God!" he choked out, so embarrassed he wanted to pass out, there on the seat. He'd tried so hard to be cool about this. Cool with Nate. Cool with his father. He'd done so good, held everything back. But now he couldn't.

Then Nate leaned over and pulled him to him, and Trevor shook and sobbed against his chest like a little kid. His nose started to run and drip on Nate's shirt and his cheeks felt as if they were burning. He cried because his father was a jerk and his father didn't love him and his father was ashamed of him and his father really *did* leave because his son was a cripple. And for the first time in his life, he cried because he couldn't get out of the chair and walk.

Nate sat there and let him cry, and thanked God he didn't say anything more about feeling sorry for him. Finally, after a long time, when Trevor couldn't breathe through his nose and his tongue felt thick, he managed to stop. He raised his head and turned away as quick as he could so he wouldn't have to look Nate in the eye. Nate Perry had been kind of his friend and now Nate would know he was just a little kid who couldn't handle his emotions.

"Cripes," Trevor said. "Let's get out of here."

Nate started the engine. "Ready to go home?"

"Do we have to?"

"No. We can go anywhere you want."

"Can we just ride for a while?"

Nate nodded and took the slow two-laner that hugged the water going out of town. For a while they didn't talk, until Trevor said, "I don't like it that you feel sorry for me."

Nate said, "You've been through a lot. I can't help feeling sorry." His voice was kind of ragged-sounding somehow. Like his throat had been kind of tight, too, which was really weird.

"I can do anything. Any damn thing I please."

Again, Nate ignored the cussing, though his mother would have had a fit to hear how he was talking today. "I wasn't feeling sorry *for* you. I was feeling sorry that you had to go through that with your dad."

"Oh." Trevor considered that. "It was rough." He was shaking and he wanted to start crying again. "Look, can we drop it, okay? It didn't work out. End of story."

Nate nodded, and they drove for a long time. The tracks of tears on Trevor's cheeks dried, making his skin feel tight. "I guess you think my dad is a real jerk, huh?" he finally asked.

"Well," Nate said, hesitating, before adding, "Yes."

"You weren't like him. Because you came back for Sara. You loved her that much."

Nate hesitated again, then turned into the next public park. There was a gravel parking lot and a boat launch. Out on the lake was a distant powerboat heading for shore. But there was nobody else.

He turned off the engine, and in a couple of minutes Trevor had to roll down his window because it was hot with the air-conditioning off. He wondered why they were stopping.

Nate draped a hand over the steering wheel. "I don't want you to think I'm some kind of hero because I came back for Sara," he said finally. "I've had to learn a lot of things about being a good father."

"But you were here to learn them," Trevor said. "And you would never have said your kid was a cripple."

"No. I wouldn't say that to anyone. But to say it to you, somebody so incredibly special..." Nate's voice suddenly went low and fierce. "See, Trevor, there are all kinds of 'crippled,' and none of them have anything to do with your legs. The person who's crippled is your father, because he has no idea what a terrific son he has."

Trevor glanced away because he couldn't exactly look Nate in the eye. There was something about how fierce Nate was being that seemed almost too much to handle.

Nate spoke again. "You've had an accident that could have made you hard and bitter. Believe me, I know. I've been hard and bitter all my life. But you don't let life do that. You just keep yourself open. You insisted on seeing your father even though you knew it might end up like it did."

Trevor swallowed hard. "Yeah. I bawled like a baby about it, too."

"You had a right. And Trev, the day you can't cry, the day you can't feel anything anymore, well, that's the day you aren't a man anymore, either. That's what I've learned."

Trevor thought about that for a while. He thought about his mom, and teasing her. He thought about his girlfriend, Ann, who wasn't just for kissing—he really liked talking to her. And he thought about Nate, and how cool it would be if this man could be his father. Not his father, exactly, because he had a father, who was a jerk.

It seemed as though Nate was thinking stuff over, too, as they watched the powerboat maneuver back into dock. Trevor knew they'd taken Nate's baby away. But he thought maybe what Nate was saying was that you had to accept stuff like that, stuff like Trevor's father being a jerk, and not let that hard knot that was in his stomach now stay there forever.

Not be angry all the time. Like his mom used to be. She was so much...gee, he didn't know, sort of freer now, and Nate seemed to be looser, too. Heck, he was here in Harborside instead of Chicago and it seemed as if he had all the time in the world. And every time Trevor saw him with Libby, he kept smiling a goofy smile like Trevor's friend Doug's older brother when he got married to Barb Fielding's kid sister.

"Am I, like, supposed to forgive my dad?"

Nate sighed. "If you can someday. If not, what I'm saying is you still have to give other people a chance, not be so afraid they'll hurt you."

"I get it."

Nate smiled then. "I'm sure you do. Now, I bet your mom will be waiting and worrying about you."

Trevor groaned. "Better get me back. Telling her everything that happened is going to take a while." He clapped a hand to his forehead and made a sound of disgust, but he didn't really mind. His mom had been there every day since the accident and he knew she'd never cut out on him the way his old man had. He never said dopey, mushy things to his mom, but tonight he was going to tell her he loved her.

When they pulled into Trevor's road, Nate asked him for his list.

"What for?" Trevor asked, fishing out the crumpled wad of paper and handing it over.

Nate smoothed it out against the steering wheel, then folded it and put it in his pocket. "Oh, I'd just like to have it. For one thing, I was thinking we could pick some of those things you can do and do them together sometimes."

Nate wanted to hang out with him? Trevor couldn't believe it. "Like go to some games or something?"

"Sure."

"But you have to be in Chicago."

Nate got the weirdest expression on his face. Kind of sad, or maybe confused. "When this current project of mine is on track, I'll have a bit more time. We'll do things together. I promise."

Trevor's father had made promises. *I'll take you to the Tiger's game on Saturday. I'll pick you up after school on Friday and we'll shoot a few hoops together in the gym. I'll take you and Doug out to Cedar Point to play the midway games this summer for sure.* That last promise had been made at the start of the summer Jonathan Samms had packed up and left.

But Trevor knew Nate would keep his promise. It was even more cool because Nate didn't have to do this stuff, like a father was supposed to. Nate Perry was busy and important. But he wanted to spend time with Trevor.

He'd said Trevor was special. So the tears sort of wanted to come again, but this time for an entirely different reason.

"How DID IT GO with Trevor?" Libby asked as soon as Nate had put one foot in the kitchen. Sara was at Kathleen's for pizza, and Libby had been walking the floors alone and worrying.

"Hi," he said instead of a reply.

She felt herself flushing. How could one little syllable always sound so intimate? "Hi."

He smiled a little, but it faded quickly. "I needed that. Trevor's father is a horse's ass who I could have easily killed with my bare hands."

"Oh, no. What happened?"

She took his arm for good measure. After he'd settled

himself into her living-room sofa and recounted what Trevor had gone through, Libby was furious.

"What did you say to Jonathan?"

He shrugged, his mouth hard and tight. "What was to say? Anything that prolonged the meeting or set Samms off might have hurt Trevor more." He paused. "Trev and I took a ride after, talked some."

"Will he be okay?"

He paused, considering. "He was hurt, sure. But he's an amazing kid. He's got strength and courage. We talked for a while and he seemed better."

Libby clasped her hands in her lap. She felt profound gratitude to Nate, both for being with Trevor during his confrontation with his father, but mostly for being willing to talk with him afterward. She wanted to know more, but Nate suddenly clammed up. For a second she was hurt, but then she realized that Nate was concealing strong emotion.

"You love that kid," she said quietly.

He looked her in the eye. "Yes."

Impulsively, she reached up and looped her arm around his neck, bringing his body to hers. Her heart was beating hard at meeting his, a good, thumping beat. "Thank you," she said softly.

"It was nothing," he said too quickly. But she looked up and saw that it was something. Their gazes caught, locked.

"I'm exhausted," he said finally.

"Emotional scenes do that to a person," she agreed with a smile. "Too tired for bed?"

The hard planes of his face abruptly relaxed as he smiled. A few minutes later, Libby led him up the stairs to her room. There they made love, so intense that they scarcely uttered a word as they joined their bodies and took comfort from each other in the twilight of the day.

Afterward, Libby lay on her back. Overhead, right in her line of vision, was a stained-glass dish chandelier made for her by Tina. Stained-glass making was an old hobby of her friend's.

Libby realized she'd made a decision. Looking up at the rose and blue glass, she got a lump in her throat, because even now she wasn't sure she was doing the right thing. Even to have this discussion would be the end of a dream, because once she'd hoped— No. That wasn't fair. Nate had come so very, very far. It was time to meet him halfway.

"Nate?" she ventured quietly.

"Um," he said, half-asleep beside her.

Libby focused on the ceiling. *Tina will still be your friend. And you might have to leave this house, full of your mother's things, and the shop you love so much, but you'll never lose your memories.* "Would you like me to come to Chicago?"

Beside her, he went still. When she rolled to look at him, he was sober, his eyes dark. "If you would. If you would only come with me sometimes."

The carefully controlled plea in his voice astonished her. He wanted her to come that badly? How come he'd never asked, then? She took a deep breath. "Not sometimes." Her hand stole over his, entwined. "For always. I was thinking I could sell the house and the shop, and open something there."

Around hers, his fingers tightened convulsively.

"What about Sara?" he asked quietly.

"We'll talk to her. It might not be easy, but we owe it to her, don't you think, to keep our family together?" He didn't answer, so she added, "There's something I've been thinking lately. Home isn't a place. I loved Harborside because my friends and family were here. Now half my family's elsewhere most of the time." She leaned in so that flyaway strands of hair lay on his neck, and she traced the stern, sweet line of his mouth with her finger. "You're my family now, Nate. You and Sara. My loyalty has to be to you."

He closed his eyes. Then he reached up and put a hand on the back of her head, slowly pulling her face to his. When their mouths touched, he made a sound, one note of thick emotion, and kissed her deep and hard and true.

Slowly, he drew back. "Could you come this Saturday? There's a party on Saturday night. I'd like you to go with me."

A party already. Well, that's what Chicago—and sharing Nate's life—would mean.

She took a deep breath. "Sara could stay with Tina this weekend. If you want me there, I'll be there."

"Thank you," he said softly. "It's going to be a rough one."

"A rough party?"

"Yes. It's at Charles Baker's house. He's got an investment consortium, and most of its members will be there. They want to talk over Iris." He rolled onto his back. "Libby, it's my last chance to pull this thing off. If not…"

He didn't finish his sentence, but he didn't have to. Panic stirred in Libby. Any society party would create anxiety in her, but this one… "I'm not sure my being there would help you, Nate. I'm not good at chitchat, I don't have anything to wear and I'm not beautiful and certainly not glamorous."

Nate swore softly. "You know," he said to the ceiling, "for a woman who can take a bunch of dried weeds and arrange them into a basket and make them beautiful, you don't seem to have a clue. I find you absolutely…" He turned, touched her hair and her cheek. "Fascinating."

Not beautiful. Not even pretty. Still, fascinating wasn't

bad. Of course, it had taken him a long time to get to "fascinating" and she'd only have one night to help Nate. But he'd had the courage to forge a family out of nothing. Could she do less than to face her own demons and help her husband?

"Well, this time, your *fascinating* wife will do all she can to wow them in Chicago."

A STRANGER LOOKED BACK at Libby from the mirrored wall in the foyer as Nate took off her black cape. The bright track lights should have shown a few freckles, that place on her forehead where she'd peeled earlier in the summer. Instead, the mirror showed a complexion that was velvety, highlighted with soft peach. A smudgy line of charcoal deepened and enlarged her eyes. Russet painted her lips and her mouth looked full and sensual. Not beautiful. But not bad, either.

Libby knew she looked the best she ever had. In desperation, she'd taken her one credit card, walked into the first classy boutique she'd seen and bought the dress the salesclerk recommended. It was a simple, tight black sheath. The dress was too short. It was a good three inches above the knee, over black stockings so sheer that Libby had worried about the damage her callused hands would do when she put them on. The stockings ended at the tops of her thighs. She usually wore tights, and these darn things felt downright weird.

Libby clutched the chain strap of her evening bag. The purse looked like a treasure chest for a doll. Of all the things she'd bought today, she was in love with only one of them, this glittering chest with its tiny lock and key. A box for Pandora, she thought as Nate greeted some guests who were also just arriving and made smooth introductions. Libby lingered as the others went ahead into a huge living

room furnished with white leather sofas and a black lac-
quered grand piano.

Nate stood behind her, gestured to the space where
brightly smiling people mingled. "Welcome to Chicago,
beautiful wife," he whispered.

The comment pleased her, but an instinctive denial
passed her lips. "Not beautiful. Just dressed up and feeling
strange."

"Hey," he said softly, and taking her hand, he drew her
down a different hallway. A statue in a huge niche was
built into the wall, and Nate pulled her aside, partially concealing her from view. The noise of the party was more
distant here.

"God, you look wonderful," he said, and he bent and
kissed her lightly on the neck. He'd been late arriving home
from the office, and she'd been already dressed. He'd had
to hurry into his tuxedo. But now that they were at the
party, he didn't seem all that anxious to go in. "We'll have
to get dressed up more often when you move here. You
have no idea how these bare shoulders..." His voice trailed
off as he used a finger to trace the thin strap.

Her skin jumped at his touch. She welcomed it, yet it
made her nervous. She had an almost perverse need to point
up her flaws, and she wasn't sure why. She looked up at
Nate—his chiseled mouth, his straight nose.

He was perfect. "This dress is so tight," she blurted out.
"The salesclerk said no panty hose, so I have these thigh-
highs that kind of pinch in the wrong place..." Oh, Lord.
She'd got over feeling awkward in the face of his perfection
long ago. What was wrong with her?

"You don't say." His breath whispered along her neck.
His voice was husky, seductive.

From behind, his hands caressed the sides of her hips,

going slightly lower as if searching for the tops of her stockings. She felt a response leap within her.

"The first time I met you, you said you'd forgotten to buy nylons." He looked down to where the black silk of her stockings met the tops of her high-heeled pumps, and his voice dropped even more. "I'm glad you're wearing them tonight."

She felt a painful squeeze deep within her middle. She remembered what she'd said, that day at the courthouse. She was surprised and embarrassed that he recalled it, too. And Nate's comment about her black silk stockings just seemed to highlight how different she was tonight.

Of course she was different. How many times did she wear a dress held up by nothing more than a couple of threads?

"You know," he whispered, "I wish we'd stayed home."

Home? His condominium had been bigger than a house, colder than a bank lobby, all sparse charcoal gray and teal and chrome. How could anyone call those huge, nearly empty rooms a home?

"Perry, there you are. Stealing a kiss already?"

Nate stepped out, drawing her to his side without a trace of embarrassment. "Randall, good to see you. I'd like to introduce my wife, Libby."

THE PARTY WAS an ordeal. Nate gallantly introduced her to nearly everyone in the packed room overlooking Lake Michigan, but everything was a whirl to Libby. Too many strange faces, too much glamour. She held her evening bag in one hand and a plate in the other, knowing she needed two hands to stand up and eat. But for some unearthly reason, she was loath to part with her treasure chest, and held on to it like some kind of talisman.

Nate had to leave her to speak with the tight knot of men gathered around the fireplace. The night was hot, and air-conditioning poured into the room. Yet on the grate, a fire was lit.

"Mrs. Perry? Libby, isn't it?"

Libby turned in surprise to find a striking redhead standing next to her. While Libby's red hair had always been an object of teasing, this woman seemed to flaunt its color—she'd chosen a dress in a shade that matched. Libby admired her brazenness, even as she looked into chilly green eyes. "I'm sorry. I know Nate introduced us, but—"

"Danielle Morgan," the redhead said smoothly, her smile coached and brittle. "So, how's married life? I just got married recently myself." With her champagne glass, she indicated a silver-haired man who was at least two decades her senior.

"Congratulations," Libby murmured.

"Oh, thank you. He's so rich," Danielle said without a trace of embarrassment. "That's why I married him, of course. He knew it. Hell, the whole world knew it." She gave a trill of laughter. Her eyes narrowed. "You, on the other hand, managed to get the best of two worlds. A rich husband. And a young, gorgeous one, too."

For a moment, both watched as Nate wove his way through the crowd. He caught Libby's eye, waved briefly, then turned away.

"Thank you," Libby said, unsure what response the comment called for.

"You know, we've all heard about Nate's marriage by now. We couldn't believe it. For a while there, everyone was talking about it."

"He does wear a wedding ring," Libby said, trying not to clench her teeth.

"Yes, and we all wonder how you coaxed him into *that*."

Libby was starting to wonder who "we all" were, but she decided it might be better not to know.

"So," Danielle continued brightly, "we wanted to get a look at the wife he's been hiding in Ohio."

Libby felt her cheeks grow hot. The cut stones of her purse bit into her palm. She put her chin up. "Well, now you've seen her."

The other woman assessed her with frank interest. "It must be the lure of the unusual. Nate has always been— shall we say—independent." She used one hand to fluff her bangs. "Of course, he's always had a thing for red-heads."

Libby's eyes flew to Danielle's hair. It dawned on her that she was looking at one of Nate's old girlfriends.

Danielle smiled wider, a slow, cruel smile. "Nate and I have been running into each other, renewing old acquaintances. If I were you, honey, I wouldn't leave him alone in Chicago all week. A man like Nate gets lonely, and there are plenty of women to console him."

Like you? Libby wanted to shriek. Suddenly, Libby felt sick. What did Danielle mean when she'd said she and Nate were renewing their acquaintance?

"Excuse me," she said tightly, and turned blindly from the window. She sensed the other woman's satisfaction.

She ran smack into a man's chest. A cracker and a stuffed mushroom flew from her plate as a tuxedoed arm reached out to steady her. "Oh, I'm so sorry," she said, and she wanted to die.

"No harm done. Are you all right?"

"Yes." Sure. How on earth had she let Nate talk her into attending this party?

"You're Perry's new wife, aren't you?"

Miserably, Libby nodded.

The man cast a sharp eye behind her, where Danielle presumably still stood. "One of the cats giving you a hard time?" He smiled, and the deep lines at the corners of his eyes crinkled.

Libby swallowed and flushed, embarrassed at how obvious this scene must appear to an experienced, urbane man like her companion.

"She's jealous. Forget her," the man said decisively. He held out a hand. "Charles Baker. I'm joining my own party late. Had some negotiations to do in the study."

Libby hurriedly set down her plate on a nearby table. This was Nate's potential new investor for Iris. His hand felt warm as she shook it, but maybe that was because her own was too cold.

"I hear you spend most of your time in the little town where Perry met you."

"Harborside, on Lake Erie. I have a business there."

The kind, rather indulgent eyes sharpened immediately "Really? What kind of business?"

As she often did when she was nervous, Libby rattled on, grateful for a good listener, grateful to get away from Danielle and all the Danielles she suddenly sensed in the room. She talked flowers, but mostly the problems with cash flow that having a business in a resort town entailed.

"I know what you mean," Charles Baker finally said, breaking in when Libby was on a roll about her plans for off-season sales. "Investing in seasonal property development has the same kind of problems."

She flushed again. Here she was going on as if she had no idea his business was much more complicated than hers. "I must be boring you," she said. She'd had secret fantasies of meeting this man and somehow impressing him, of helping Nate win Baker's confidence. Instead, she'd been talking about inventory overflows!

"So, how goes it?" Nate had come up, a glass of wine in each hand. He held one out to Libby, who accepted it and took a large, unladylike swallow.

"Just talking to your wife," Baker said. "How refreshing to meet a woman running a business. And not consulting or being on the board of directors of Daddy's company, either. Why didn't you tell me your wife ran a shop?"

Nate flashed Libby a look of surprise. She took another swallow of wine, not sure if he was pleased. Well, she'd done the best she could. She was no flirt, and if that's what Nate wanted, he would be sorely disappointed.

Nate took a sip from his own glass, then said lightly, "My wife is a woman of many talents."

Sure. The charming thing to say. Without even knowing exactly why, Libby felt her teeth clenching.

Charles Baker looked them both over. "Well, Perry, all I can say is that it took you long enough to grow up, but I'm glad you did. When a man is investing in another man, he likes to see him exercise good judgment, make good choices in both his public and his private life."

Nate went still. "Investing? Then you've decided to come in on Iris?"

Instead of answering right away, Baker turned to Libby. "My wife, Carol, is over by the windows, talking to the caterer. Why don't I introduce you? Then I think you'd best excuse your husband and me. We've got things to discuss."

"THEY'RE IN! I've got Iris licked." Only a half-dozen steps into his condominium, Nate picked her up and whirled her around.

"Wonderful." Libby made a grab for enthusiasm. After all, this was her life now.

"Charles Baker was so taken with you, said he was glad I'd picked somebody like you."

Well, at least Charles Baker had seen she was different from the Danielles. And Libby was the one Nate had married. He'd paid no attention to Danielle at that party. In fact, he'd been nothing more than superficially charming to the other women.

"Oh, baby," he murmured, and his breathing picked up. He splayed a warm male palm over her bare back.

A shiver went up her spine, despite her mood.

"This dress is..." His voice trailed off into a husky whisper. "I don't know which I want to see more, you peeling down that little bodice or you showing me the tops of those black stockings."

Heat poured within her, embarrassed heat, aroused heat. He pulled her to him, and his own arousal was blatant and demanding. His hands on her hips, he started to draw up her dress. The sensation of his hands on thin nylon, and then, abruptly, on the bare skin of her upper thighs, nearly drove her wild.

She kissed him with utter abandon, needing him, claiming him, pressed tight to his legs and chest, her fingers in the layers of his hair. She loved him. And if the price of having him was sharing his life here, so be it.

Impatient now, he shoved her tight skirt higher, to her waist. He pulled down her panties, and she kicked them off. She was frantic, desperate to make love with Nate and blot out all these confusing feelings. "Now," she said, and it was both whisper and moan.

"Yes, now." With a little hop, she wrapped her legs around his waist. The shock of her bare, most sensitive flesh on the fine weave of his trousers was like a fan on flames. He was so...hard.

Taking a couple of steps, he pressed her to the wall of the foyer. The crystal chandelier in front of her glittered in a thousand colors. She closed her eyes on the sight, but still she could see pinpricks of light against her lids. Nate's hands came between them, tugging at his own clothing. A stud or two clinked, rolled on the marble floor. His zipper came down, and then he was inside her.

Her body closed around him and she held on for dear life. Before, their lovemaking had been intense, but it had always happened lying on her bed with the door closed. There they had to be careful; they were parents. Here they were only lovers. One thrust, two. That was all it took, and she was convulsing around him.

Right as it happened, he put his lips against her ear and whispered, "I love you."

CHAPTER SIXTEEN

THE REAL WORLD came back slowly to Libby. First there was the chandelier, the high light of the foyer as she opened her eyes, then the scent of sex. She was half-dressed, jammed against the wall, held up only by Nate, who was shaking and breathing as hard as she.

He loved her. He loved her!

Warmth shot through her in a giddy rush, replaced just as quickly with cold.

Which Libby did he love? The real Libby, who baked bread and talked too much and chose sunflower nightgowns and dahlia T-shirts? Or this Libby, the one who wore black dresses that were too tight to be comfortable and balanced champagne in one hand and a plate of crudités in the other?

He moved back, and with his hands to steady her, she slid slowly down.

"Are you all right? I didn't hurt you?"

He'd never asked before, because he'd never needed to. Their lovemaking had been so hot and abandoned. So hard. He'd taken her against a *wall*, for Heaven's sake, and she had wanted it.

Her mind refused to dwell on all the times he must have made love—had sex—against the wall of his foyer.

"Sure. Yes." Unsettled, she picked up her cape from the floor and then her treasure chest from the console. She opened it and took out her credit card, lipstick and two tissues, all the tiny purse would hold. She turned to find him watching her with an intensity that was almost blinding.

"Did you hear what I said, there at the last?"

Her lips were tender from his mouth molding so hard to hers. "Yes."

"I didn't..." He swallowed. "I didn't say it only because I was caught up in what we were doing. I meant it." His eyes took her in. "I love you."

She didn't say anything. Her throat felt too tight.

He waited a beat more, and when she didn't respond, his mouth turned straight and grim. "I thought that was what you wanted to hear."

"Why did you wait until I came to Chicago to say it?"

He came toward her, his arms out. "It's just that when you said you'd come here, and then, at that party, you convinced Charles Baker to take a chance on me—"

"Wrong answer."

He stopped abruptly. Slowly, his hands fell to his sides. "What's the matter with you? This is supposed to be a celebration."

What *was* the matter? She'd volunteered to come. Suddenly, she knew the answer. "It's because you love me only this way, Nate. You love me only because I've passed the Chicago test. Because I managed not to embarrass you at the party."

"I'm proud of you."

"Are you proud of me in Harborside?"

"Well, of course, but here everything's so important—"

"More important than your family?" She felt tears start in the corners of her eyes. *More important than the happiness of the woman you just professed to love?*

"Libby," he said slowly, looking past her, taking in his surroundings. "This is who I am."

Her heart started a peculiar, irregular thump. "So in Harborside, when you came to Sara's rehearsal, when you helped Trevor through the incident with his father, when you tried the square dance, when you...when we first...that wasn't you?''

She had him. For a moment, he visibly wavered, his eyes confused. Finally, as if it didn't matter, he said, ''Sure, that was me, too.''

But it mattered. And suddenly, she was angry. All the understanding she'd tried to give him, every time she'd dared to hope, all mixed together in a powerful anger.

''You love me this way, Nate. Well, I love you *that* way.'' She looked down at her dress. ''This isn't the real me. In this dress, here in this house, I feel like a fraud. Like an actor in one of Sara's plays.'' She drew a deep breath. ''And it hurts me and makes me angry that you prefer me this way.''

Unable to bear the intensity of his gaze, she pushed past him into the living room. She stumbled a little on the un- expected step, having forgotten that his living room was sunken. Anyway, she couldn't see too well with her eyes full of tears.

''Please,'' he said, and the raw, almost desperate way he said the one word tugged at her heart.

''I made a mistake.'' Despite her best efforts, her voice quavered. ''I should never have come here. I don't wear black dresses. I don't wear lacy lingerie or sexy night- gowns. After all, you saw me one night before I bought that green nightgown. Do you remember what I was wear- ing?'' Her voice grew tighter. ''Yes, it's a test, Nate. Do you remember?''

''I don't take tests.'' His expression was taut and dan- gerous.

''You don't remember.''

Abruptly, he slammed a fist down on the table. The thick

glass of the tabletop shivered, rattled a Lalique sculpture. "You were wearing a nightgown with a sunflower as big as a dinner plate splashed across your breasts. Hell, you think I don't remember? I dreamed about taking that thing off you for a month afterward!"

Oh. For a moment she hoped—but his recollection didn't change anything, not after tonight. "You'd rather have me in a cocktail dress, impressing your friends!" Both their voices had risen now.

"I like you that way, yes. I like you in black, I like you in sunflowers, and I like you in nothing at all!" Unexpectedly, as if he'd just now realized he was yelling, his voice dropped. "I love you." Almost tentatively, as if he'd forgotten how and was just relearning the movement, he held out his hands, palms up.

At the gesture, the tears in her eyes spilled over. She was unable to hold back her pain. "I bet Danielle Morgan doesn't wear sunflowers."

"What's Danielle got to do with this?"

"You tell me, Nate."

He looked confused for a moment, before comprehension dawned. "Did she say something to you at the party?"

Oh, God. Was it true then? "Did you have an affair with Danielle?"

"Is *that* what she said?"

"Is it true?"

"No, it's not true!"

She searched his eyes. Under the circumstances of their marriage, she could forgive him, hardly blame him. But it still hurt.

He took a few steps toward her, put his hands on her shoulders. "Listen to me. I didn't sleep around on my first wife and I don't sleep around on you."

She felt suddenly limp, and she wanted someone to hold

her. Her best friend. Funny, she thought now with a touch of hysteria, that person was Nate. "You might have had a right," she whispered finally. "We were married, I should have let things happen naturally. But all my life, I've just wanted somebody to love me the way I am. For me, not for who they wanted me to be."

"Look." He spread his hands. "I admit, there were women in my life. Maybe not as many as you think." He shrugged, looked away quickly. "But I was single, and they were single. And I can't change what I did then. I can only tell you that I'm trying now."

"I'm trying, too. But I can't be what you want. I thought I could, but I...can't."

Her words seemed to hang in the air. For a long moment, they stared at each other. Libby's throat was unbearably tight.

"So," he said, and that coolness, that utter control was back in that one word. "Where do we go from here?"

"I don't know," she said miserably. "I just don't know."

NATE DIDN'T KNOW, either, but he learned one thing in the next two weeks: they couldn't go back to the way things were. In desperation, he'd fallen back on old routines. Friday nights to Sunday afternoons in Harborside, the rest of the week in Chicago.

It was terrible. How had he ever thought this was a good solution? When he was in Chicago, he thought about Harborside, wondering what *she* was doing, whether she was having a good day in the shop, what was going on with Sara. Then when he came in on Friday nights, he felt as awkward as a boy, as unwelcome as a stranger among old friends. Why couldn't he say he'd missed her, that he'd missed them?

He knew why. Because he'd offered his love for the first time in nine years, and she'd rejected him. Rejected his life.

Now it was Saturday, Harborside again, and the tension was thick. Once he would have fled to his makeshift office upstairs, or gone out for a sail. Now, teeth gritted, he endured being downstairs this hot afternoon, going over cost projections for a new project, one that was so massive in scale that it would leave Iris in the dust. A man had to keep building, and each project had to be bigger.

Sara had picked up on the tension in the house and was stuck to Libby like glue. Libby sat at the dining-room table with some ledgers from the shop. Sara sat next to her. She was supposed to be reading, but she kept interrupting. She'd gone on and on about a fight with Kathleen, then about her horse, and now she was starting on the play.

"The seam in my costume has a rip, under the arm. Nobody can see it, but I know it's there. Can you fix it?"

Libby looked up. "Sure. Later."

"If you can't fix it, Tina maybe could."

"Um," Libby said, her pencil stopping on one of a line of numbers.

Libby looked uptight. Lines marred her forehead, and she'd pulled her hair back into a ponytail as if she couldn't cope with it today. She'd said little to him. Last night, he'd snuck into her dark room like a thief, the first time he'd gone to her bed since Chicago. He'd wondered if she'd throw him out, but instead in the dark they'd held each other with bruising force. He'd whispered, "I love you," and she'd whispered, "I love you," but neither had any solutions and Nate had the terrified feeling that she'd stopped trying to find any. If Libby stopped trying...

Afterward, he'd said he couldn't sleep—the truth—and

he'd walked her beach in the dark, and then he'd returned to his own room for the night.

"I wanted to practice my lines for *Fiddler* today." Sara again.

"Maybe Kathleen would like to do that," Libby said, looking up with a frown. "You guys could make up. You always do."

"Kathleen doesn't like acting. Actually, I'm pretty mad at Kathleen. Like I told you, she—"

"Well, one of your other friends, then."

"*You're* the one in the play."

"Sara, I can't. I've got income tax forms I have to get done by midweek. I've got to work, honey."

"You're always working," Sara grumbled.

"Sara," Nate finally said. "Stop bothering Libby."

Both Libby and his daughter looked over at him in surprise. Usually he let Libby handle Sara, but the girl was bothering her, and Libby had just said she needed to work. He dropped his eyes back to his own figures.

Sara fell into a sulky silence. Nate couldn't focus. Instead he looked out the windows of the small living room. Out on the street, a couple of boys went by on bikes, followed by a black-and-white mutt that had patches of summer mange. The air was sultry, unbearably still. The clock ticked slowly. Nate rubbed the back of his neck. What was he doing here? He didn't belong here. Funny how not belonging gave him such a hurt, way inside. He pushed the thought away. Maybe a sail, after all, then an early trip back to Chicago.

Sara closed her book. "Lib, we could do one of our songs. You know, for the chorus at the wedding. 'Sunrise, Sunset.'"

"Not now, Sara." In exasperation, Libby threw down her pencil. "Why don't you go look for shells? Why don't you go in-line skating, or listen to your CDs, or go out on the sunporch and practice your lines by yourself?''

"I don't want to do stuff by myself. I'm bored." She gave a long, dramatic sigh. "It's boring in this house, boring, boring—"

"Enough," Nate snapped. "That's enough, Sara! Now go find something to do!"

She stared at him defiantly, holding her hair up above her neck. "It's too hot to do anything outside."

He gritted his teeth. "You didn't hear me, I guess. Now I'm telling you again. Go...find...something...to do, and leave Libby alone!"

Sara leaped to her feet. "Why are you sticking up for her? You're mad at her, so why are you sticking up for her?"

Libby put out her hand, but Sara shrugged it off.

"He's not mad at me," she said. "Not exactly."

"So why is everybody tiptoeing around this house?" Sara faced him, but her lower lip wobbled. "Something's going to happen. I know it! And I *hate* you!"

Her steps pounded through the kitchen and sunporch and they both heard the door to the beach slam shut.

Nate raised his eyes to Libby. She stood and swore softly, and shut her ledger with a snap.

"What did I do?" Nate asked.

"For God's sake, Nate," Libby said sharply, and then she headed upstairs. A moment later, he heard the shower start.

He sat still, listening to the damn clock by himself. And then he went out the front door, fished out his car keys and got into his Jag.

He drove aimlessly, shaken. What had Sara meant, saying something was going to happen? He didn't know, but he felt it, too, an almost unbearable tension. Sara had never been angry at him before. Scared of the newness, sure. Distant, certainly. But he'd never yelled at her before. She'd never yelled at him.

I hate you.

He loved them both, but his best efforts seemed always to fail.

He got back at dusk. He wasn't sure what the welcome would be, so he went in quietly. Libby was on the phone, but she hung up quickly and came into the living room.

"Have you seen Sara?" she asked, her eyes wide with concern.

"She's not here?"

"I haven't seen her since she went out to the beach this afternoon. Her bike's still here, and I've been calling her friends. She didn't come back for dinner, Nate, and it'll be dark soon."

His gut clenched. But he made sure his voice was reasonable. "Maybe she just needed to go somewhere to cool off." After all, he told himself without much conviction, hadn't he spent the last few hours doing exactly that?

"Sure, be reasonable," she said, and her voice shook.

He was getting more scared by the minute. Libby was pretty relaxed with Sara, treated her as half grown-up. If Libby was worried... His tight stomach turned, and then he knew an old sensation, an almost unbearable fear for his daughter's safety, a sensation he was able to contain only with rigid self-control.

He made a grab for control now, but for some reason gaining it was harder than it used to be. He reached out to Libby, grabbed her shoulders and hung on for a moment. "We'll find her. After all, everybody in town knows her. People will look out for her." Thank God they were here in Harborside, not in Chicago. "Who've you called?"

"Kathleen's mom, all her friends. The Romers, who live

way down at the end of the beach. I don't know who else to call."

He didn't, either. "Stay here and wait by the phone in case she calls. I'll go out in the car and look." He didn't add that he'd just driven through town and hadn't seen a sign of Sara. Harborside wasn't that big. But there wasn't much here that could harm a ten-year-old.

Except the lake. The water.

He forced himself to remain calm. "Call Tina and see if Sara's been hanging around Bittersweet Point." At the Point, there were all kinds of machinery, pits in the dirt, lots of things that could injure a child.

That thought was bad enough. The second was worse. For the first time, he faced the idea that she might have run away, might be far away, in trouble and out of reach.

He drove every road he hadn't driven that afternoon. They were few, but it took some time because he scanned the roadside in the gathering dusk, the high weeds, the dark woodsy areas.

When he got back to the house, Libby met him in the driveway. "Tina and Trevor just got home," she told him tersely. "Trevor noticed right away your boat's missing from the dock."

Oh, God. "Sara's afraid of the boat. She'd never take it out." But he met her eyes in the dark and they both had the same thought. Sara was no sailor, but she had some experience with powerboating; every kid in Harborside had. And his boat had an inboard motor.

"Get in," he said, reaching over and pushing open the passenger-side door.

When she was seated, he headed for the yacht club.

Libby spoke. "I called the sheriff, and they've notified the Coast Guard. But I want to be there, too, Nate. I have to look. So I called Rob Johnston at the yacht club and he's going to let us borrow a powerboat.''

Nate nodded.

Unexpectedly, her hand stole between the seats, took his. Hers was icy, his way too hot. She squeezed, and the gesture brought tears to his eyes. He blinked them away. He couldn't give in to emotion. Sara might be out there on the black water. But he was aware that this time his fear for his little girl was shared by someone else. That sharing was almost overwhelming, but after a moment he released her hand. He needed to concentrate on his driving.

ONCE ON THE WATER, Nate headed for the nearest group of islands. Dark had fallen and there was only a sliver of moon. The lights on shore were a thin strand, a few other boats the barest floating glimmers.

"The Coast Guard will check these islands first thing," Libby said in a hopeful voice.

"Yes."

"Would she have enough gas in the tank, do you think, to make it to the islands?''

Libby had just given voice to one of his worst scenarios, that Sara would run out of gas and be floating helplessly on the water somewhere, or that she'd do something incredibly risky like try to raise the sail.

"I can't remember how full the tank was," he said tersely, and she was silent.

The Coast Guard was already near the largest island, moving slowly along the shoreline. That island was touristy. Crowds had spilled over from inside the bars to the tables set up by the water. Boats of every description were tied up.

Nate gave the docks a quick glance, but didn't spot his

sailboat. "I'm taking her farther in. Do you think she might go to that island where we had the picnic?"

Libby grabbed his hand, squeezed hard in hope. "Maybe she would. Yes. You know how dramatic she is, how something like going back there might appeal to her."

"But we were in a storm that day."

"But before that, we had so much fun. We were a family there."

Nate maneuvered the powerboat carefully. He remembered where the major sandbars were, but the waves shifted the bottom all the time, and you never really knew what was underneath your craft as you approached shore. Just another thing to worry about, he thought, sick with dread.

When he was in close enough, they scanned the shoreline. The island was used only by day sailors, so there were no facilities, and therefore no lights.

But... Yes! Yes! Nate's white boat was tied to the dock, its sails still furled, its mast gleaming dully.

Hands on the wheel, Nate stood. "Sara!" he called.

Libby cupped her hands around her mouth and added her voice to his. "Sara! It's Libby! Are you there?"

A small figure stood on the edge of the dock, waving. As Nate got the boat closer, he could hear her calling for Libby.

The rush of relief flashing through him buckled his knees, and he sank heavily back into the seat.

As soon as he docked, Libby was scrambling out of the boat. Sara rushed into her arms, and she held her tight. "Oh, I was so scared," Sara cried.

"Shh, baby," Libby crooned, rocking her in her arms.

Nate tied up the boat and got out on the dock.

"You're not mad?"

"I'm so glad you're all right," Libby said fiercely.

Nate's heart was in his throat, watching the scene. His

daughter's curls mingled with Libby's, and the natural way they held each other tugged at his insides. God, he loved them both. If something had happened to Sara... Unable to even fully voice the thought, Nate clenched his fists against the strength of emotion.

"I got scared," Sara said. "I got here okay, but it took so long. I didn't know how to make the boat go fast. Then when it was getting dark, I tried to start a fire, like I saw once on TV, but it didn't work." Fresh sobs shook his daughter.

"Shh," Libby murmured again. "I'm here."

"I was afraid to come home on that...*boat*."

Thank God she hadn't tried to start back in the dark. Nate cleared his throat. "You would have run out of gas, Sara."

She raised her head for the first time and looked at him. Libby's arms were still around her. "I banged up the boat, getting it in," she said in a small voice.

He hadn't even begun to think of the perils of docking. Sara falling from the boat, hitting her head, smashing her hands between the boat and the dock. His legs started to shake.

"That's all right," Libby said soothingly.

"It was just that...when everybody was being all snotty with each other... Heywood used to do that, he'd get drunk and then we'd just kind of *know* he was going to say mean things, and me and my mom would try to be quiet. But today I thought, get it over with, get all the mean things out, and then he did yell..." She buried her face in Libby's chest.

Nate's heart hurt, a physical pain. He'd done this. Sara's running away had been his fault because he'd brought back memories for Sara of Heywood Clark. Had he yelled at her? He'd been angry, but now he didn't even remember yelling.

Libby let go of Sara, but reached out to gently stroke his daughter's bangs away from her forehead. Sara turned to look at him. Expectantly. He knew what he was supposed to say, those things Libby was saying that somehow he couldn't. The fear, the utter terror and sense of loss that he'd held at bay for the sake of the search was still there, like a fist in his chest.

"Never go out on the water alone again, Sara. You could have drowned. You could have..." He couldn't give voice to all the possibilities. "Do you know how terrified we were?" His tone was harsh. He didn't mean to be harsh. He wanted to do what Libby was doing, soothe his daughter, hold her. He'd learned to do that these last few weeks. But now he couldn't move.

And with the knowledge that he couldn't move, couldn't be what Sara needed in this moment, he knew he'd made a decision.

The right decision. The decision that was killing him inside.

ON THE WAY HOME, Nate told Sara in short, halting sentences that he wasn't angry at her. With real vehemence, Sara had vowed never to scare them again.

At home, Libby made Sara a sandwich, and then sat on her bed for over an hour. Finally, Sara fell asleep.

When she got downstairs, Nate was waiting. "Is she all right?" he asked immediately.

Libby nodded, suddenly weary. This had been a terrible day. The last two weeks had been terrible, and something had to change.

"Walk with me?" Nate asked, and his voice was so sober, his mouth so tight, that she had a very bad feeling.

He led her to the water's edge. They stood together, looking out over the water he loved, the water that could turn wicked so easily. The foundations at Bittersweet Point gleamed in the night.

"The condos are going up right on schedule," she said, nervously trying to fill the uncomfortable silence that had fallen between them.

"And they're all filled, much more quickly than our projections would ever have indicated. You were right about families needing someplace." He paused. "You were right about a lot of things. And wrong."

"Wrong?"

"Wrong about us," he said quietly. "Wrong to think we could be a family."

"Oh, Nate, I—"

"Wait. I have to say this fast. I'm no good for you or Sara. You love so easily, Libby. You touch people so easily, you go so comfortably through life."

"We love you." Her hand came out to touch his. Gently, he pulled away when she would have entwined her hand in his. He couldn't say what needed to be said, or endure what needed to be endured, if he let her touch him.

"Today proved that Sara is better off without me. I know how her stepfather hurt her, and I acted like him today."

"You're not like Heywood. For Heaven's sake—"

"I reminded her of him. And then tonight, when we found her, I couldn't touch her again. I couldn't reach out and say the right thing. What if you hadn't been with me? How would she have felt, alone and scared with a father who..." He couldn't help it; his voice started to break. "With a father who couldn't take her in his arms when she needed to be held?"

"Nate," she said, her voice breaking, too, "please let me touch you. Let me love you."

"It's better if you don't. Too much has happened to me. And I do better when I concentrate on things. I can't hurt things."

"They can't hurt you. Listen. You think you were wrong with Sara today, but you acted like a father in a real family. Real families argue, get on each other's nerves, get angry when they've been worried. Real families fight, disappoint each other, and then they make up and go on."

"I wasn't what you wanted in a husband." He faced the water.

"No," she said softly. "But you're the man I love." She paused. She was so sure she was right that Nate could be part of her life here, part of Sara's. Nate was a man who felt deeply, just held too much on the inside. She swallowed and said what she had to. "I'll come back to Chicago. I'll try again."

"You wouldn't be happy there."

"I can try," she said, her voice so very thick. *Don't start crying,* she ordered herself. If she couldn't reach Nate in the next few moments, she'd lose him. She struggled over her next words. "But I agree, we might not be happy there. I'd come easier if I knew that's what you really wanted out of life. But you've been happy here, Nate. You've fit in, you know people, they want you to be part of something. Maybe something smaller than what you're used to, but something fine and valuable and real."

He turned to her. "I'm a millionaire developer. The papers call me ruthless and coolheaded. It's what I am," he said simply. "It may not be what I want now, but it's what I've become. It's what I can handle, it's how I excel. Your way is too..." He swallowed. "Hard on the heart. And I'd break your heart and Sara's in the end."

She cried then. She couldn't help crying because he was breaking her heart here and now. "You'll have to tell Sara.

I've tried to make things easy for you, but I won't do it this time."

"Oh, God, Libby, do you think this is easy? Leaving you is the hardest thing I've ever done." He crushed her to him, holding tight, his breathing harsh and unsteady.

"You could take a chance. Why give up on us now, when it just might work out?" She was desperate to convince him, but she had no more words.

"The hurt will be worse later. For Sara. For you." He paused, but he didn't add what she'd thought he might—*for me.* Instead, he said very, very quietly, "You knew all along I'm no gambler."

For a timeless moment they held on to each other.

When he pulled away, his voice was cool, in control. "Forget the prenuptial agreement. You and Sara will have everything you need for the rest of your lives. I do want visitation spelled out, however. I just... I trust you, but I need my rights to Sara."

CHAPTER SEVENTEEN

SARA WAS ANGRY. She refused to visit Nate after he moved back to Chicago a month ago. The three performances of *Fiddler on the Roof* came and went. Libby dropped out of the chorus, unable to bear being in the play, but Sara performed like a trouper. Sara didn't, however, invite her father to be part of the audience.

Over at Bittersweet Point, Nate's condominiums were going up. The rough-sawn cedar siding fit into the setting so well that the condos were barely visible from the water. The sugar cube was torn down, and Tina and Trevor moved to town, to an old place that was awkward for Trevor. But the arrangement was temporary. Nate had offered Tina a job as live-in manager of the Point, so Tina and Trevor would be moving into one of the new units as soon as it could be completed.

One night, Tina made a casual reference to something Nate had said.

"What?" Libby asked quickly, even though the comment had nothing to do with her or Sara. She just wanted to hear his name again, know he was safe and happy in Chicago, in the life he'd chosen.

Tina repeated what Nate had said, then added, "If you want to talk to him, give him a call."

"I can't. He left me, remember? You were right all along." She couldn't help the bitterness.

"Libby, one thing I've learned is that you've got to keep

fighting for what you want. If Nate's what you want, fight for the guy. Don't let your hurt blind you to the good things in life like mine did for so long.''

Libby just shook her head

And today was the worst, the absolute worst. At the shop, Nate had served her with divorce papers. They were accompanied by a dispassionate letter from the ever-efficient Marta Wainwright. The terms were more than generous, the letter pointed out.

Libby didn't want Nate's things. She wanted Nate.

Sara came in from school, in a purple shirt and matching jeans, and in her silver sneakers. A summer's wearing had made them dingy. ''Before you ask, I don't have *any* homework. I stayed in at recess to do my math so I can help you with that harvest thing you're doing with the leaves.'' The paper leaves Libby had ordered for a fall wedding fascinated Sara. She charged around the counter, dropping her book pack midstride. ''How many can I use?''

Libby smiled a smile that suddenly felt a bit watery. Nate might be gone, but he'd left something infinitely precious behind. His daughter.

''Hey, what's all this?'' Sara picked up the papers Libby had left by the telephone.

''Sara, we've got to talk.'' Libby reached for the papers, but Sara pivoted, still reading.

''It's about the divorce,'' she finally said.

Libby said, ''Yes, but your dad wants to see you anytime you're willing. I can show you the part where it says he wants the maximum visitation—''

''Forget it. How will he have time, anyway? Trevor told me Dad has a project going that's like a whole rain forest in a hotel.'' She dropped the papers. ''Trevor also says he seems sad.''

Tina had said the same thing to Libby.

"I want him back," Sara said suddenly. It was the first time since Nate and she had had their talk and he'd packed up for Chicago that she had said such a thing.

"I do, too," Libby admitted, deciding there was no point in hiding her feelings. Sara was too perceptive.

Sara picked up a gold and rust leaf, twirling it by the stem. "I said he was like my old dad, but he isn't," she said finally. "He's nothing like Heywood."

"I know."

"I love him." Sara appeared engrossed in the leaf.

Libby choked up. Darn, she needed to do better, for Sara's sake, but nowadays her emotions lay so close to the surface.

"So how do we get him back?"

"It's not that easy, sweetheart." Libby needed to be honest. Sara needed to understand, first and foremost, that Nate loved her. "Nate loves you. He's always loved you."

"Trevor says that's why he came back."

And why he went away. "Right." Despite her best efforts, her voice was starting to thicken, so she lowered it. "You see, your dad was hurt a lot as a little boy and he didn't know how to live in a real family, and then when your mom took—when you had to go into the witness protection program, Nate lost you, and you were precious to him. So he told himself he was cold inside and nothing could touch him there. So even though Nate loves us, he thinks he's bad for us because he can't love us enough."

"But he does love us enough."

"Yes. Oh, yes. But he can't see that."

"Well," Sara said slowly, "maybe we could prove to him somehow that he does know how to be part of a family." She turned earnest eyes to Libby. Blue eyes. Nate's eyes, wide and deep with a grown-up intensity. "Remember when he tried to help me learn to sail. And he made breakfast and he helped me with my lines the night of the play rehearsal. Does he remember all those things?''

Libby nodded, but she was suddenly struck by the thought that Nate didn't know what those things really meant to her or Sara. Burned breakfasts. Carpooling. The simple things that went into making a family.

But how to make him see? Proof, Sara said, and looking down at her divorce papers Libby had an idea. She pondered for a moment, but a moment only. She hated to risk hurting Sara. But wouldn't Sara be hurt worse if they didn't take one last chance? And Sara had a special maturity that came from living with a difficult stepfather, of losing her mother, and of forging a new family with Libby. Yes. If Judge Wyatt was willing, perhaps they could prove it, after all.

NATE COULD HAVE BEEN late, because Charles Baker and his investors wanted to go over a mock-up of the new project. But even though he'd spent a hundred hours in preparation, he found himself making excuses. He was required by the court to be in Harborside for the final hearing for his divorce—and he was going to be there in plenty of time. He would see Libby again, and he couldn't wait, even though he knew seeing her only meant that the end had come.

He had to see Sara, too. He'd talked to her on the phone, but she wouldn't come to Chicago. She wanted him to come to Harborside. And Nate would, as soon as he could bear to make the trip. Maybe he'd take one of the condos on Bittersweet Point on a permanent basis, a place to see Sara if she continued to refuse to come to Chicago.

The courtroom was as he remembered it—old and majestic, with high ceilings, worthy of a big city. He wondered about the people who had built it. They must have done so with high expectations, sure that Harborside would grow someday. But it never had. Now Nate thought with a rush of unwanted sentimentality that maybe the town founders would be proud of the independent people who called it home.

The courtroom had been the beginning of his dream of a family. So it was fitting that the dream would end here. Nate clenched his jaw, searching for his self-control, his distance.

It was hard to look at Libby. She smiled at him nervously, as his own eyes took in every detail. She had on a new green suit. It seemed not her style, until he got a peep of the shell she wore underneath. Some sort of leafy print. *Okay.* His Libby.

Only not his Libby, because he was at his table with Marta, and she was alone at another table. He frowned. Why didn't she have her lawyer with her? Even though the property settlement wasn't contested, she shouldn't be without legal advice. Protectiveness rose in him, until he realized he was trying to protect her from himself.

Judge Wyatt took the bench.

Nate rose with Marta and Libby, then sat down when directed to do so. "Well," Judge Wyatt said finally, looking down over the bench with a stern countenance. "I thought when you two married that we'd seen the end of this bizarre case. Apparently, I was wrong. Ms. Wainwright."

Marta stood. "Your Honor."

"Mrs. Perry has elected to act as her own attorney today," the judge said.

"Mr. Perry would prefer it if Mrs. Perry were represented," Marta told him. "In affairs of this kind, sometimes a more…impersonal approach is better."

"I don't agree," Judge Wyatt said flatly. "Now, your petition cites irreconcilable differences."

"The grounds for divorce aren't contested, Your Honor."

"Oh, but Ms. Wainwright, they are. Mrs. Perry has chosen to fight the divorce."

Nate peered at the judge, trying to understand what was going on. The judge was smiling at Libby. Nate had a sense of the surreal. But he took the stand at Marta's direction and prepared to give testimony as to why he and Libby couldn't live together. He answered Marta's crisp questions. Yes, he had never really made Harborside his home. Yes, he'd kept his home in Chicago. Yes, he and Libby disagreed about many things. What were those things? He looked over at Libby. She was staring at him.

Actually, he thought in some surprise, they were more in sync than he'd ever imagined. Basically, they agreed on the importance of family. After all, that's what had finally made him realize how bad he was for her. They were one in their love for Sara. They both had guts. He in business, she in life. Hell, they even shared a love for the water.

He shook his head. What was he supposed to say? Irreconcilable differences. *She takes chances, risks her heart. I don't gamble.* Suddenly, that sounded...cowardly.

Somehow, he got through Marta's questions. But he fisted his hands, surprisingly shaken, when Libby got up to do her cross-examination.

"I only have a few questions, Your Honor," she said in a clear voice. Then, when she moved, her suit jacket came open. And there it was, splashed boldly across her front— a mammoth sunflower.

I like you in black and I like you in sunflowers...

He cleared his throat.

"Mr. Perry," Libby began. "Isn't it true that despite

what you testified to here today, the real reason you don't want to stay married to me is that you don't think you can be a family man?''

God, she didn't mince her words. "Yes, that's true."

"And because you think you don't fit in here in Harborside, and in some misguided attempt to spare Sara and me some unformed, future hurt, you think it's best to get out of our lives now?''

"Objection to the word *misguided*," Marta said, getting to her feet.

"Sit down, Ms. Wainwright," the judge said. "Answer the question, Mr. Perry."

So Nate said, "Yes." He had been so sure he was doing the right thing that night on her beach. Over and over in his mind in the month since he'd left, he'd heard Sara's "I hate you." But to try to explain today in this courtroom... Nate started to sweat.

"No further questions."

In great relief, Nate took his seat. Marta made a short speech and then rested her case.

The judge asked Libby if she had any witnesses. Libby said she had four. "First, I call Trevor Samms."

As Nate sat there in shock, Trevor wheeled his chair into the room and took his place near the witness stand. In a loud, clear voice, he raised his hand, took his oath and began to tell about his father and that heartbreaking meeting at the motel.

No, Nate wanted to say. *Don't make him tell how humiliated he was that day.* But Trevor did. He testified to his anger and embarrassment. He talked then about how Nate had been there for him, how he'd sobbed on Nate's chest and Nate had driven him for miles as he'd calmed down and reconciled himself to his father's rejection. Nate wondered why the kid was making it sound as if Nate had done so much. It had been Trevor who had shown extraordinary courage.

"Mr. Perry told me that I should go ahead and feel things, that it was okay for a man to feel, to hurt, to cry."

Nate had said those things. He remembered that moment in the car with painful poignancy, so sure then—thanks to Libby—that he'd learned something about sharing feelings.

Libby took a few steps toward the witness stand, until Nate could only see the proud line of her back and the back of her head, where strands of red tangled in a fiery glow. "Do you have an opinion on what kind of father Nate Perry would make?"

Trevor turned to the judge. "Mr. Perry would make— is—the best father on earth."

"Thank you. No more questions."

The funniest thing started to happen to Nate. He could hear the roar of wind, like the breeze that caught his sails, and he could smell the fresh water–laden air that was ever-present in the unpolluted air of Harborside. Frowning, he looked up at the stained-glass windows that were sealed closed.

Then Libby said, "I call Sara Perry to the stand."

Quick as a wink, Marta was on her feet. "Sara is only ten years old, not old enough under Ohio law to make any choices about her custody—"

"Sit down, Ms. Wainwright." The judge scowled at her.

Nate got to his feet, too. What was Libby thinking, putting his daughter through this hearing? "Your Honor, my daughter's been hurt enough by this entire process. She shouldn't have to testify."

"Sit down, Mr. Perry."

"Your Honor, with all respect, we're talking about my daughter here—"

"Sit down!" the judge roared. Then, slightly softer, he

said, "Really, Mr. Perry. Sit down. I've got some things to say to you."

Nate sat on the edge of his seat.

The judge took off his glasses and leaned forward over the high bench. "When you first came to me wanting your daughter, I wondered about you. I knew who you were and where you came from, and I knew you were a man who got whatever he wanted. I couldn't help but wonder—and worry—if you wanted that little girl only to prove that nobody could take her away from you. I'm glad to know I was wrong. Because you've just demonstrated that you do care for Sara. And because of that, I'm going to let her try to knock some sense into you." He stacked a sheaf of papers. "I don't know if you're a praying man, but I am. I guess sometimes a little child really *does* need to lead them." He turned to his bailiff. "Go get Sara Perry."

When Sara was led in, her white face made Nate want to go to her immediately. She gave him a tremulous smile, and his heart squeezed painfully. Sara took the stand, and Nate didn't miss the little thumbs-up sign she and Libby exchanged. So *Sara* had something to do with planning this fiasco of a hearing?

"Well," said Sara in answer to a question from Libby that Nate had apparently missed, "he makes breakfast on Saturday mornings. It's a pretty gross breakfast," she said earnestly to the judge, before quickly adding, "But he tries."

He tries. Was that enough? Once he'd have said no way. But maybe...

"Then he drives me to horseback-riding lessons. He had his assistant do all this research into saddles, and he bought me the safest one. Not the coolest, though." Again she looked at the judge. "But he tried to get something cool and safe, too."

She testified about the sailing trip, the picnic, the storm. To Nate's utter astonishment, she said he was a hero. Then she talked about the play practice, about how he'd gotten up in front of all those parents.

He had done all those things. And they apparently meant more to Sara than she'd ever let on at the time. Hell, she wouldn't even touch him back then, and here she was saying that she remembered all those things and they were special.

"See, Judge, the thing is—"

"He tries," the judge finished for her, smiling.

"Right. I think a really, really good father tries hard. And my dad does."

That roaring was back, a good, fierce, cleansing wind. And with it Nate felt a rush of feeling so deep and true that he wondered if he'd ever known what love really was before. With that feeling came a heady rush of belonging, of happiness. He stood, his legs trembling under him. "I want to testify," he said.

"Sara's still on the stand."

"I want to testify. I want to…say some things."

The judge looked over to the other counsel table. "It's up to Libby—Mrs. Perry. It's your case, Mrs. Perry. Do you want Mr. Perry to testify?"

Libby's eyes met Nate's. He tried to communicate without words his love for her. *Please.*

"Okay," she said, and he heard a breathless note in her voice. "I had a couple of other witnesses—Kevin Smithson, Tina Samms. I was going to get the caller from the square dance, but he was out of town, and then I thought of a lot of other people…" As if realizing she was rattling on, she sat down hard.

Nate exchanged places with his daughter. Out of the corner of his eye, Nate saw Marta practically slumped in her chair. Well, he thought, if she wanted to be his attorney, she really needed to learn that things were different in Harborside.

He raised his right hand, prepared to take the oath.

The judge said, "You don't have to do that again, Mr. Perry. You're still under oath from your previous testimony."

"Give it to me anyway. I don't want there to be any doubt about what I'm going to say." The bailiff stepped forward and Nate repeated the oath.

He fixed his eyes on Libby. "I just want to say that I've learned something here today. I think it was something I should have learned a long time ago, because my wife and my daughter sure spent a lot of time teaching me. I was a slow learner, I guess. But what I've learned is what love means. Love means you take chances. You risk everything. I love my wife and my daughter and I can't imagine how I thought I could live without them."

The courtroom was utterly still. Libby sat forward in her seat, her hands clasped hard in front of her.

"And I want to live in Harborside."

Libby jumped to her feet. "Nate, you don't have to say—"

"No, Libby, I'm the one testifying here." Nate motioned to the judge.

With a grin, Judge Wyatt said, "Sit down, Mrs. Perry."

Mrs. Perry sat.

"I've got a great assistant. He wants to make something of himself, and I could sell the business to him. Favorable terms. And I could use the proceeds to invest in things that are a little smaller. Resorts geared to families." At his own words, Nate felt a hundred pounds lighter. The people who depended on him would be in good hands with Jeff. And

Nate could start living again, in a little place called Harborside.

"I want to see the sunrise from our old sunporch, and walk on everybody else's beach without being accused of trespassing. I want to have homemade pie in the Shoreline and help my wife shop for organic flour and go horseback riding with my kid. I want to put in a hard day's work that means something to real people, and then sail on a hot summer's night, without worrying what'll be in my fax machine when I come back. I want to be a big fish in a little pond, I guess, like a friend of mine once said."

The judge motioned for his bailiff. "I think he wants to dismiss the case."

"You're damn right I do. I want my wife and my daughter."

He got up then, came around the witness stand, and held out his arms. In a rush, Libby and Sara mobbed him, and he wrapped his arms around them both. They were warm and alive and so much more important than any tower of steel and stone he'd ever built.

"Do you mean it, Nate? Oh, I was so afraid." Libby tucked her head against his neck.

"I'm the one who was afraid. But you both took a chance on me. How could I do less than take a chance on love?"

EPILOGUE

Ten months later:

"There it is. All finished." Nate gestured to indicate the living room in the newly completed model condominium at Bittersweet Point.

Libby looked around. The living room had been designed to be white and spacious. But with lots of prints on the walls, a few brightly colored cotton rugs on the floor, and some handmade pottery in the bay window, the effect was rather cluttered. The furniture was wicker, its cushions a green flowered print. "Nice," she said. "Was it done up by one of those sophisticated city decorators of yours?"

They both laughed. "Not exactly," Nate said. "This time I used the decorator who knows how to make a place seem like home." His laughter faded away, and he gave her a smile. That smile wasn't practiced at all, but gentle and genuine.

Libby blushed. He'd insisted she decorate the model condominium because the concept of Bittersweet Point had been her idea. "So what do you think of the decor, Nate?"

"I like it. It suits the place."

Bittersweet Point now was a sweep of rustic waterfront condominiums, set back into the woods. Simple paths made of wood chips led to the beach. There too, the area had been left natural, except for a playground area that had been built near the water's edge. The Point was crowded this time of year, because—except for the unit they were standing in—the condos had all been sold to families with young children.

The condominium on the end had a ramp and a boardwalk instead of a chip path, and the walk led right down to the water's edge. When Nate had built the unit for Tina and Trevor, he'd made sure that Trevor could get down to the beach.

Now Nate was using the condo Libby had decorated as a model for his next project. That resort was more modest than Bittersweet Point, set on a quiet, out-of-the-way island in Lake Erie. Nate envisioned it as a hub for families who liked to sail, and he planned docks and a simple clubhouse, but none of the fancy amenities that would take the cost of ownership out of reach of the average family.

He still worked too hard, Libby thought, but he was slowly learning how to relax. These days, she could easily coax him out after dinner for a swim or a walk with her and Sara.

Libby walked over to the sliding doors and glanced out. Sara had come to the Point with them, and now was out wading in the lake, in a pair of cutoff jeans. She had something in her hand, probably a new shell or rock, but her attention was focused on a gang of boys who were playing volleyball.

Nate came up behind her and looked over her shoulder. "She's growing up," he observed. His voice softened. "And I think every day how lucky and blessed I am to be here to see that. To have you and Sara—all of you—to love."

Libby's heart squeezed, both at Nate's words and the easy way he spoke the feelings in his heart. Almost unconsciously, her hand went to her stomach, a touch for their growing baby.

He planted a soft kiss on the back of her neck. "Thanks for agreeing to go to Chicago with me this weekend."

Libby held back a sigh. She wasn't really looking forward to the dedication of the Iris Complex, but Nate thought they should go to support Jeff. For all its problems, the completed Iris complex was a gleaming masterpiece, a testament to Nate's vision in design and his good judgment in giving Jeff a chance. Nate retained a financial interest in the resort but had sold most of the business to his former assistant. Everybody was happy with the results.

"I was thinking we could buy you a new dress for the round of parties after the dedication," Nate said.

"I couldn't fit into that black dress again for sure," Libby said with a rueful smile.

Nate's arm came around her, cradling her stomach, feeling the little mound low in her belly. She put her own hand there again, over his. "Maybe it would be a good idea to shop in Chicago," she conceded.

"Yes. A new dress. One with flowers." His voice whispered along her neck. "Big, humongous flowers. A dress that's easy to take off. We'll come back to our room early, and I'll tell you again how I like you in black, and big, big flowers and then in nothing but bare skin. How does that sound?"

It sounded downright wonderful. Most things these days were wonderful.

"And then when we're done in Chicago, maybe we'll take a vacation."

"Nate, we can't take a vacation now. You know how busy my shop is in the summer."

"A vacation," he insisted. "A short one. I have this great spot picked out. It's a resort with a lot of amenities. Blue sky, woods and sand and clear water, and the place we'd be staying in has all this art on the walls..."

"Sounds a lot like Bittersweet Point," she observed.

"That's because it is Bittersweet Point." Slowly, he turned her to face him. "I bought this last condo to surprise you. That's why I wanted you to decorate it."

"You bought this place? But why on earth...? We live right across the cove."

"I figure, with a baby on the way, and Sara turning into a teenager in a few years, and with my building projects and your shop, we'll want someplace to get away once in a while. Spend time alone together."

That sounded heavenly. "Yes, but...here?"

"Why not right here? After all, is there any place in the world better than right here? Better than very close to home?"

HARLEQUIN SUPERROMANCE®

COMING NEXT MONTH

#758 BEAUTY & THE BEASTS • Janice Kay Johnson
Veterinarian Dr. Eric Bergstrom is interested in a new woman. A *beautiful* woman. He's volunteered his services at the local cat shelter she's involved with. He's even adopted one of the shelter's cats. But he still can't manage to get Madeline to go out with him. That's bad enough. Then Eric's twelve-year-old son comes to town, making it clear that he resents "having" to spend the summer with his father. Well, at least Eric's new cat loves him....

#759 IN THE ARMS OF THE LAW • Anne Marie Duquette
Home on the Ranch
Morgan Bodine is part-owner of the Silver Dollar Ranch; he's also the acting sheriff in Tombstone, Arizona. Jasentha Cliffwalker is a biologist studying bats on Bodine property. Morgan and Jaz loved each other years ago, but it was a love they weren't ready for. *Are they ready now?* They'll find out when a stranger comes to Tombstone, threatening everything they value most.... By the author of *She Caught the Sheriff.*

#760 JUST ONE NIGHT • Kathryn Shay
9 Months Later
Annie and Zach Sloan had married for all the right reasons. They'd fallen in love and neither could imagine life without the other. But those reasons hadn't been enough to keep them together. Then—six years after the divorce—a night that began in fear ended in passion. And now there's a new reason for Zach and Annie to marry. *They're about to become parents.*

#761 THIS CHILD IS MINE • Janice Kaiser
Carolina Prescott is pregnant. Webb Harper is the father. After his wife died, he forgot all about the donation he'd left at a fertility clinic. Due to a mix-up, Lina is given the wrong fertilized egg—but that doesn't make her less of a mother! Both Lina and Webb have strong feelings about the baby she's carrying and the ensuing lawsuit. Can their growing feelings for each other overcome the trauma of the battle for custody?

1998

SUNDAY MONDAY TUESDAY WEDNESDAY THURSDAY FRIDAY SATURDAY

Keep track of important dates

Three beautiful and colorful calendars that celebrate some of the most popular trends in America today.

Look for:

Just Babies—a 16 month calendar that features a full year of absolutely adorable babies!

1998 CALENDAR

Just Babies

16 months of adorable bundles of joy!

Hometown Quilts

1998 Calendar

A 16 month quilting extravaganza!

Hometown Quilts—a 16 month calendar featuring quilted art squares, plus a short history on twelve different quilt patterns.

Inspirations—a 16 month calendar with inspiring pictures and quotations.

Inspirations

A 16 month calendar that will lift your spirits and gladden your heart

Steeple Hill™

◆ HARLEQUIN®

Value priced at $9.99 U.S./$11.99 CAN., these calendars make a perfect gift!

Available in retail outlets in August 1997. CAL98

HARLEQUIN WOMEN KNOW ROMANCE WHEN THEY SEE IT.

And they'll see it on **ROMANCE CLASSICS**, the new 24-hour TV channel devoted to romantic movies and original programs like the special **Romantically Speaking—Harlequin™ Goes Prime Time.**

Romantically Speaking—Harlequin™ Goes Prime Time introduces you to many of your favorite romance authors in a program developed exclusively for Harlequin® readers.

Watch for **Romantically Speaking—Harlequin™ Goes Prime Time** beginning in the summer of 1997.

If you're not receiving ROMANCE CLASSICS, call your local cable operator or satellite provider and ask for it today!

Escape to the network of your dreams.

See Ingrid Bergman and Gregory Peck in *Spellbound* on Romance Classics.

WELCOME TO *Love Inspired* ™

A brand-new series of contemporary inspirational love stories.

Join men and women as they learn valuable lessons about facing the challenges of today's world and learn valuable lessons about life, love and faith.

Look for:

The Risk of Loving
by Jane Peart

The Parson's Waiting
by Sherryl Woods

The Perfect Wedding
by Arlene James

Available in retail outlets in August 1997.

LIFT YOUR SPIRITS AND GLADDEN YOUR HEART with *Love Inspired* ™!

Steeple
Hill™

LI-997